Mistresses of the Macabre

edited by
Lori Michelle

DARK MOON BOOKS
an imprint of Stony Meadow Publishing
Largo, Florida

Mistresses of the Macabre

ISBN: 978-0-9885569-5-9

dark moon

www.darkmoonbooks.com

Contents

INTRODUCTION

WOMEN HAVE WRITTEN horror for longer than it's been a recognized genre, and we've lived with horror for as long as we've walked the Earth. Let me explain.

The obvious connection that women have with blood—menses—curses us all. So often, men are surprised—and horrified—to discover exactly what goes on between our legs on a regular basis: the shedding of linings, the gushes of blood, and the pain through which we suffer time and again, as predictably as the rising of the moon. We hide it so well, most of the time.

This monthly blood-letting has long been a mystery that has inspired fear, prejudice, and superstition. It has helped to solidify the line between men and women, and it has been used as an excuse for keeping women out of "men's business."

Richard Webster, speaking about historical superstitions in the *Encyclopedia of Superstitions* (Llewellyn Publications, 2008), says, "People looked at a menstruating woman with horror and awe, because although she lost blood, she continued to live. Menstruating women had to remain out of sight, as it was thought that they brought potential danger to the whole tribe. Even making eye contact with a menstruating woman was considered dangerous."

But not all the damage was done by men. In proceedings of the Royal Society of Medicine, 1915, Raymond Crawfurd wrote an article entitled "Of Superstitions concerning Menstruation." In this article, he describes how British farmers' wives believed that a "menstruous woman" could not be trusted with milk because once she had touched it, it could no longer be churned into butter. They clung to this belief, despite the evidence to the contrary.

Women have carried the mark of "uncleanliness" since before the Middle Ages. Judaism, Hinduism, and Islam have histories of labeling women as "unclean." Leviticus 12 (Old Testament) warns that a woman who has just had a boy child remains "unclean" for seven days afterward (as she is during her customary impurity [menstrual cycle]). This state is contagious, thus explaining why boys aren't circumcised until the eighth day. The boy child is infected with his mother's impurity until then.

For thirty-three days after giving birth, she is forbidden from touching holy items or even entering the sanctuary. And, if the woman had a *girl* child, Heaven forbid, then she remains anathema for twice as long, sixty-six days. She must suffer a forced separation from her family and friends during this time, and anyone who attended her was considered tainted by her and must have cleansing rituals performed upon them.

Catholicism persecuted women as well. In 1140 AD, the *Decretum Gratiani*, a collection of Canon law, stated that God had not made women in His image, but had made them "weak of mind." The Church banned women from teaching scripture to parishioners, distributing communion, becoming priests, and even from touching any of the holy accoutrements of a priest's garb and tools. It wasn't until 1983 that the Catholic Church finally lifted many of these primitive restrictions.

Even in this modern day, among the more radical religious right, some still believe that painful childbirth was a burden placed upon women when Eve was banished from the Garden for her sin. Genesis 3:15 says, "To the woman He said: 'I will greatly multiply your sorrow and your conception; In pain you shall bring forth children; Your desire shall be for your husband, And he shall rule over you.'"

Whether any of these Biblical laws and warnings were intended as censure or simply as health care advice, the fact remains that they set the tone for the treatment of women through many centuries. Time and again, uneducated men—who did not experience menstruation or childbirth—assigned mystery and magic to them, but not in a good way. A woman's holy role in procreation did not raise her up in their estimation. Instead, they painted her as unclean and unholy, and eventually, they called her a witch and burned her at the stake. Even now, women are associated with the moon, like many creatures of darkness: lycanthropes, vampires, and lunatics.

Over the millennia, men have thought of women as objects that can be owned—collected—and have subjugated them to slavery in forms both subtle and overt. The practice of public sexual harassment, groping and rubbing, intended to humiliate and dominate a woman is still called "Eve teasing." The implicit idea is that the woman somehow deserves this disrespectful treatment and was teasing the man with her womanly wiles, inherited from Eve who tempted Adam.

Many women who have ridden a subway train in France or Italy have witnessed, if not experienced, this disgusting behavior. In 2004, I myself was in a jam-packed (no standing room left) subway train in Europe, and I saw a man rubbing his crotch purposefully and continuously against a teen-aged girl's backside. She couldn't get away from him without making a scene, and she was obviously unwilling to do that, despite how uncomfortable she was. I could tell she was suffering in silence, waiting for her station.

I intervened and gave her my seat. The man was frightening to me, and I wasn't even the one he was assaulting. He used fear to take advantage of the poor girl. I remember thinking later how sad it was that I, a foreigner in that country, was the only one who took action to rescue her. It would appear that "Eve teasing" is so commonplace that objecting to it isn't worth the possible conflict.

Western society has been male-dominated for millennia, and women have been relegated to the kitchen and bedroom. The attitude, so persistently propagated through generations, that women are the weaker sex, that they're unholy, have less value, and are property to be owned has at least one extremely serious outcome: violence.

Violence against women comes in many forms, it's always horrific, and it starts when we're young. In an article entitled "Not a Minute More: Ending Violence Against Women," the United Nations Development Fund for Women estimated that 1 in 3 women around the globe will be beaten, raped, or otherwise abused during her lifetime.

In 2007, there were more than 500 rapes per day in the United States. The CDC released the results of a survey in 2010 (The National Intimate Partner and Sexual Violence Survey) that reports, "Nearly 1 in 5 women in the United States has been raped in her lifetime. This translates to almost 22 milllion women . . . " By contrast, they say, "Approximately 1 in 71 men in the United States reported having been raped in his lifetime." That's about 1.6 million men.

Most female victims of rape experience it before they're 25. Usually, they knew their attacker, 91.9% of the time, and more than half of the perpetrators were the victim's partner or ex-partner.

Think about it this way. Given these statistics, at least one of the writers in this anthology, and probably more than one, has survived sexual abuse and/or violence. Or, at least one of your female friends has.

Let's take it up a notch. Every day, three women in America are murdered by their boyfriend or husband. What could possibly be more horrific than being murdered by someone you love? How about being sold into slavery or prostitution by a parent? Human trafficking doesn't just happen in Thailand, India, or other far-away places. It happens in the Western world as well. ABC News printed a story, written by Russell Goldman, about how the Internet has become a place for parents to "sell" sexual encounters with their children in exchange for drugs, money, or tickets to the big game.

Why stop there? Honor killings have reached the United States. Some cultures believe that it's better to kill your daughter than to allow her to date outside the approved list. This clash between the Old Ways and the modern Western world is so harsh that it results in dead young women. Hina Jilani (human rights activist) says, "The right to life of women in Pakistan is conditional on their obeying social norms and traditions."

Honor killings are often associated with Muslim cultures, but Shahrzad Mojab, a professor of Women's Studies at the University of Toronto has said that followers of Hinduism, Islam, Sikhism, Judaism, and Christianity have also committed them, rationalized by their religious beliefs. According to Mojab, honor killings have even been around since before any major religion existed.

Thomas Reuters Foundation determined the five most dangerous places in the world for a woman to live, and they were, best to worst: Somalia, India, Pakistan, Congo, and Afghanistan. In India, a woman is expected to bring a dowry (a financial wedding gift) to her husband when she marries. If the husband feels the dowry was insufficient, he kills his bride. In 2001 (not 1401), the Indian government logged more than 7,000 dowry deaths. One method used by these disappointed husbands has an official name, "Bride Burning," and it involves kerosene.

If they don't kill them, they maim and disfigure them to coerce the family to pay more or punish them for not paying enough. "Acid throwing" is popular, the acid usually splashed in the victim's face with the intent of permanently scarring and mangling the tissue there. The message here is clear: "I own you, and I can do anything I want to you." This type of assault is so prevalent that there's an international organization dedicated to its victims: the Acid Survivors' Trust International. Every year, globally, more than 1500 people suffer this kind of attack, and 80% of them are female.

Honor killings, dowry deaths, and maimings imply that the woman did something wrong and thus had to be punished. But, there are even worse things being done to women to prevent them from *ever* doing anything wrong.

In many countries, including first-world Western countries, the practice of female genital mutilation (FGM) remains alive. According to the World Health Organization's Fact Sheet #241 (February 2013), it's estimated that over 140 million girls and women worldwide are suffering from the consequences of FGM.

FGM is genital mutilation perpetrated upon women for no good health reason, and it's nothing more than an extreme form of discrimination and controlling abuse. Culture, not religion, keeps the practice in place, and it's usually performed when the girl is less than ten years old.

The partial or total removal of the clitoris is intended to dampen the woman's sexual enjoyment, to free her from her libido, to help her resist illicit sexual temptation, and to increase her loyalty to her husband. Sometimes, parts or all of the labia are removed, or cut and repositioned to create a smaller vaginal opening, often leaving only enough space for the menstrual flow.

The procedure is carried out by traditional circumcisers, although an alarming trend shows that 18% of all FGM are done by actual health care providers. It's driven by social pressure from communities and older family members (often women themselves who had it done to them). Some feel it has to happen in order to prepare a girl for adulthood and marriage. It derives much of its rationalization from beliefs related to what constitutes proper sexual behavior, premarital virginity, and fidelity. In certain cases, it's all about maintaining cultural ideals of femininity, cleanliness, and beauty.

Horror. Women live with it. And that's what makes them such great writers of it. What they haven't experienced, they can extrapolate and imagine, because something in their world has given them a hint of what the greater experience would be like. Women bring this to their horror stories, the pain, the fear, the feeling of being physically dominated by a stronger individual, and the vulnerability we've all known.

The stories in this anthology deal, whether metaphorically or directly, with the trials and tribulations of being a woman. It kicks off with "My Left Hand," by Charlotte Jones, a tale that—at its core—is about how our bodies betray us, a feeling most women know intimately. As you read on, you'll travel through atypical stories of abuse, the things we'll do for love, and the sacrifices we make for family.

"Orbs," by Chantal Boudreau shows the obsessive nature with which men hoard and attempt to gain complete control over physically beautiful women. In "Playdate," the repercussions of a distant tragedy continue to ripple through a young girl's life, and in "Out with the Old," a woman trades in a new model for the old comfortable one. To cap it off, Joanna Parypinski offers us "And One for the Road," a reminder that none of us are immune to the trauma that comes with the horrific events that occur in our lives.

Horror, sometimes brooding, sometimes screaming, flows through these stories from beginning to end, a constant reminder that these women writers have a deep connection with it.

And now, I feel I've done my job of preparing you to take the journey through this anthology. Like women, each of these stories has a different terror to tell. You'll find both depth and breadth carefully built into each tale by these Mistresses of the Macabre. Evil exists, but we can take back the night and make it ours. Let's do it.

Angel Leigh McCoy

My Left Hand

CHARLOTTE JONES

I KNOW THAT sound, the sound of no good. It twitches, rustling the sheets, but then it quiets down, making me more nervous. Constant vigilance is what's required to keep that . . . that thing away from me. Tonight, with the midnight train, my ordeal will finally be over. At least, that is my hope. I glance at the clock. Another hour-and-a-half to go. Just as I begin to doze off, there is movement again. I'm on my back, so I roll to my right, yank my elbow to drag it closer to my body and then roll back as fast as I can, trapping my left hand beneath me, smothering it under my silk nightgown.

* * *

It started yesterday during my normal morning routine. I'd let Peanut, my Jack Russell, out to roam the yard and sat at the kitchen table drinking my first cup of tea while reading the international section of *The New York Times* about the rising tensions with Iran. When I finished the article, I flipped the page, scanning for the next item of interest—something about the Greek debt crisis—and I made a mental note to call my broker and make sure I didn't own any foreign bonds. Out of nowhere, my left hand reached out, set that section aside and reached for the travel section. At first I thought it was a subconscious move, maybe my brain had registered an article of interest. But no, I'd already read about the California wine country. So, with my right hand, I returned to the international news.

My left hand suddenly grabbed and crumpled the paper, wadded it into a ball. I watched, astounded. Like it wasn't even my hand. I quickly rose from the table and went to the sink where I forced the hand under cold running water until it quieted down.

The rest of the day was normal. Both hands cooperated to clip on the dog's leash. Both hands worked well together to chop some vegetables for dinner.

Just a little twitch or a tic or something, I rationalized. I must have imagined the incident this morning. Nothing to worry about. But just in case, I tied the hand to the bedpost with a belt over night.

The next morning, my entire left arm was numb and tingly, and with the sun bursting through the window, it all seemed so silly. Crazy ol' bat, that's what I was. After breakfast, I took advantage of the unseasonably cool weather to work in the yard. The weeds were taking over the roses and my goal was to clear them out and lay down some new mulch before lunchtime. I'd nearly forgotten about the previous day's disturbance with the hand and, indeed, it worked swiftly and deftly, right alongside my right hand, tugging weeds and deadheading the flowers. You might say I was keeping an eye on it, though, bracing for a scratch or two when it brushed close to the thorny stems, but I managed to finish my work unscathed.

After lunch I decided to give myself a well-deserved manicure. That's when the trouble escalated. My left lay quietly enough as my right hand pushed back the cuticles, trimmed the nails and painted them a cheery peachy-red shade of "Cha Ching Cherry." But when I switched the tools to my left hand, it attacked my right, gouging the scissors deep into the back of my hand and spilling the nail polish all over the bathroom vanity. Now I had confirmation that something was wrong, but what to do? I considered calling my doctor, but he already thinks I'm a hypochondriac. I can hear him asking if I've been taking my anti-anxiety medication. So I treated the wound myself with hydrogen-peroxide and a stiff martini. Unfortunately, the left kept dipping its fingers into my drink.

That evening, right hand still bandaged, I decided to grill a steak. While I ate, Peanut sat at my feet, begging for scraps. Before I knew what was happening, my left hand grabbed the steak knife, turned the tip toward my face and tried to stab my eye. It took every ounce of strength in my right hand to keep my left at bay. Peanut jumped up with his forepaws on my thigh and barked viciously at the hand. I finally was able to bash it against the edge of the table until it let go of the knife. The dog snarled every time my left hand came near him.

I began to visualize the railroad track behind the house. Every night at midnight, the train ran by. Ideas began to coalesce into a plan. Not wanting to arouse the suspicions of my left hand, I stuck to my routine and was in bed reading by 8:30 p.m.

* * *

At 11:25 p.m., my alarm clock jars me out of dosing. It's time. I roll off the hand and rise from my bed. I tell the hand I can't sleep, that I need a breath of air. I casually slip it into the pocket of my robe where I feel it clutch and crumple the Kleenex planted there to keep it occupied. If I can convince the hand we are only going for a stroll, perhaps I can tie it to the track before it knows what's happening. The hand is unusually docile at the moment. Maybe it knows what's coming; maybe not.

I fill the dog's bowl with kibble and make sure to leave the front door unlocked, in case this goes badly. I double-check that the instructions for my executor are on the kitchen table.

As I make my way out the back gate and toward the track, it occurs to me that maybe the hand is simply restless. Maybe it wants to get out of this boring small town and go places, do things, and have a life of its own without being tied to me. I recall it reaching for the travel section only yesterday. I can understand wanting more out of life. Perhaps it knows this journey is in both our best interests. Compassion dictates that I change my plans, so I drop the rope my right hand is carrying. The left doesn't seem to notice.

Standing by the track now, I see the headlight at a distance. The train always slows as it enters town, and I must wait for it to reach my side of town. It seems to take forever before I can hear the clickety-clack and feel the rush of wind.

As the train approaches, I tell my left hand, "You know what to do." The cars pass, and the hand hangs limply at my side. With the end of the train nearing, the hand comes to life and reaches out to grab the handrail of the final car. I run alongside to keep up for a few steps, but then stumble, my feet dragging the ground. Struggling to keep from falling under the wheels, I feel my shoulder joint begin to loosen. The pain is more than I had anticipated, and while I hadn't planned to lose the entire arm, I know I must rid myself of this monster.

As the train picks up speed, my left hand's grip tightens. The skin at my shoulder begins to tear. Finally falling away, I roll down the embankment and rise to my knees. I will my right hand to clasp what remains of my left shoulder and stem the flow of blood.

It disobeys, sadly waving goodbye to its partner.

The Mistakes

HOLLIS JAY

SLIT. The house stood crouched in darkness. No one came there anymore. She could still hear their laughter hovering above the ground, keeping them far away. She knew they could only hide deep inside. Heavy and thick dust held the seams together now. Once when mother was alive, she danced. They used to twirl with her, round and round until they felt as if they would fall to the floor. Father left a long time ago. The noose was heavy when they found him. Years ago, mother told them that he would return. She asked them to close their eyes and imagine their father smiling in front of them, holding them in his arms. That was before the gun went off, before the splattering of blood against the ceiling fan that slid down the wall.

Furrow. Mash. Then they were all alone. They sat. Staying inside. Holding each other through the shadows. Keeping each other sane. Sometimes, the corners of the house would talk to them, whirling up a story for bedtime and whispering deep dark fears.

"You know they never wanted you."

One would whisper to the other. Sitting on the cold pantry floor. Shivers creeping through her dress and up the back of her spine.

"I was always the pretty one."

Lying to each other. Telling each other the truth. Shifting in their seats and holding their breath until the sunlight shifted on the floor. There were still pictures on the walls. They could see their mother, beautiful in her white wedding dress cascading down the stairs. A blue brooch in her hair and curls tumbling down in long and round rolls.

"They used to love each other."

"Like us?"

"Like us."

Furrow. Chop. Their father's smile dwindled over the years. At first he would play. Hide and go seek at three in the afternoon, around the corner and through the garden. Top hat and cane. Just like old times.

"Ladies and Gentlemen. Boys and Girls. Look to the stage to your left. Notice the amazing, the awe inspiring . . . "

Sometimes mother would join in, just like before.

"I wish we were back in the ring."

"They would never take us now."

They would run in circles . . . fast and then slow . . . slow and then fast . . . until their legs wore down and they couldn't support anything anymore.

"That was when the trouble started."

"He liked me first."

Kisses in an old stagecoach. He promised that he would never tell. It would be their secret. Just a few times, all alone. He gave them presents and held their hands. A blue brooch for you. Candlelight outside. Warm hands and warmer hearts.

"It's all your fault."

"He loved me. I know he did."

Mother kept quiet at first. Holding her tongue. She still came in to wish us good night and pleasant dreams. Cookies and milk on a silver plate.

"We were her stars."

Mother had been a singer before. She had stood on stage all aglow, lit up by the limelight. Everyone loved her. Her voice rose above the club and kept her safe. Money came in and she was given enough to live, to survive and not to leave. She met father there. In the back of the club, before the beginning of her show. While she pulled up her stockings, he came to her door with flowers and candy. She didn't like him at first. No sir. He wasn't looking for a good girl. He wanted someone who drank Gin and cursed. She wanted to get married and stay a good girl.

"He forced her into it."

"No, he didn't. Our father was a good father, a kind father."

"You only think that because he gave you her brooch."

Rip, Trim. When mother had loved them, she made them new clothes. The sewing machine would go all day long. Pitter. Patter. Her foot would pump against the seams. Father would play. He would hold them down. He would push and pull. Staring into the walls, they could see father swaying there waiting for them to come and cut him down.

"Hold his feet."

"No. You hold his feet. I'll hold his head."

"You're not strong enough for that."

"I'm stronger than you are."

They set him down on the hard wood floor. Mother asked that he be placed face down. She didn't want to see the smile on his face. They clutched together. Listening to mother. It was all their fault. They had driven him to it. If it hadn't been for the baby, he would be alive. They seduced him. They held him down and forced him. He had always been a weak man. They swayed against the force of her words. Their small hands grasping. Rubbing her stomach, she wondered when the baby would come. But, mother had another idea.

Slitting. Snipping. Mother took their hands and led them outside. Where everyone would laugh. Where everyone would stare. It had happened once before. Father had wished for them to go to school. They needed to leave the house. They needed to interact with children their own age. Mother tried to warn him. She tried to stop him, but he pushed until she was tired and she gave up.

He took them one morning. It was dawn when they rose. Mother made them pancakes with maple syrup. It ran down her lips and into the corners of her mouth. She licked them clean. They dressed well that morning. Yellow dresses with their brown shoes. Hair pulled back into a loose fitting ponytail that rode down her back with the spurs sticking into her spine.

Mother was supposed to go with them, but she didn't. She knew what would happen. That's why she didn't go. She knew what they would do to us. Father didn't love us. He always let them point and stare.

"Step right up folks. Step right up. Stare into the minds of horror."

They would pay their money and sit in front. Always in front. One man's mouth dropped open. One woman's heart stood still. The children were the worst. They would laugh and throw stones. But, father always let them stay. Once a boy snuck into the tent. He threw stones at our heads and caught me in the eye. We tried to push him out. We tried to tell father. But, he was collecting more money. Mother had left us alone. She could never go to our shows. She only went once.

Nip, Insert. She stood with us on stage remember. She held your hand. She bowed with us afterwards. I thought she liked being with us on stage. I went to go tell her we liked her too. She was crying so hard. I never saw her cry like that before. Father told me that she cried all night. She only cried like that one time before.

"When was that?"

"When she found out she was pregnant."

Mother didn't tell anyone. She went to the doctor in secret. She had always been a good girl. No one must know. No one knew until the end. When the doctor told her she cried. Father was there. Father held her hand and bought her flowers. They were blue. She took those flowers and had them dried. He took them to a jeweler and made them into the brooch.

"Why do you still wear that thing?"

"It reminds me of father."

"You know he never loved you."

She married him that week and decided to have us. The doctors told her that we might not live. But, they were wrong. Accept, you came out backwards. No, I came out forwards. I'm older. No, you're younger. We came to this house that very day. Father bought it and placed all of mother's things inside as a surprise.

"He loved her."

"No, he didn't. He loved me."

They were happy for a little while. Remember our room. Pink with ribbons and bows and little heart shaped flowers. Things were simple then. Mother would braid our hair and put it into ringlets. I would lie in the sun when we were younger and curl my hair on the tip of my finger. No one saw us. Yes, no one saw us. Until father needed money. So, he went to the circus. But, they wouldn't take us. So, he went to Mr. Richards. Mr. Richards took us in. He made us a part of the family; a part of the act. Mother was so angry. But, father told her that they needed the money. So, she went along with him. She agreed. I was scared at first. The stage was small and close to the strangers.

"I was never scared."

"Yes, you were."

"No, I wasn't. I was brave. I made father proud."

Carve. Chop. Remember the dog. I remember. She was curly with a fluffy tail. You let her get into trouble. You let her eat the candy. It wasn't candy that she ate. Molly ate the poison. The poison that mother wanted to feed to us? Yes. That poison. Mother was so mad. She found out about father, about the baby and she couldn't stand us. Molly was so cute. Father found her for us. On Christmas Eve. No one wanted her, so he took her home and we fed her turkey and ham with warm bread and gravy. She was brown with large and deep brown eyes. She smelled like honey. We would play with her when she was younger. She would run across our beds and try to grab our pillows in her mouth. Before the baby came, mother would play with us. Before, the baby came, father was alive. He would run circles with us in the garden and no one would know. I would hug him and hold Molly and we would kiss her together and she would lick our hands. On long summer days, I would play with her and hold her in the grass. I loved her.

"More than you loved father?"

"More than I loved father."

"She never let anyone hurt us."

"She never left us alone."

When did mother buy the poison? One day, old Dr. Wallace. Her doctor when she was pregnant took her by the arm and she told him everything. She told him about father. She told him about how we played and of Mr. Richards and the stones. He tucked the poison in the palm of her hand. She took it from him. Mother never loved us.

"Yes, she did."

"She tried to kill us. Twice."

"But, she was desperate."

That night she made us soup. Our favorite; chicken with noodles. Your stomach had grown by then and everyone could tell. I could tell. Mother could tell. Molly could tell. Having had litters of her own puppies, Molly would sleep with you at might and rub her small face into your pillow. Do you remember the puppies? Until father took them away. I would hold them and throw them up in the air and catch them again. We would play with them every day. Then, father sold them to Mr. Richards. We never saw them again.

The soup was served with bread. Fresh from the oven with patterns of butter heavy and glossy. But, I wasn't hungry. And neither was I. Molly licked the bowls clean and died in the middle of the night. I was the one to find her. Alone in the corner with her tongue sticking out cold and blue. Mother wanted us to be alone in the corner with our tongues sticking out cold and blue. She never loved us. She was afraid.

The house pierced through the cold rain. It sat overhanging the town lonely. Its arms, its trees pushed up to the stars. Inside there was no light. Only steel. The children were so hateful. Yes, they spit on us and smiled. Like father smiled? Yes, like father smiled. Down against the hill no one thought of them anymore. Most guessed that they were dead. Then, mother got the gun. She buried Molly in the ground beneath the old chestnut tree which no longer produced. She buried her there and didn't even allow us to put up a cross. Pulling us inside, remember? Up the stairs and into our rooms. She made us get down on the floor. I ripped my dress and tore my stocking. She made us close our eyes, and then the gun. The noise! It was so loud! The baby pushed against my stomach. She knew. It heard the shot. We took mother to our garden. She was heavy, so we dragged her by her feet. The blood sifted out, like powered sugar on French toast. We buried her next to Molly. We buried her without a cross.

Pierce. Mark. We kept father. He turned blue. We held him at night when we grew cold. No one came back to the house. Mr. Richards never came back. Dr. Wallace never asked mother if it worked. We were alone. I changed father's clothes. I shaved him and trimmed his beard. When the baby came, he was there. I pushed so hard. I thought that the whole village would hear me. I thought that they would come running. But, no one did. Her head came out first. She was blue and cold. I held her hand and watched her open her eyes. Then, she closed them once again. We took her and placed her next to father. We placed her in his arms.

Kerf. Groove. It was then that I came to hate you. I knew that you had taken my baby's life. You were responsible. I could hear you plotting against me through the walls. I could feel you breathing on me when we slept. You would never leave me alone, even when I wanted to be with father. It was always you. You. Who got in the way. I could have had a family. A family of my very own. Father would have had another act. My daughter and I.

"Step right up folks. Step right up. See the amazing Samantha and our daughter."

We could have ridden horses and eaten waffle cones for desert. We could have been happy, but you kept everything from me. I could feel you watching me while father gave me my brooch.

"It wasn't his brooch to give."

Where I would walk, I would hear your footsteps clamoring behind me. I could see your face in my mirror. You never left me alone. Father told me. He would whisper again into my ear. He told me that you were the one. You were the one that caused all of our trouble. Mother and you.

"Mother loved us."

"Mother was afraid."

"I am afraid."

"You should be."

The house held them inside. Father lay against the floor. His eyes to the wood grain. Do you remember our first love? Do you remember Tommy? He wasn't like father. He was tall and long. His legs were lean. His eyes were wide and blue. The fine blonde ambers of his hair would glisten in the wind. Tommy Richards. Mr. Richards's son. But, he didn't love us. No, he didn't love you. You with your big eyes, all shiny and new. You with your freckled face. I waited for him and he never came. He was supposed to meet me down by the river before the baby was born. He said he loved me.

"He lied. Don't you see that now!"

"You're the liar. You're the one that told father."

"I didn't mean to, but he had to know. He had to know that he was going to be her father too."

I walked the river with my belly exposed and felt the cool rush of air hit against her and he never came. Tommy and I kissed once. We stood behind the racks at the show and our lips met. His were thick and rough, like callused knuckles against my skin. I held him a long time until Mr. Richards saw us. His eyes turned flame red. He turned on a dime and pulled us apart. I screamed and father came running. It was the only time that he tried to protect me. Mr. Richards told father what he had seen. What everyone knew. Father was angry. I was only to be his. He wanted Tommy to go away. But, I loved them both. Tommy promised to take me away. But, you ended all of that talk.

Nip. Prick. Father yelled at me. He told me that I didn't love him. He told me that Tommy didn't love me. He yelled loud enough for mother to hear. Mother knew about the blue brooch. She saw him give it to me. She knew everything soon enough. Father wasn't quiet. That was when you told him. We had been to Dr. Wallace a few days ago to check on your spine. You were having pain and I wanted to make sure that you were all right. The pain was causing you to become dizzy.

"I didn't tell father."

"Yes, you did."

"No, I didn't. Dr. Wallace did. Mother did. I didn't."

"Blame everyone else. That's just like you."

"Don't take responsibility for your actions."

"But, you don't know. I promise. I'm not lying."

Your spine was curving. It was making an uneven circle. Dr. Wallace checked us. He checked you and then me. He found out. He told us. I was scared, but you said . . .

"We'll get rid of it. We'll bury it under the chestnut tree. Father will never know. Mother will never find out. We'll keep it a secret."

So, we went home. But, Mother knew.

"Dr. Wallace told her. See. See."

"No, she knew because she was a woman. She knew because she had once been pregnant too. She knew because she was our mother. A mother."

So, she asked us and we denied. We told her that she was wrong. We told her that father was in the right. We told her that nothing ever happened and that she was mistaken. She yelled back. Right in our faces. She told us that we were the liars. That we were the mistakes. She went to father. Father cried. He told us he couldn't deal with another birth, another show. He told us that he hated us and that he used us only for money.

"So, maybe you didn't tell her. But, you were a problem, the problem for me. For me and father. For me and Tommy. For me and the baby. You got in the way of everything."

Father was quiet after that day. He didn't talk to us. He didn't talk to mother. Mother gave us treats and treated us like children, but I wasn't a child anymore.

"She was only trying to protect you."

"Well, she was too late."

"She wanted the best for us."

"No, she didn't. She wanted us dead. Father told me."

When mother discovered she was pregnant with us, she sat in a warm tub for hours. Lathering up with soap and lavender, she took a long hanger and stabbed deep up inside until she saw red. Father found her. He pounded open the door. He fished her out of the water and took her to Dr. Wallace. He saved her and us.

"What if we shouldn't have been saved?"

"What if we shouldn't have been saved? Do you think that we should have died?"

"Maybe."

"Well, maybe you should have died and then I could have lived."

"Not without me you wouldn't."

Slash. Section. The rain stopped. A cold and harsh wind blew through the house, as if they were lost at sea—a ship without an anchor. Father spoke from upstairs. He spoke in a language that only

I could hear. He demanded for justice. He didn't want to die without a reason. He kept me safe and held my hand as I cut. He tried to keep me steady as mother crept along the floorboards, holding the baby while Molly danced at their sides. Mother slid without using her legs now. A hole in the back of her head where her brain would have been gooey and black and set with clotted blood. Molly held up by mother. Her hands stuck through rotted fur and flesh, blue and bulging. Molly's eyes were sliding around in her sockets now. Mother's jaw was loose. Some of her teeth were missing. Perhaps they were under the chestnut tree and all the while I kept hearing Mr. Richards go on and on and on in high and great booms.

"Step Right Up Folks!!! Step Right Up!!! See the freaks of nature. Pay a dollar and see it all!!!"

They threw rocks at our heads and most of the time, fruit. Father would sell rotten apples in the tent. Mr. Richards thought that it was a good idea. The apples would leave bruises on my face. I would look over and see the apples hit you too. Shards of white and yellow, like a gun shot flying through space. It would hit you, hit us, and we would buckle. Down we went. Like the first day of school, when Michael Buckman attacked us. Then, everyone else followed. I only knew his name from the teacher. She called him that when he got into trouble. For the first hour, all I heard was his full name as the teacher put check marks on the board. One mark, you're warned. Two marks, you have extra homework. Three marks, you go to the principle. During recess, he turned on us. We stuck out. We were different. He hit you first. He swung at me and missed. You fell down. I fell down and then they all started. They kicked and hit and tore and bit. They pulled your hair.

"I thought that we were going to die."

"I knew that father would save us."

"Father didn't always save us. It was mother that time."

Mother had been watching. She saw him knock you down. She saw me fall too. She ran over and pushed him down. She protected us and pulled him by his long hair.

"She protected us when father didn't."

We never went back to school after that day. Father kept us at home. Lessons at home were fun. Mr. Richards told father that he didn't see why we needed an education, but father ignored him. Everyday, we went to school in the garden. We learned our alphabet. We learned to read. I learned to sew. Father even told us how to gut a fish and where to slide the knife.

"Mother never taught us anything. She tired of us and tried to kill us."

"But, father never protected us. He never protected you."

Father's corpse spoke upstairs. It told her that she was a liar. It told her that he loved her and that he would never leave her. She could feel him dancing on the floor above, his feet pounding out the waltz. They used to dance, all of the time. Sometimes, mother would watch. Sometimes, she would wear the blue brooch with her hair down long.

Stab. Slot. Even now, she didn't need her. She and father would do fine without her. Long cuts. Short cuts. She winced in pain at the slight of the blood, but sooner or later she would be finished. Sooner or later they would be separated. She pulled at her sister, her conjoined twin and tried to remove her like a slab of beef. But, she wouldn't budge. The blood poured out. She tried to push it back inside. She tried to lap it up, to swallow it whole but she couldn't get it quick enough. Stitch. I'll stitch us back up. Slowly, Samantha wiggled down on the floor. Blood poured now. I can make it to the sewing room. Everything will be all right. Her other half was silent now. Their spine semi-fused, semi-broken held together by mire strips of skin pulled to and fro and set itself up and down. The sewing machine was in her sight. She was the strong one. She could do it. It was her that father had loved, not Amanda. She pulled herself up to the seat, blood coating every strand of fabric. She held her sister up and tried to thread the needle. Her eyesight was dimming. She was becoming cold. Just one more stitch. I can do this. I am the stronger one. She stitched again and again until the room went numb. Her hands collapsed at her sides, and she fell from the chair against her sister's side.

"They can bury us underneath the chestnut tree. Right next to mother. Right next to Molly. And father will join us soon."

"Step right up folks! Step right up!!! See the amazing Willow twins joined at the bottom of their spine from birth. Freaks of nature!!! Step right up folks!!! Step right up!!!"

The Sadistic Chessboard

NADIA BOULBERHANE

IT **ALMOST LOOKED** out of place in the red-carpeted dining room, as she entered "Chez Alain," the most over-priced French restaurant in the city. Her black stiletto heels made a strong imprint in the carpet, and her matching black Vera Wang dress with a slit just above knee looked too dark for the events of the night. The tables were wooden and painted black all coated with white table cloths over the top.

A man in a white shirt with a black vest and bow tie approached her. She was wearing the stilettos, so she appeared taller than him, but the heels were the only reason.

"Bon soir madame," he approached her. "Do you have a reservation for this evening?"

"I'm meeting someone," she replied to the host.

"Yes, and the name of your party?" He furthered.

"MacAvoy," she said clearly.

"Certainly," the host went on smiling. "You are Madame Anderson?"

"Yes," she replied as plainly as possible.

"Right this way," he smiled all the while.

For fraction of a microsecond, she almost thought that the host might have been staring at the v-line on her black dress, but there were other things floating around in the universe of her mind that superseded a simple "check out" from a man with an excellent French accent.

Tara Anderson followed the host down the beautiful red carpet and through the ocean of white table cloths. Then, they made a left turn, and they climbed a small set of stairs, also coated in the luxurious red.

Once they approached the top, the moonlight sky awaited them, and they were standing upon the grounds of a terrace. The rooftop of Chez Allain served as a private dining area. There was only one single table surrounded by a pattern of patio stones.

Tara felt the cold breeze slap her in the face, and she felt it was too cold to dine outside. However, once again, there were other ideas and motivations for the night that didn't involve the forecast. The table on the terrace didn't have a white cloth. Instead, it was just an elegant blackwood, and the man that sat at the table wore a black Brooks Brothers with a light blue button up shirt and no tie.

"Voila Madame," the host said. "Your server will be right with you."

He made a simple gesture and Miss Anderson took her seat. The man across from her with his dark hair, tanned skin, and very light beard cracked a smile that was almost too wide.

"Why did you choose the name MacAvoy this time?" She asked.

"It sounds so innocent," he almost gloated. "It reminds me of a character from a folk song. It's the same with the blue shirt. It just feels so harmless"

"No," Miss Anderson turned down the idea. "I didn't come here tonight to talk about the colors of your wardrobe. You know why I am here, and I don't want to waste any time."

"Well, we have to eat first," MacAvoy hummed. "I took the pleasure of ordering. It was so difficult to select the wine. I wasn't sure if I should go with the Milbrandt Cabernet Sauvingon, which looked dreadfully in poor taste, should I go with the Bordeaux Letoure, second most expensive one on the list. However, the real clincher was when I saw they carry Layer Cake wine . . . Layer Cake. I just love the sound of that. It sounds so indulgent and appealing. It's almost like a surprise and an adventure in the labeling department. I have to warn you it's very economical, and I take no shame in saying that; it's just I don't want to alarm you with any surprises. I also had the pleasure of ordering dessert. The server wasn't too happy when I told him we were only staying for dessert, well just wine and dessert, but he can always find some other form of employment. I ordered the Grenoble raspberry mousse cake for two . . . "

"Hey . . . MacAvoy or whatever . . . " She cut him off. "I am not here to talk about cheap wine, and I am not here to eat."

"Well, it's part of the game," MacAvoy insisted. His face fell flat and devoid of emotion.

"You know exactly why I'm here," she snarled.

"Well, I don't exactly appreciate your tone Miss Anderson," he spoke slowly and precisely. "Oh, look our server is here. That's what happens when you order ahead."

Miss Anderson could feel the sense of discomfort and the sense of annoyance piling up at her. She stared at MacAvoy, and as he put on a show for the server; his face almost glittered. Before she knew it, there were two plates in front of them and two glasses of wine poured. It felt like a blink, but that's how the mind worked when it was preoccupied.

"What are you waiting for?" MacAvoy returned to his flat tone of voice. "Eat."

"I told you. I'm not here to eat," Miss Anderson snapped at him again. "I am not here to drink wine. I am here to . . . "

"Eat it because I told you to," his voice remained lifeless, but he raised it a little. "Please and thank you of course."

She stared at him, and their eyes locked. Neither one wanted to turn away. Then, she grabbed the fork next to her, and stared down at the mousse cake.

"Stop," he ordered.

She obeyed.

"With your hands," he directed her.

"No," she replied. "Stop wasting my time. There is no point to any of this."

"There is a point," MacAvoy orated. "You know just as well as I do that if you don't play, you lose. You don't even know what's at stake, so you have to play. If you are going to play, you'll have to do what I say. If you walk away, you'll never know what's at stake, and you'll not be able to play. Then, you will lose."

"I understand all that," she said sincerely, "but you can do better than this. Are you a demon, or are you not?"

Miss Anderson almost expected MacAvoy to sound offended as she called him by what he really was. However, he sat contently like a gargoyle statue. It wasn't the first time she had a dinner date with this demon, but she hoped it would be the last.

"I don't always love a challenge," MacAvoy explained. "In fact, most times it's annoying. I'm impressed so far Miss Anderson. I mean that honestly . . . well, as honestly as a demon can be. I've dealt with mathematicians, astrophysicists, even strategic analysts for the military, and none of them ever prove to be any fun. They also always lose, yet somehow a New York City accountant and stock trader outwits them all, and knows exactly how to appeal to me. After our last encounter ended in a draw, you've seen what I can do. Well, you've seen part of what I can do. A demon can always do a little more than what the human knows. Do you even know what demons are Miss Anderson?"

"Tell me what's at stake," she stated. "Mr. MacAvoy, it's not every day that a demon challenges me to a battle of wits, but I have to confess that I could not care less about your personal . . . or demonic characteristics. I don't care about eating cake. Tell me why I am here."

"I already have." He shouted. "You were a little slow this time Miss Anderson. I have made it clearer than day. If you wanted to know what you're playing for, what you seek to win, or more specifically what you stand to lose, you have to obey me. With that being said, I was going to give you a small easy task, such as nothing more than eating a piece of cake. What is the human saying? Starting small?"

"I understand that MacAvoy," she said, "but if I have you . . . starting small . . . then, you will keep me here all night, constantly adding on tasks and challenges and minute details to distract me from knowing even what I'm supposed to do."

"Fascinating," he licked his own teeth. "I feel almost duped. Whatever shall I do? I was going to go easy on you, but you've declined."

His eyes made contact with hers.

She tensed, and he noticed.

"What shall I have you do then?" He asked. "Disrobe yourself? Walk along the terrace in the nude?"

Her lips formed into a flat line.

"Perhaps, I shall tell you to sit perfectly still, and that's it," his voice didn't indicate if he enjoyed it too much, or not at all.

He laughed at his own comment. Then, he rose from the table and slowly walked toward her, making sure he made eye contact.

"Stay still," he gloated.

His dark tanned fingers ran along the skin of her neck. Then, with the outside of his fingers he stroked her cheek. There was no point in hiding that he enjoyed the sight of her cringing and startling, and as he ran his fingers lower, he decided to run just to edge of her bra line.

"You're the one who is going to do it for me," he decided at last. "Remember, if you don't play, you lose. Now, show me your breasts."

MacAvoy walked back around to his seat at the table, and he waited for his opponent to make her move. MacAvoy seemed content.

Miss Anderson could see he had made up his mind. Her body felt cold, and it wasn't because of the outside air. She gazed around at the rooftop, and then, she gazed at him. Was anybody watching? Would anybody see?

There was a small trickling of drool at the side of his lips, and she could only guess that it wasn't about human anatomy. It was about embarrassment. He was fantasizing about her discomfort, not her nudity.

Miss Anderson's face relaxed, and she reached into her purse, removed a blue ink pen. On the palm of her hand, she scribbled.

"Your Breasts"

The writing was smudged and crooked on her skin, but the demon in human form sitting across from her understood the message.

"You said show me your breasts," she began, "and there you have it . . . I have shown you 'your breasts.' What do you think? Do you like them? Perky? Firm? Now tell me what I'm playing for."

"A girl," MacAvoy replied.

"How old is she?" Miss Anderson asked on instinct.

"17," MacAvoy answered.

"What do you want with her?" Miss Anderson asked.

"If you lose, she loses," MacAvoy laid out directly.

Miss Anderson bit her lip.

"What does that mean?" She demanded.

"You and I are going to play the game," MacAvoy announced. "After all, we've already begun. If you win, nothing happens, but if you lose, and there is a high possibility that you will lose, things will not go nicely for this 17-year-old girl."

Miss Anderson felt the blood turn hot.

"Stop drawing out all your sentences and tell me straightly," she spat at MacAvoy. "Are you going to kill her or not?"

"Every time, every single unforgettable time," MacAvoy grumbled. "Why do you think it's death that one plays for? There is no point to play for death. Why play for it? Miss Anderson, I'd expect more out of you. You should know that the death of a person is going to happen no matter how many games you win, and no matter how many games you lose. Winners die. Losers die. All humans will die, but if you had something that was worth avoiding until death, wouldn't that be worth playing for? Wouldn't that be worth winning?"

Miss Anderson waited.

"She's 17," MacAvoy repeated. "She's a virgin. By your standards, most would say she's gorgeous. She has that curvaceous figure, large breasts, golden blonde hair, thick red lips, intelligence, and early admission to Princeton University, which I am not sure why that's so appealing to the male audience, but it seems to make the lads go wild. See Miss Anderson, if you lose tonight, this girl is going to get raped."

Miss Anderson waited again. She forced herself to listen.

"I am going to rape her myself," MacAvoy continued with a smile. "Some say demons are beings of evil. Some say demons are beings that are made of fire. Some say demons are made of all the dark feelings: sins, and hatred in the world that every person fears. Imagine if they were all true Miss Anderson. Imagine how much a demon can do, how much pain this little blonde virgin will feel . . . and that's just before I'll rip her breasts from her body with my teeth . . . and you thought it was death? Death is nothing compared to misery in life."

Miss Anderson wished she could just sit there like MacAvoy and have an emotionless and untainted view of the game, but she had played once before, and MacAvoy, using another name, and her had ended in a draw. She had no choice but to play, for if she didn't, MacAvoy would do the things he had described.

She had to win.

"Who is this girl?" Miss Anderson asked.

"Are you serious?" MacAvoy shouted.

"Who is she?" Miss Anderson restated.

"I'll never understand how humans think," MacAvoy avoided the nature of the question once again. "She's a girl. She's a human being. She has type o negative blood. There's nothing else you need to know. Well, there is nothing else I will let you know to be more specific. You see, when you lose Miss Anderson, this girl is going to feel more pain than anyone you've ever known and all because of you. It has nothing to do with her. She isn't here right now. The only thing that matters is that look on your face. It's about those little quivers on your cheek. You lose. She suffers, yet she hasn't suffered yet, and you suffer now. My my."

Miss Anderson had to play.

"Make your move Mr. MacAvoy," she continued the game.

"Think of this as a game of chess," MacAvoy unraveled. "You have three moves to put the king in checkmate. You like the stock market, and you're an accountant. You like numbers. You know numbers. Well, I'm thinking of a number. You have three moves to get the number. If you don't get the number in three moves or less, you lose. The girl loses too."

"What's the range?" Miss Anderson jumped on instinct.

"Between one and unlimited," MacAvoy answered with a laugh. "Silly goose, that'd be too easy."

Miss Anderson had to think. She had to think. MacAvoy had been right. Her teeth were grinding together against her lips. She had solved so many equations in her life. She could calculate her accounting formulas with the slightest of ease, but they had structure. They had order. This was just complexity and chaos. It could literally be any number. Was MacAvoy leaving this up to chance?

Of course he wasn't. MacAvoy was demonic, but he was also looking for an opponent. He wanted to relish the victory of a challenge, and he had openly said Miss Anderson had come closer than anyone else. There had to have been clues. She remembered if she thought out loud, MacAvoy might give away some kind of a signal.

"I walked up to the terrace," she began to ramble. "There are two chairs and one table, that's three. The server came with two glasses of wine, and two desserts. 3 + 4, 7.

That's it. Lucky Number Seven. It's seven."

"Incorrect," MacAvoy shot her down. "Two more moves Miss Anderson."

"Too simple," Miss Anderson mumbled along. "Of course, you wouldn't do something regarding observational materials. You're a sadistic freak. You want to do something ridiculous. You knew you couldn't pick something as simple as seven. You are not going to go for something complicated such as 486,234."

"Is that an answer?" MacAvoy teased.

"No!" She roared back. "It's obvious, but not superficially obvious. It's simple, but it wears a complex face. It's essential, but it's often ignored. It's famous, yet it's overlooked."

Her face lit up.

"It's Pi," she deduced. "3.14159265 . . . "

"Incorrect again," MacAvoy cut her off before she could continue the sequence. "Poor little blondie. However, I am so curious what her skin tastes like . . . especially below the waist. Want to give me another number, so I can go interrupt her slumber?"

Miss Anderson ignored MacAvoy's laugh. She had blown it. What had she been doing? She had been absolutely idiotic, two numbers both between 1 and 10. It didn't take a mathlete to understand that probability was not on her side with that. There was only one more move.

She had to think, but all that was on her mind was the girl. She couldn't put a face on her, but she was imagining the blonde hair, the soft body, a smile. This couldn't happen. She couldn't let this happen.

Why couldn't she think of numbers?

"You're a demon," Miss Anderson restated.

"Clearly."

"You're a demon," she said again. "I was right. You're trying to nail me with the obvious, and you're trying to humiliate me. You know I care about the girl, but you don't care about the girl. You just want me to be wrong. You'll do almost anything for me to be wrong."

The muscles on her face began to feel a slight feeling of excitement.

"You are a demon," she said once again. "You think you're superior to me in all forms of intelligence, and I know you're just toying with me now, but there is a specific number I'm supposed to find. You wanted something that would embarrass me. You wanted something that would humiliate me and make me bear the guilt for the rest of my life, but you are a demon. You don't play by human rules. You don't play by any substantial rules. You even set this up. A number between one and unlimited, there are no real parameters. There are no real rules. You knew that there were no real rules, and you didn't have a specific number in mind once I started the game. Therefore, you were going to take one of my previous wrong answers and make it the correct answer on my third guess. You were going to say that I was wrong because the first two times the correct answer would have been 'undetermined.' It is only upon my third response that there is a single precise answer. You would have picked seven or you would have picked Pi, but in fact, you made one small error MacAvoy, or whatever you choose to call yourself. I kept talking, and you kept listening. You still wanted to embarrass me. You still wanted me to lose, but you made the smallest mistake once you entered into a world of rules and parameters. Mr. MacAvoy, I guessed two numbers seven and Pi, but you have picked a different number. I complicated your equation. You wanted to taunt me just a little more. I said 486,234. Then, you asked me 'is that your answer?' I replied 'no.' You wanted to find the one that would nerve me the most. As soon as I said no, you chose that as the number. I've got you MacAvoy. Yes, that's my answer. The number you had chosen out of all infinity is 486,234."

She paused to take a breath. The feeling was exhilarating. She had to be right. It all made sense. It fit the motive, and it fit MacAvoy's game. She knew it. She had done it.   MacAvoy was silent, and his eyes were wide, but once again, Miss Anderson couldn't get a clear read.

"Well?" She barked. "Was I right? I was right. I knew what you were doing."

MacAvoy continued his silence

"Say something," Miss Anderson demanded. "What was the number? What was the number?!? Was I right?"

MacAvoy leaned forward, and he picked up his glass of Layer Cake wine, and he swallowed it down. His lips came together in a slight puckering motion. Then, MacAvoy rose from the terrace table on the rooftop of Chez Allain, and he headed for the door, which lead back down to the red carpeted dining room and the ocean of white tablecloths.

"What are you doing?" Miss Anderson shrieked. "Where are you going? Say something. Was I right? Tell me the answer. Tell it to me. Was I right?"

MacAvoy stopped in his tracks, and he turned around and faced Miss Anderson with that ugly, arrogant, distasteful smirk on his face.

"Yet look, now you've forgotten all about the girl," he called to her. "Goodnight Miss Anderson."

"Was I right?" Miss Anderson shouted back. "Was I right? Was I right?"

"Maybe," he said. "We'll see."

Then, he walked away.

The Hangar

MELISSA CLARE WRIGHT

NORA WALKED ALONG the train tracks, seeing how long she could balance on one rail. She'd rushed along the first section of tracks, hoping no one would warn her off them, and most of the town was far behind her now. Out here the area was industrial, large warehouses and factories scattered on her left, fallow fields protected by low strings of rusting barbed wire on the right.

If she turned around, the tracks would lead through town and out west. Last summer Nora and her best friend, Jessie, had walked as far as they could out that way. In the trees bordering the tracks, they'd seen beer bottles and the ashes of former fire pits, and they'd made up stories of who might be living out in the wilderness, what they might be up to. The girls walked so far and paid so little attention to the time that they'd had to call Jessie's mom to come get them when they realized they wouldn't be able to retrace their steps before dark. Jessie's mom had looked momentarily stern, then laughed. Nora hadn't told her parents about the expedition at all.

Last summer, Jessie had seemed as into their exploration as Nora was. Together they walked forgotten roads and trekked through neglected woodlands, trying to uncover all the secret corners of their town. This summer Jessie usually wanted to go to the mall instead. And today, she'd point-blank refused to come.

Nora stared at the shiny metal of the rail under her sneakers and wondered what Jessie was doing right now. Maybe making out with that long-haired bozo outside the mall. It was much better to be here, outside in the sun, going somewhere you'd never been, maybe about to find something exciting. Nora was almost glad Jessie wasn't with her. Jessie spent a lot of her time these days yapping about the other people they knew, or talking about what high school would be like. Nora didn't look forward to high school. She looked forward to whatever comes after.

The tracks curved east up ahead, through a scraggly stand of thin trees that had somehow escaped the farmer's clearing on one side and the industrial encroachment on the other. Nora liked the bends the best, when the forests and hills hid what came next along the route. The factories and buildings to the east didn't continue this far, and Nora hoped the trees would screen the train tracks from the fields, although from the looks of things no one really plowed or worked out here anymore.

Nora stopped where the trees bracketed the tracks and raised her face to the hot sunshine. She closed her eyes and inhaled. This was escape. It was quiet, like the end of the world.

When she opened her eyes and lowered her gaze, she could see beyond the edge of the residual forest. There was a building on the left, partially screened by trees. She hadn't noticed it before.

"Fuck." Nora, though genuinely annoyed, savored the flavor of the illicit word in her mouth. Jessie would have rolled her eyes at the obscenity, but Jessie wasn't here. What was here was a big fat building that looked like an airplane hangar.

Nora continued up the tracks toward the building. Maybe it was abandoned.

It sure *looked* abandoned, she noted as the whole of the structure came into sight. It was maybe fifty feet from the railway tracks, and not quite big enough to house full-sized airplanes, the type Nora took when her parents sent her off to visit her grandparents. But it was big. The rounded roof, like half a cylinder laid on its side, looked like it was made of some kind of metal, but the sides were crappy wood and cinderblock. Everything was painted a kind of faded beige, dirty and chipped in places. The end closest to Nora had several multi-paned windows, high up underneath the curving roof line. The wall below the windows was twenty feet or more of empty beige paint. One lengthwise side of the building was also visible. Here, several windows nearer to ground level had been covered over with plywood; only their upper portions remained unobstructed. A small wood door and a larger, newer looking garage-style door of metal sealed the entrances to the decrepit building. There were no other buildings nearby.

Nora moved off the track and through the brush that divided the old hangar from the rails.

The ground sloped downward into a gulley that ran between the railway tracks and the cracked and blasted asphalt that must have once served as a parking lot for the abandoned structure. The gulley was choked with weeds taller than Nora, but most of them cracked and broke as she passed, cloaking her in their fuzzy, clinging seeds. In the spring, she'd have been ankle or even knee-deep in mud, but now everything was dry and dusty. She climbed the farther, lower slope to the level of the parking lot. The asphalt was so cracked that in some places it was broken into fist-sized chunks, and in others, small bushes had pushed their way through to the sky. Most of the bushes appeared dead; the hot, dry summer had baked them in place, their scrawny roots not strong enough to pull nutrients from below the manufactured surface.

Nora stepped out of the underbrush and onto the warped pavement, looking up at the looming structure as she did. The afternoon sun hit the remaining glass in the multi-paned windows and reflected back at her. The building looked blind and somehow angry in the glare, and Nora hesitated. As she stood, transfixed, wondering if the building would notice her when the sun left its eyes, she registered the sound of an approaching car.

"Shit-tastic," she muttered watching the puff of dust advance toward the hangar. She wasn't sure if she was trespassing, but Nora didn't want to run into *anyone* way the hell out here. She melted back into the weedy ditch, flattening herself onto her stomach so she could watch unseen.

The vehicle, an old Ford pickup, arrived in a plume of dust and foul-smelling smoke. The thump of the local 'modern rock' radio station—which insisted on playing Nirvana constantly, as though Kurt had died just yesterday—poured out the windows then halted abruptly as the driver cut the engine.

Voices rose over each other, an unintelligible teenage cacophony. It seemed to be all guys in the pickup, four or five, although Nora couldn't see for sure.

The driver's door opened and a slim boy in jeans and a t-shirt emerged, his voice rising over the babble. "I think there's something really frying under here."

He walked to the front of the truck and leaned over the hood, sniffing the air. His pals, three of them, tumbled out of the truck.

"Why does Doug always get shotgun?" one of them complained, stretching.

"Because you're the runt," said a blond-haired boy, who'd emerged from the front passenger seat.

"Because Adam is secretly in love with him," said a lanky boy in a Cubs hat as he pulled himself out from behind the blond.

The blond—Doug, Nora presumed—gave the boy a whack on the back of his head, knocking the cap off into the dirt. "And because you're the runt," the boy said, stooping to pick up the hat.

The three passengers made their way toward the building. They seemed to scan it, top to bottom, left to right, as they approached. Like they were planning an assault.

Doug-the-blond tried the handle of the wooden door. He said something to his companions, but he was too far away for Nora to hear. They took turns throwing their shoulders against the door, like cops in a TV show, but it must have been more solid than it looked. They gave up after a couple of tries.

Closer by, the driver, Adam, popped the hood on the truck and bent over it. He held one hand by his waist and used the other to poke at the truck's insides. Every now and then he glanced up at his friends, one of whom was now stomping his foot against the wood door.

"Hey Ad-man," called the boy in the Cubs hat. "Leave the truck. I wanna get in here."

Adam looked up. "Smoke it outside, asshole. There's something wrong with my truck." He held the dipstick aloft and swatted it in the direction of his friends. If he was the most mechanically inclined of the bunch, they'd be walking home.

Cubs Hat looked at his friend for a moment then pulled a tin out of his back pocket. He extracted a slim roll—cigarette or, Nora assumed, joint—from the tin and passed it to Doug, who sparked up. The boys passed the joint back and forth, inspecting the door. Suddenly Cubs Hat started to laugh.

"Mother*fucker*!"

Adam looked up. "What?"

"Get over here." Cubs handed the remains of the joint to the Runt and stepped forward.

"What?" Adam took a few steps toward the hangar and stopped. He looked up at the façade, then glanced down to his friends. Nora had the impression that he didn't really want to go closer.

"Fuckin' door opens out," Doug called to Adam.

"You guys are stupid," Adam replied, taking a step backward. Cubs and Doug took turns yanking on the door handle. Adam turned his attention back to the truck.

Doug placed a foot on the doorframe and pulled with both hands. Wood splintered and the door pulled away from the frame, sending

Doug sprawling in the dirt. Cubs and the Runt hooted with laughter, but Adam didn't look up. He stood with his head bowed, gazing into the engine compartment and not moving.

Nora scooted forward a bit on her stomach, but she was at the wrong angle to see into the building through the open door.

Doug and Cubs Hat strolled through immediately. The Runt hung back, sucking down the remains of the joint before tossing it to the shattered asphalt and turning to follow. He took one step and stopped, his head moving forward on his neck, a puzzled gesture. From the hollow depths of the building Nora heard an echoing shriek.

"Doug?" said the Runt. He moved to the doorway and stepped over the edge. "What are you do—"

It was as though someone in the building grabbed his shirt front and heaved him into the interior of the hangar. His screams mingled with those of his two friends, carrying on for several seconds after the others abruptly cut off.

Nora's body turned to stone, lying immobile in the thin underbrush. It wasn't just the screams that scared her, or even their sudden end. It was Adam, who stood stalk still at the front of the truck, his back to her and his head down. He stood that way a long time, long enough for Nora's body to melt from stone to jelly, and pain to begin prickling through her muscles as she willed them not to go to sleep.

She looked from Adam to the open door. The boys didn't emerge. Nothing crept out. Yet.

Finally Adam moved. Nora held her breath, but the boy didn't turn around. He walked slowly toward the open wooden door and stopped several feet away. Adam flicked his gaze left and right over the structure but seemed to avoid looking directly at or through the open door right in front of him. Seconds later he reached out with his fingertips and knocked the door shut. Then he raised his leg and stomped the flat of his boot against the wood, the door settling with a clunk into the splintered frame. Adam ran, weeping, back to his truck. He could have looked up and seen Nora at that moment but didn't. The hood of the truck slammed down and the engine fired up. The radio, now playing an old song by the Offspring, buzzed from the windows and faded with the cloud of dust pushed up by the vehicle's tires.

Nora waited until the sounds, both musical and mechanical, had faded and the dust was mostly settled out of the air before she climbed carefully to her feet, brushed the dirt and dry grass from her front, and approached the building.

She considered the possibility that the boys knew she was there, some middle schooler they thought it would be fun to play a trick on, but discarded the idea before it was fully formed. They'd had no time to confer. The boys arrived on this spot with the intention of going in the building—it was like they'd been here before but hadn't managed to force the door. Their entire purpose was to check out the place. Except for Adam. He seemed to know better.

There was something bad in there. Nora, at not-quite-thirteen, was halfway between the adult ability of convincing herself that everything was fine when really it wasn't, and believing that maybe there really were fairy rings in the middle of some forest outside of town. She strongly suspected there was a monster crouched inside the hangar. And she wasn't going to leave without having a look at it.

She cast a glance toward the rutted track that disappeared into the field, presumably ending at some more heavily trafficked road and a way into town. The truck was long gone and the summer afternoon was silent. The end of the hangar closest to the railroad tracks had all those multi-paned windows, but so high up she would need a crane to peer inside. Nora stepped across the cracked asphalt to the longer edge of the building. The side with the door.

The big, garage-style steel door was closest to her, but it had no cracks or windows. Nora inspected the three windows at eye-level between the garage door and the wooden door the boys had used. The plywood covering the lower two-thirds of each was free of splits or handy knot-holes. Glass showed at the top, above Nora's head, and she glanced around for something to stand on—an old tire or oil drum didn't seem unlikely—but there was nothing but dry plants and crumbling pavement.

At the wooden door, she paused. It was shut, but the wood around the latch was splintered where Doug had wrenched it apart. There was a good chance she could just open it and take a look inside. Nora reached out her hand, letting it hover over the handle. What would happen if she pulled? What if she stepped inside? As though in response, a low moan, like someone coming gradually and painfully awake, drifted to her ears. She snatched back her hand and moved past the door to the next window. This one (and the next five, marching in a row to the end of the building) was also mostly covered in plywood. But here the nails were pulled out of the frame on one side and Nora was able to dig her fingers under the edge and pull, exposing a gap. She pushed her face to the opening and looked inside.

Much of the building was hidden from her constrained angle.

What she could see was a cavernous space lit by the fading afternoon sun, which poured through the upper windows and painted squares of light on the opposite wall. The floor was a wide stretch of cement, unbroken by walls or furniture. A crumpled form, still wearing a Chicago Cubs ball hat, lay sprawled at the edge of her field of view. His body was painted with shadows, and it took Nora a moment to notice that he was missing a leg.

The moaning came from someone else, out of sight to Nora's right. The Runt pulled himself into view, his breath coming in watery sobs. He didn't seem to be able to get his knees underneath himself to crawl properly; he was using his forearms and fingers to pull his body across the floor. Nora could see something bulging and glistening from his abdomen. It left a wide, red smear across the concrete floor as he moved.

The Runt seemed to have lost track of the door. He was moving resolutely forward, but in front of him was nothing but the blank wall of the hangar. Every now and then he would look up, as though searching the sky, but Nora could make out nothing but the high metal ceiling.

The sound of the Runt's body scraping across the concrete drifted out the window, muffled only by his ragged sobs. Nora didn't hear the sound that made the Runt look back over his shoulder. The noise he made in response wasn't a scream; it was a choked cry of fear and despair. His body was jerked into the air, the bulge at his abdomen falling apart into coils and loops of red. Something held him aloft; something Nora couldn't see.

She stumbled backward from the window and fell on her back, staring at the door. The screams from inside faded away, gradually, like a voice disappearing along a tunnel, and she climbed to her feet. She stared at the plywood a moment, before creeping back up and putting her eye to the gap. The one-legged corpse lay alone on the floor, a red smear leading past him. She saw no other bodies. Nora backed away from the window and looked around. Using her fingertips she pried a chunk of asphalt from the ground and quietly edged up to the door, setting it in front, like a doorstop. It was a flimsy barricade, but it was only after placing it there that she was able to turn her back on the building and run.

***

When adults come face to face with the unexplainable, they bury the memory and convince themselves it didn't happen the way they remember. When twelve-year-old girls experience something momentous, they tell their best friends. So that's what Nora did. Maybe it was an attempt to get her friend's attention away from the long-haired boy she'd met in the mall.

Jessie 'ooh-ed' and 'ahh-ed' then giggled a bit. It was clear that she didn't really believe her. It didn't help that Nora was having a hard time putting into words what she'd seen. She found herself not really *wanting* to describe it.

"Don't laugh, Jess. There were bodies in there, I swear."

Jessie got quiet for a moment. "For real?"

"Seriously, I'm not kidding you."

"I want to see them."

Nora should have expected this. Of course Jessie would want to see for herself.

"It's pretty far along the train tracks . . . "

"We'll drive. Jay said his friend Chris just got his license."

Mall boy. Great, now it would be a field trip with Nora as tour guide.

"I don't think it's a good idea to—"

"There'll be four of us," Jessie said. She had that tone of voice that meant her mind was made up. "We'll watch each other's backs." Probably she craved the idea of something interesting happening in their boring town. Nora couldn't blame her. These things always seemed exciting until you experienced them in real life.

"There were four of them, too."

"But we'll be on our guard. It's fine. The guys will be so excited. You know, Chris said he thinks you're kind of cute. I told him you're fourteen." Jessie laughed and Nora surrendered. There was a good chance she wouldn't be able to find it from the road anyway.

But they did.

Aided by GPS and online maps, after only a few wrong turns on various dirt roads, Nora could see the building appear in the distance from her spot in the front seat.

"It looks old," said Jay from the back. "It's weird that it's not on Google maps."

Jessie grabbed the phone and poured over the images, exclaiming about how weird, how *crazy* that was. Nora ignored them, her attention on the hangar.

Away from here, she'd almost managed to convince herself she'd imagined some of it, but the sight of the building made her want to jump from the still-moving car and run back the way they'd come. This was a terrible idea.

Melissa Clare Wright

"Guys . . . really, let's just go, okay?"

Jessie and Jay paid her no attention, wrapped up in some mindless conversation of their own. Chris looked over as he pulled into the empty remains of the parking lot and cut the engine.

"So you claim some guys were murdered in there?"

Nora nodded. Jessie had given them details on the way there, spinning a lurid story of corpses strewn about inside. She made it sound like Nora had discovered the scene of a grisly murder, moments after it occurred. She also made it sound like Nora was making everything up.

"It was bad," she whispered, breaking the unwritten rule to play it cool at all times.

"Don't worry, I'll keep you safe." Chris smiled and climbed out of the car.

"Oooh . . . Look, she's so scared . . . " said Jay from the back seat. "Some crazy man in there is gonna eat us."

Jessie laughed and the two climbed out of the car, holding hands as they moved toward the building.

Nora followed. "Don't open the door," she said in a low voice, reaching out and catching Jessie by the shirtsleeve. Jessie laughed and pulled away.

"You're really nervous, aren't you?" Chris said, glancing between Nora and their friends.

She nodded.

"If there are bodies in there, we'll call the police," he said, taking her hand and pulling her toward the others, who were wandering along the building's façade, looking for a place to peer in.

"It's all boarded up," Jessie complained as they got closer.

"Right here," Nora said, indicating the loose plywood over the window nearest the wooden door. She hung back as Chris stepped forward and put his eye to the gap. Jessie and Jay crowded forward behind him.

"It's empty in there," Chris stepped back and Jay took his place. "At least the part that I can see."

"Yep, empty," confirmed Jay. He moved back for Jessie to have a look, but Nora pushed past her and peered inside.

They were right. Through the window she saw the cavernous interior of a deserted industrial building. No furniture obstructed the smooth, dusty concrete floor. No bloodstains, no bodies.

"Nice gag," Jay said, smirking at Nora. "You totally had Jess fooled."

Jessie looked at Nora reproachfully, but Nora didn't respond. Could someone have cleaned up all that mess?

"Let's go inside," said Chris. "It's a pretty cool old building." He moved to the door as he spoke, and kicked the asphalt block away from the bottom of it.

"Don't," Nora said immediately. When Chris put his hand on the door she noticed the cracked frame, the newly-exposed wood still bright. *I didn't imagine it.*

Jessie laughed, a little harshly. "Don't be a baby." When Chris opened the door, she was the first one through.

Jay and Chris were close behind, but although Chris trailed a hand out behind him for Nora, she stayed where she was, standing in the doorway, watching Jessie.

The other girl's momentum propelled her several yards beyond the door before she drifted to a standstill, looking around with her mouth slightly agape. Jay, rushing in behind her, tripped and went sprawling. Chris stepped past them both, looking around with eyes wide.

"Holy shit! Where . . . ?"

Jay looked up and around, but didn't get off the ground. "Whoa . . ."

"What do you guys see?" called Nora from the door. She wondered if they were making fun of her.

"Nora?" Jessie looked in Nora's direction, but a little past her.

Chris looked in the same direction. "Where's the door?"

"Right here," Nora said. "Some joke, guys." But she didn't move any closer.

"I don't like it here," Jessie said, almost whispering. She grabbed onto Jay, who had finally gotten to his feet beside her.

Chris was wandering off to Nora's left. "Far out . . . " she heard him mutter under his breath.

Nora stepped toward the entryway then stopped, hovering right on the border. She stepped backward again and studied their faces. Fear on Jessie's, awe and apprehension on Jay's. Chris had his back to her, but she was staring right at him when it happened.

"What the fu—" He cowered, then was jerked upward suddenly, toward the ceiling of the hangar, although caught by some invisible hook. It wasn't invisible to Jessie and Jay. Both looked up and screamed, their voices mixing into an oddly musical harmony.

Shadows wreathed the roof of the hangar, and Chris's body melted into them, vanishing from Nora's sight.

　　　　　　Melissa Clare Wright

"Oh my god, oh-my-god, ohmygod . . . " Jay was muttering, faster and faster, staring up at where Chris had disappeared. Nora could see a wet stain spreading on the front of his jeans.

"Where's the door?" Jessie was in tears. "Nora, where the fuck is the *door*?"

"Here," Nora called. "I'm right here!"

Jessie turned toward her voice and sprinted toward the door. At the last minute, Nora realized that she wasn't running directly at it. She was going to hit the door frame. Or the wall.

But she didn't. Before Nora could open her mouth, Jessie had shot past the entrance and seemed to keep on going. There was no crash, she didn't bounce off, she was just . . . gone.

"Jessie?" Nora called. "*Jessie!*"

Jay remained immobile in the middle of the room, looking up at the ceiling and muttering under his breath.

Nora moved back to the door and hesitated. She cupped her hands around her mouth again and yelled Jessie's name. There might have been a response, but it sounded faint, far away. Nora wrapped her arm around the doorframe, as though it was a dock and she was entering the water, not knowing how to swim. She stepped over the sill and into the hangar.

She was outside. The ground was unnaturally flat, like polished green-black stone, or glass. It stretched out to the horizon where the land met a poisonous-looking yellowish-green sky. In places the sight lines were broken by massive blocks that might have been buildings or solid stone, their sides washed in sickly light. Shadows lay in strange directions across the land, like lakes of black ink spilling in random directions from the base of these monoliths. In the distance spindly shapes like deformed trees slowly writhed and twisted upward into the strange, still sky.

The air held a noxious glow, not bright but so pervasive Nora found herself squinting. And the *smell* . . . Like overripe fruit and the kind of toxic chemicals that would eat you slowly from the inside out. The ground nearby was speckled with circles, increasing in size as they swirled out like a nautilus from a central point just beyond the hangar entrance. *Like a target*, Nora thought for a moment, as her mind veered and swung, unfocused and trying to make sense of this place. The circles looked manufactured, some rising as smooth cylinders and others etched into the ground. A few were holes of inky black big enough for a person to fall into. *Dots mark the spot.* Nora looked up from the weird ground, fighting the urge to run.

Jay stood only a few yards away. He had stopped muttering, but still gazed wide-eyed into the sky. Nora looked in the same direction, but it was empty. There was no sign of Chris.

Nora looked back over her shoulder, expecting to see the shining rectangle of the doorway, opening out on cracked pavement and sunshine. Instead, she saw the landscape continue on behind her. Jessie stood at a distance, her arms around her waist as she wept.

"Jessie! Here! The door is here!" As Nora called, she scanned the terrain around her friend. It was much the same as the view in the other direction, except that the sky was not empty. In the distance, tiny spots of black swept through the poisonous yellow, wings clawing the sky.

"*Jessie!*" Nora meant to yell again, but the name came out as a hiss. She tried to force her voice louder. "This way, run!"

Jessie looked up, her eyes wide. Nora looked for the doorframe again. Her arm was curled around it, and she could feel the wood pushing into the bend of her elbow. But the arm disappeared at the bend, as though sliced by a guillotine.

Beyond, Jessie broke into a stumbling run.

Nora turned. "Jay. *Jay!*"

He turned slowly and looked at her. "Did you see it?" He pointed vaguely toward the distant horizon. His hand shook so violently that he could be indicating the entire landscape. "It was . . . it got . . . "

Movement behind him pulled Nora's gaze from Jay's swaying form to one of the dark pits beyond him. If the walls of the hangar existed, if this were someone's virtual reality torture chamber, it would have been beyond the far side of the building, about ten yards from where Jay stood. Something poked its way out of the darkness. It was as thick as Nora's wrist, but knobby and came to a point. It scrabbled and clawed the smooth stone at the edge. Another followed and Nora thought at first they were the legs of a spider. Two more legs joined the first couple to scrape and click on the ground. It would have to be about the size of a cat. Then she saw the arm disappearing back into the darkness and realized she was looking at a clawed hand, ashy black, with more fingers than she wanted to count.

"Jay, come on!" Without waiting for a reply, Nora swung herself through the doorframe she could feel but not see, and stumbled backward, falling onto her back hard enough to knock her breath away.

She was out.

A sob of relief escaped her, and for seconds she looked up at the cloudless blue sky, her mind blank. She scrabbled to her hands and knees and, crouching, peered through the door. The strange landscape had vanished. Jay stood alone in the middle of the hangar, still looking vacantly toward the door.

"Jay! Jessie! Come on!" Nora cupped her hands around her mouth and screamed, but didn't put her head beyond the door. It occurred to her that something could come up behind her in there, with her head in one place and her body in another. For a moment she pictured the teenager Adam coming back and rolling her headless corpse the rest of the way through the door. He hadn't gone inside. Had he known what his friends would find? And still he didn't stop them?

Jay turned toward Nora's voice. He stepped in the direction of the door, but a noise, inaudible to Nora, pulled his attention behind him. To the hole that Nora could no longer see.

He shrieked. Nora screamed for him to run, but Jay was already in motion, charging forward, away from the hole. Like Jessie, his aim was off, and Nora, still calling to him, reached a hand beyond the doorframe, giving him something to aim for.

Jay corrected his course and reached out. For a moment their sweaty hands met and she pulled, still on her knees in the dirt. Jay's face broke through into the afternoon sunshine beyond the door and Nora saw relief flicker on his face for an instant before his eyes went wide. His body was jerked backward, and his hand slipped out of her grasp.

She reached out for him. She called. She cried. But she did not go through the door to help him. Nora watched as Jay was dragged, struggling across the concrete floor of the hangar. As he neared the opposite wall he started to fade. Shadows reached out and wrapped around his writhing body, and Nora didn't see him any more.

Jessie should have come into sight by now. She knew the direction to go. Did she see what happened to Jay, and go some other way? Nora stayed where she was for hours, calling to her friend until her voice was gone and her throat felt cracked and bloody. But Jessie never reappeared in front of the door. Eventually golden light pierced the multifaceted windows nearest the train tracks. It was late.

Nora looked left and right, pulling her eyes from the interior of the building. Her neck creaked and started to spasm. The parking lot looked still and normal in the afternoon light. She pulled herself to her feet, wincing as blood returned to needle her extremities. She sobbed occasionally as she pulled the door shut. One final look inside, but Jessie wasn't there.

Nora pulled the chunk of asphalt back across the pavement from where Chris had kicked it, and positioned it in front of the door. She knew she'd dream that night of her friend, pounding on the door, begging to be let out. But the dreams would be worse with the door left open.

Still limping from the pins and needles, Nora shuffled through the ditch and up to the train tracks. She looked back at the sedan, probably belonging to one of Chris's parents, sitting in the overgrown lot. She wondered when they would find it.

Movement pulled her attention from the car to the corner of the building. A figure, standing still in the shadows, moved into the parking lot, toward the car she was watching. It was the boy, Adam, from the day before.

He looked up at her and waved. With the setting sun in his face, she could see his smile. He seemed pleased. Grateful even. Nora turned and fled down the tracks, toward town.

Melissa Clare Wright

Orbs

CHANTAL BOUDREAU

IHAVE A secret, or maybe I should say, "eye" have a secret—heh heh. I've always enjoyed a good pun. The only way to preserve my sanity in my line of work was to find some sort of levity. Humour was one of the few things that might distract you from what you were doing. You couldn't look at what you were working on as a human being. They were a subject; your job was a matter of science and everything you pulled away from it was just pieces of an intricate puzzle—or a little round miracle from God.

I confess; I am an enucleator. I'd also call myself an oculophile, but there's nothing sexual to the attraction, just a deep-rooted love. My fascination with the orbs started long before I did what I do now. I spent twenty-five years working in the M. E.'s office and I looked into a lot of glassy-eyed stares during that time, but I was taken with eyes even before that. Several events as a child, from a scene I witnessed on a TV show where someone tossed acid in another person's face, to stumbling across a rather gruesome morsel of road kill where the carrion eaters were pecking at those juicy little globes, seeded my obsession. Time allowed it to flourish.

We are surrounded by an amazing number of references to the orbs in popular culture. The eyes have it. Beauty is in the eye of the beholder. The eyes are the window of the soul. Seeing things through someone else's eyes—it would seem that I am not a lone man possessed. Eyes are everywhere. You see them on TV, on billboards, in magazines, even staring out at you from the back of the bus. Sure, those irises have been airbrushed and the pupils artificially dilated, for sexual appeal, but I could still sit and stare at them for hours. Powerful . . . seductive . . . mesmerizing.

Did you know your eye is composed of over two million parts? So many rods and cones—it's an organic phenomenon.

I'm the type of personality that feeds off of outside influences, but never directly. I kept my passion hidden from even those closest to me. My parents and siblings never suspected. When I was a teenager I admired the orbs from afar. I observed others eyes unnoticed, scrutinizing them when I could and fantasized about holding those spherical wonders in my hands when I couldn't. Selecting a career path was simple. I set my sights—heh heh—on becoming an eye care professional, an optometrist, an ophthalmologist, an ophthalmic medical practitioner, it didn't really matter which at the time. My parents were thrilled I wanted to attend med school and went to great lengths to support my endeavours. Their son, a doctor? It was a parent's dream come true.

Only, I didn't end up choosing any of those options. While I was in the middle of the introductory phase of my education, pre-med, I came to a conclusion while working with the cadavers that were a part of the curriculum. What you could do with the eyes of a living person was limited. You couldn't pluck out those jellies as Cornwall had done to Gloucester in King Lear . . . a classical reference, although I would never consider them vile. You couldn't jiggle and roll them in your palm like marbles. You couldn't hold them up to the light to get a really good look at their colour. You had to be careful and leave everything intact. Not that I didn't want a profession that required finesse. I'm a tactile man with a refined sense of precision, but I wanted to be able to immerse myself in my work. Being an eye specialist of any variety wouldn't allow for that.

Did you know that your tears contain natural antibiotics? That's to keep them sound, and sensual. Even the highest quality of saline solutions doesn't properly emulate them.

Becoming a medical examiner, on the other hand, offered me much more freedom. On solo runs, I could prod and pry to my heart's content and in some instances it was actively encouraged that I handle the orbs directly. It was such an occurrence on my first day at work that I believe was what sealed my fate. Given my predisposition to eyes in the first place, imagine my reaction when the initial case they brought in was the fatal victim of a domestic dispute who had been blinded before being murdered. Both eyes had not been destroyed in the process. A vindictive wife, charged with psychotic rage over adultery, had gouged one of her unfaithful spouse's eyes out before plunging a knife through the empty socket into his brain. As I stared at the one fixed eye, and the one bloodied, lolling globe, my imagination ran wild.

How had she overpowered him? He was not a small man, and unless she had been a monster of a woman, she would not have been able to out-strength him. Had she launched herself upon him while he slept, weapon in hand, and struck before he had had a chance to defend himself? Had he been falling down drunk and clumsy in his attempts to avoid her? Any sane man would fight to keep his eyes in his head.

The average person blinks ten thousand times a day. You blink more when you're nervous—like now.

I gazed upon the one good eye. It was a plain brown—an ordinary colour. I took the greatest pleasure in orbs of unusual design. This was not one of them. Despite that, the moment was still one I would treasure.

It was an exhilarating experience. I got to finger the eyes. I was required to examine them very closely. I was like a child with the toy of my dreams and the work associated with such play was secondary. Those around me did not recognize the nature of my interest. I was the new kid, an eager beaver with the need to prove myself. As far as they were concerned, my enthusiasm was all for show, to strengthen my position in the lower ranks and perhaps open a route to somewhere higher up someday. I had my eye on the prize, you could say—heh heh.

I was in my second year at the M. E.'s office when I met my wife, Muriel. She worked for a franchise store selling eyewear: glasses, sunglasses and their accessories. I was walking past their store front on my way to work one day when I saw her perched in front of a customer. She was adjusting a pair of glasses on the young man's face, peering into his eyes. The vision took my breath away. I had to stop and stare. Most men would have considered her homely, heavy-set with a large nose and plain brown hair, but it was her eyes that had me enraptured. As I looked at her through the window, her irises seemed to shift in colour every time she moved—first grey, then green and finally blue, with a hint of yellow at their centres. I immediately fell in love with those eyes, and I had to meet her.

Staring into someone's eyes without talking for several minutes can increase feelings of physical attraction. If you don't believe me, you should try it.

My vision was twenty/twenty at the time, but I still managed to produce an easy excuse to go in. Summer was upon us and I needed optical protection. Eyes are prone to damage from UV rays. I went in on my lunch hour, on a quest for shades and seeking a date with Muriel's eyes. She was shy and avoided my stare, but she was flattered by my flirtation and quickly accepted my offer for dinner that night. I was not hard on the eyes—heh heh—yet.

I toiled hard to seduce those orbs with their alternating colours. The rest of Muriel was just along for the ride, a necessary accessory to the only part of her with any real value. Of course, I had to charm the person in order to maintain my ties with those eyes—sort of like showering the ugly best friend with compliments for the sake of the favour of your true love. I forced her to look at me, even though she kept trying to glance away. I don't think the woman was accustomed to such attention because she soon found it difficult to hide her reciprocal infatuation from me. She didn't realize that I only cared about two things, and that the rest of her was just fleshy baggage.

I proposed to Muriel's eyes after six months of dating, and married them after six more. That was how our lengthy and reasonably pleasant relationship began. She was always grateful to have an attractive and successful husband and I had all I needed from her whenever she looked my way. We had three children together, with all but the youngest sharing her strange eye-colour, those of my last born being a lack-lustre dark blue. In a way, their existence lessened my interest in Muriel somewhat, because their eyes made hers seem not as special, no longer unique. No one suspected the reasons behind the diminishment of my fervour towards Muriel. They assumed it was the typical response to a lengthy pairing: we were aging, I was bored with her and bearing children had somehow marred her youth and beauty. We fell into that customary state of pleasant contentment and casual apathy that most married couples eventually achieve.

Don't look so surprised. Eyes are closely linked to many social signals. They are our primary tool for relating to others. For example, I knew you were interested the moment you looked at me. I used that to lure you in.

So that was my life for twenty-five years, and nobody suspected that anything was out of order. On the outside, I was a hard-working pillar of the community. I raised my children, I loved my wife and I was a charitable man—but I hadn't become a collector yet, and I still had plenty of opportunity to do what I loved most. Locked up in my harshly lit space with the body laid out on the cold slab, I would fondle those things that appealed to me most. Not in an obscene way, understand. As I mentioned, I never loved them that way, more like one might gingerly handle a valuable artefact or a rare jewel. That's what they are, after all—precious gems generated by the human body. As foul as the rest of our flesh bags may be, the eyes are a true measure of beauty.

Blue-eyed couples actually can have a brown-eyed child, despite what people think. Eye colour is determined by multiple genes. It's a complex process.

No, I couldn't take any of my work home with me while working in the M. E.'s office. If I had yearned to collect kidney stones, they never would have been missed but the eye is essential to the man. I could not send corpses away with the lids sagging into empty sockets or use some reasonable-sized replacement that might be detected by the undertaker. I would have never been able to explain just cause for the switch, so when I was done with my playthings, I had to bid them adieu. Twenty-five years of pleasure followed by loss. Twenty-five years of ups and downs until my retirement.

When it was suggested that the time had come for me to pass on my role to a deserving younger man, I objected at first. Abandon the only way of satiating my very particular desires? The idea frightened me, even though I had known it would come to that some day. Financially, I was in a good place, and my family pointed out it made sense to retire while I was still young enough to enjoy it. I yielded to the combined pressures of co-workers and Muriel, who had long since left her job and was watching our youngest prepare to leave for college. Dread of an empty nest had set in, and she was tired of spending her days alone. She didn't really have much in the way of friends; she was never a social butterfly.

Some butterflies have eyespots on their wings, possibly to startle predators. I could never find eyes frightening.

I'll admit, initially, I didn't handle retirement well. I moped sullenly about the house, getting underfoot unpleasantly rather than providing Muriel with anticipated companionship. Eventually, it was all too much for her. She sat me down in front of the computer and instructed me to keep surfing until I found myself an acceptable hobby. She had insisted that she would not give me leave to rise from my chair until I at least had some idea of a new way of occupying my time.

I wasn't sure where to look, at first. When Muriel had left the room, I started browsing sites associated with eyes. Most of them were related to optometrists, or things like designer contact lenses.

Personally, I couldn't understand the need to artificially change eye colour. Even the most common of iris shades had their own natural appeal. The false displays from the contact lenses looked ridiculously fake. I could tell someone was wearing them from across a crowded room and they made my stomach turn.

Rene Descartes came up with the concept of corneal contact lenses. "Eye" think therefore "eye" am—heh heh.

Ploughing my way past those wretched sites, I soon found myself navigating through pages that presented me with prosthetic eyes, and even artificial orbs intended for use in taxidermy. That notion brought me to a screeching halt. Taxidermy—an odd hobby, but one that seemed fitting for an ex-medical examiner. It would be a far cry from people, but at least it would allow me to handle eyes again, even if they were only the organs of lesser animals. Beggars can't be choosers, and I was a desperate man.

I ordered how-to manuals, downloaded instructional videos and ordered a selection of supplies. It took a fair amount of practice, but before I knew it, I had my own little business on the go, one that fed my habit to a minimal degree.

So how did I go from that to becoming a collector, you ask? I'm getting there; we still have time.

It began with a dead cat—an odd cat with spectacular eyes, brilliant green flecked with orange. I could not find a match from the various suppliers I used and decided that in order to present a proper life-like preservation of this family pet, I would have to redesign one of the existing glass models myself. I placed the eyes in a jar with a special solution to keep them moist and firm. I use a similar solution with preservative properties in all of my jars.

Having multiple colours in a single eye is called heterochromia iridum. When the secondary colour is in the middle of the iris, like mine, it's called central heterochromia.

I used those orbs as a reference while I painted in the appropriate striations. It was pure bliss, staring at the jar that stared back at me. I had an excuse to ogle them for hours and when I was done I was proud of my craftsmanship. After inserting my work into the mounted cat, I couldn't bring myself to discard the original eyes. I placed the jar on my shelf, so I could peek at them whenever I wished. There was such a feeling of satisfaction leaving them there. They belonged there, and I wanted more.

I probably would have left it at animals. I'm really not a sadist. I just love what I love, and do what's necessary to be able to pursue my passion. I craved the human eyes, though. They're different. It's an irrational longing, I know, but as Gilbert Keith Chesterton said: "There is a road from the eye to the heart that does not go through the intellect." Still, I would never have gone that route, not without sufficient prompting . . . and then something drastic happened.

I had gotten into the habit of prepping all of my glass inserts for a perfect match and preserving in jars all of the eyes that they were replacing. Several now lined my shelves. That day when I emerged from my workshop, Muriel's scintillating eyes were tearful. She had been having health issues and the doctors had performed a series of tests. Cancer, they had told her, and it was spreading. They planned various forms of treatment, but they would have to remove multiple tumours, and the first operation would involve the extrication of one of her shade-shifting eyes.

At first, I was devastated by the idea of such a loss. Then I realized that it did not have to be a loss at all, that I could simply add hers to my collection, but I would need a reason why I must have it, so I begged her to allow me to design her replacement. She agreed to it, too overwhelmed by the idea to care. She just thought I needed the task as a distraction, to cope with the situation.

I still lost one of her eyes, the remaining one when her cancer finally took her, but the first one is still up there, in a jar. Can you see it?

The problem was, as soon as I had my first human eye, I couldn't stop there. It was like having a piece of really good chocolate or a tasty potato chip. It's impossible to stop at only one. But how would I manage to collect any more? I fought the urge at first, and then . . .

The fellow was a hiker, heading into the mountains, just like you. He was only passing through town, and no one expected him to stick around, so no one missed him. He had the most amazing eyes. Jonathan, I think he said his name was. Those are his orbs on the top right-hand side. The clearest example of central heterochromia I possess. They're a wicked hazel with the pupillary section such a vibrant emerald green that they stopped me dead in my tracks. We got to chatting, and when he heard about my taxidermy shop—well, I guess he had a morbid sense of curiosity. He had time to kill before the shuttle bus to the foothills arrived. I brought him to my home and served him the same blend of tea that I served you, with that addition of several rather special ingredients.

It took some time before anyone noticed him missing. People assumed he had just gotten lost in the mountains. No one keeps track of who is actually on that shuttle bus. A few discarded belongings for rescuers to find, and voila! One hiker gone astray—never to be found.

You'll notice eight jars on that shelf beside the beloved eye of my Muriel, and sixteen other orbs with irises of spectacular colour. If I wasn't so particular, my activities would draw suspicion, but I don't just take any eyes. I'm a proper collector and I only take those that are unique. No plain old browns or baby blues for me. As fussy as I am, there is sometimes a period of several months between great finds. I'm a connoisseur; only the best will do. I keep myself occupied with my taxidermy while waiting for someone like you to come along. They won't notice that you never got on the shuttle bus either.

I can see you growing drowsy and starting to nod off. The tea I gave you causes a mild paralysis, that's why your limbs won't work, but I also mix in a strong sedative, a pain killer and a gentle hallucinogenic. You'll soon be drifting happily in a mellow dreamland, and you'll forget all of this. Like I said, I'm not a sadist. I just love what I love . . . and your eyes are an incredibly striking shade of violet . . .

Weaving Tangled Webs

DIANE ARRELLE

Sept. 15

THIS IS VERY difficult. Dr. Allen feels that a journal will help. He said I suffer from stress. Can you imagine that, stress? If only Dr. Allen knew the truth, then he'd realize a journal could never be enough.

What the hell, I'm willing to give this a try. Maybe putting my life down on paper will get rid of some of this pent-up frustration.

This is almost fun. After I'm done I have to find a good hiding place so Troy never sees it. I certainly don't want him to know I went to Dr. Allen about my sprained wrist. He'd be furious if he found out I wasted some of the grocery money on myself.

Do I start writing about my life from day one? I was born on the poor side of town to . . . I have lived my life as a statistic: child of an abusive alcoholic, married to an abusive alcoholic . . .

Nah, this is silly, Dr. Allen said to write about my daily life, so here goes.

Today was kind of standard. Troy worked late, went out drinking and still isn't home so I know tonight will be all right. The brats are quiet, I think they're in bed or else maybe out robbing a bank. I don't care, just so everyone leaves me alone.

I guess autumn is almost here because I found another spider in the laundry room. Ugly bastard! I wonder why they're so godawful ugly. If there is anything I hate more than my life, it's those eight-legged nightmares.

I stood next to the dryer and watched it scurry across the top. At first I recoiled, edging away from the small black thing. If it had been any bigger, I would have been terrified, but it was tiny and I felt in a brave mood for a change. I thought about killing it, but didn't. I don't know why, but sometimes I feel sorry for the really little guys. I sometimes wonder if they feel as frightened of me as I do of my world.

I didn't kill it, but I gave it a stern warning. "Stay out of my way or you are going to be dead meat," I said and wondered, *could I get locked away for threatening an arachnid? Is there is a government agency to protect household infesters?* Sparing its insignificant life made me feel powerful, like I was in control for once.

Sept. 16

Today life went from pathetic to intolerable. Troy woke up with a hangover (no big surprise there). He was exceptionally miserable and I tried to tiptoe around him until he left. Only it didn't work, he found my house-cleaning annoying.

I was on my knees washing up the spilled juice, cereal, and assorted unidentifiable foods off the floor when he walked into the kitchen. He poured himself a cup of coffee and obviously didn't notice me stooped over. Tripping over my feet, he stumbled and dumped most of his coffee on my back.

"Shit, woman!" he yelped wiping at a few dark brown spots on his shirtsleeve. "You trying to kill me?"

Incapable of answering, I blinked tears away as fiery pain etched a red welting design on the skin across my shoulders. *I hate you,* I thought, rolling over to rub my burned skin in the cool soapy water puddled on the floor.

That was a mistake. I saw it coming, but didn't have time to roll away. He kicked me. That son of a bitch kicked me in the ribs while I was down. And for doing what? For cleaning up the filthy mess his rotten kids leave every morning before they go off to mug senior citizens or maybe actually attend a day of school.

I tried to draw in a breath but couldn't. He had booted the air right out of me. For a moment, dark spots danced in front of my vision. I thought I was going to pass out but fought to draw in some air and stay alert.

Slowly, it seems to get slower with each assault, I worked my way up to my knees, then to my feet. As I stood there swaying, holding my bruised side, I tried to decide whether I should run away or kill him.

"Mandy!" he bellowed. "Just don't stand there like a useless piece of garbage. Fix me another coffee and iron a clean shirt. Fast!"

Decision made, I walked over to the coffee pot right next to the knife drawer. Slowly, ever so slowly, I poured him another cup and carried it over to him. It made me feel a little better to annoy him by moving in slow motion. Then I ironed his damned shirt.

Yes, I know I'm weak and the bastard needed to be punished, but it just wasn't in me. I don't think I am capable of hurting a bug.

Sometimes I envy the female spider who can bite off the head of her mate without blinking an eye. Now, there is a woman who doesn't get dumped on. I think I'd like to come back my next life as a black widow. Yeah a widow sounds really good, especially a poisonous one.

Troy put on his shirt, came up close to me and raised his arm over his head. I cringed; ready for the blow I knew was coming.

POP! His shoulder cracked loudly in the silent room and he lowered his arm. "Ah, that's better. Well, guess I'll go now," he said and bent over to give me a sloppy wet kiss. Then he went off to his little executive office at the bank.

I sometimes think his mood changes have nothing to do with aspirin. I think he just does it to torture me and keep me off-guard.

I think I like writing everything down like this. It helps me channel my anger. I can hate the words instead of everything else around me.

Sept. 16/17 (3A.M.)

Well, here we go again. I couldn't sleep so I decided to finish writing about my day. I guess I'll pick up where I left off.

I finished cleaning the kitchen and started on the powder room. I was just about to scour the sink when I saw "it". Revulsion clutched my stomach, squeezing it, forcing my breakfast back up my throat. I whipped my hand away from the porcelain bowl, terrified "it" would leap off the drain stopper and start ripping the flesh from my arms.

"It" sat there, still and silent. I felt like taking off my shoe and smashing its dime-sized black, furry body to a pulpy green and yellow mush. Could it possibly be the same one as yesterday? Although it looked like the same kind of spider, this one was bigger. Big enough to scare me. I watched it with distrust, waiting for it to make a move toward me.

Suddenly one thread-like hairy leg lifted then the other seven followed. As "it" scurried up the rear of the sink, I backed off, cowering. Then the truth hit me, "it" was afraid too. To that disgusting awful spider, I was the monster, just like Troy was to me.

With a surge of understanding, I decided I could be generous to a fellow creature, even one as grotesque as this arachnid. "I warned one of you guys yesterday, but I'll give you one more chance," I said picking up a wad of tissues. "But this time I mean it. Get out of my house and stay out!"

I gingerly grabbed it with the tissues, holding it at arm length in case it attacked. I decided it was a she and added, "Go out and kill a mate or two for me." Then turning around, I heaved it out the open window giving the tissues a couple of good shakes.

I was brimming with compassion as I called, "There you go, little sister. Have another shot at life and make it better than mine."

Only I wasn't as gentle as I thought and one skinny twitching leg stuck to the tissues. So much for compassion.

When Troy came home he acted like nothing happened earlier. Once again we were a perfect family. Except, that when the doors were closed and the blinds drawn, the maid/whore/punching bag were packaged in one convenient sack. That's what I feel like most of the time; a shapeless, useless, burlap sack laying by the side of the road waiting to be kicked or run over by the eighteen-wheeled semi called life.

As I tried to fall asleep, I recited my usual mental chant, *another day concluded*. That's how I spend my days, counting them off, waiting for the final victimization.

Sometimes I try to recall bright moments, but they were too few and too often snuffed out, just like Denny. Even from the beginning Troy and this marriage were hollow and joyless. On our first date, Troy forced me to have sex with him. I had been a 23-year-old virgin on a blind date. After that night I was a victim of date rape. Mom helped a lot. She alternated between calling me a tramp and telling me how lucky I was that someone could like a plain, spineless, old maid enough to make it with her.

Even back then, I was already beaten, both mentally and physically. I was totally submissive to my existence. There was no fight in me, just acceptance of whatever fate handed out.

Troy knew when I didn't turn him in and actually agreed to go out on a second awful date, that he had found the perfect wife. Yes, the perfect wife: dull, mousy, scared of everything, I was that special someone to raise his kids. I'd cook for them, clean for them and cover up for them whenever they'd go on one of their juvenile crime sprees.

We both knew what we were getting with each other, but marriage seemed a better alternative to spending the rest of my days caring for Mom. Fat, crippled by decades of alcoholic abuse, she'd crippled me mentally. Beating me and browbeating me until I was too afraid to think for myself. The few times I did fight back, I paid dearly with broken bones and shattered spirit.

It seemed that I was doomed to wait on her forever and then came Troy. True, he was cruel and explosive, but his viciousness wasn't aimed at me like hers was. He didn't hate me personally, only life. He hated life's blows and took them out on me.

I guess I've been writing a long time. My fingers and wrist ache and the sky is starting to get light. I think I'll quit and try to get some sleep.

Sept. 17

I did fall back to sleep but had an awful nightmare. I dreamed I was wrapped in spider webs, caught in yet another trap. I spent the morning resting as soon as everyone left. In the afternoon I went upstairs to clean some more. It seems that cleaning the house is the only thing that keeps me sane. I can scrub away all my bitterness and hurts for a while. I can feel accomplishment in a clean home, it was something I had never had growing up.

Mom, the drunken pig, never cleaned, never cooked and never cared. She never cared about me or Denny. I don't even remembering her crying at his funeral. Of course I don't remember much about that time. I had to be drugged because my constant sobbing interfered with her stricken mother routine. Denny—handsome, blond, big brother, Denny—was the only person who ever really loved me and he died. Sent to the store for a bottle of booze, he never came home. She didn't care that she made him go out in storm for her scotch. She didn't care that a car smashed him, smashed his bike. She never cared.

I cared and everything died with him.

So now I clean, every day, religiously I scrub and scour looking for a ray of hope in the sparkling white enamel. I went into the twins' room, a nightmare of junk, crumbs and wet sheets and started to strip the plastic lined beds. Those two monsters were every stepmother's worst nightmare. No wonder their mother abandoned that family, two bad seeds and a rotten pod.

As I pulled the urine-stained sheet off of Ricky's bed, movement caught my eye. There was another spider, black and velvety, sitting on a corner of the mattress. This one had to be the big brother of the one from yesterday, at least the size of a half dollar.

Dropping the sheet, I slowly backed out of the room and closed the door. I ran downstairs and grabbed the bug spray then dashed back. Gingerly opening the door, I found the bed empty. Giving a spritz just to be on the safe side, I slammed the door and let the sheets dry on the floor. I wasn't going back in there. I was afraid it was the same spider, feasting and growing on the hate in this place. Maybe growing on the hatred it must feel for me since I crippled it.

It seems that I am becoming obsessed with spiders. This is silly, but I wonder if it is coincidence that the spiders keep getting bigger or does this house generate enough negative energy to cause a monster to grow. I'm afraid, more afraid than usual. What if that spider really is growing? What if, what if, what if? I don't have any answers and I guess I never will.

Sept. 20

Thursday, two days ago, had to be the absolute worst day of my life. It was the day that all my nightmares came true all at once. I can't believe I'm still sane and functioning, but maybe I'm not. Maybe this is the ramblings of a madwoman. I don't know anymore. Am I free or am I being hunted. Who knows?

Thursday she (it) appeared next to the washing machine in the laundry room. Oh I know now that it's her and she's going to get me. She got big, a real growing girl. About the size of a saucer, I found her on a strand of silk hanging right over the washer, bouncing in front of my face at eye level. I turned to run and bumped into Troy who came home early from a late liquid lunch.

I screamed, not sure what to be more frightened of. Which was the more monstrous. Troy snarled and shoved me into the washer. I felt the metal and knew I would have a few more bruises before he finished. "God, you're an ugly thing," he muttered, his breath stinging my nose. "Why'd I ever marry something as pathetic as you?"

I knew what was coming, he loved angry sex. It was the only way he could get hard. The more he hurt me, the harder he'd get. "You're not even fit to take care of Ricky and Nicky. Why, you're not fit to live!"

He grabbed my neck and suddenly I knew he was really going to kill me. All the other times were just practice, this was the real thing.

"Stop!" I squeaked, unable to fight off my own death. "Stop, that hurts!"

His grip tightened, I could feel his fingers digging into my flesh. The bones in my neck were grinding together and it was only a matter of seconds before the vertebrate crumbled to splintered dust. As the pain and pressure increased on my collapsing windpipe, I feebly tried to slap his hands off. I needed to breathe.

I was dying, and the worst, the most degrading thing about it was he was getting off. The tighter he choked me, the harder he was grinding against me. He was breathing heavy, a track of spit running from the corner of his mouth down into the stubble on his chin. And he was smiling, panting, coming. My God, he was coming!

That was worse than anything, worse than death! The bastard was not only murdering me, he was depriving me of every last dignity.

I wasn't going to die that way! I refused. For the first time in my poor excuse of an existence, I fought for me. I grabbed at his hands trying to pull them away but couldn't. I slapped at his face but things were blurring, growing darker. It was ending and I knew I had lost.

My last thoughts were that I had finally fought back. Some solace, huh? Then out of the blue, that spider fell from above onto my face. It scurried onto his hands and it was really odd but just as consciousness faded, I noted that it only had seven legs and an oozing stump.

I wasn't quite out completely. Suddenly, I heard Troy bellow like a wounded animal and I felt myself slide down as the pressure disappeared. Sitting on the floor, propped against the washer, I gratefully gasped air, amazed to be alive. My vision slowly returned, and I was alone. Troy was gone; all I could see was a trail of blood droplets leading away from the laundry room. "I hope it's his," I mumbled as I rubbed my agonized throat.

I remembered that spider, the one with seven legs. If it were the same one, growing bigger every day, it was going to get me. I had ripped off its leg. It may have been during an act of kindness, but I maimed it. It was going to get me.

Pushing myself up, I staggered out of there as fast as I could. I had to escape. I had to get away from that madman and the spider. I really did want to live. I really did. If I survived, I swore I would get help. I'd learn to love me. Even if no one else in this entire world could find in their hearts a place for me, I'd love me.

I'd spent my whole life wanting love, searching for it, settling for anything, any tidbit of affection. This whole situation was my fault. I stayed with Troy even though I knew he was horrible and cruel. I knew he only wanted a slave for those kids, those nasty, hateful kids. All these years and all I had to do was walk out that door. Well, I would now. I was going.

Only, he grabbed me from behind as I reached for my pocketbook in the living room. He spun me around and I saw his hand was wrapped in a blood soaked handkerchief and there was a bleeding red welt on his cheek. "Where do you think you're going?" He snarled as he wiped at his face with his shirtsleeve. "Look at me! This is your fault! That spider bit me. It's all your fault! Filthy house, I always said you were useless!"

He was insane, I could see it in his eyes and he was still going to kill me. As he raised his hand to slap me, I nailed him, kicked him where it did some good. I was done being battered. If one of us was going to die, it wasn't going to be me.

I grabbed my pocketbook and ran for the door. I would have made it if those kids hadn't jumped out of nowhere and tripped me.

"We hate you!" They both shrieked and started kicking me.

I remembered the times they burned my clothes, cut me with a knife, killed our neighbors' pets, set the school on fire, and kicked and hit smaller kids.

I jumped up and punched them. First Nicky, then Ricky. I really wanted to let them have it, but it was too late. Troy was on his feet and coming for me. I looked around desperately, saw my only escape was back to the laundry room. I ran for it. I was more willing to face that spider then them.

I slammed the door, locked it, and moved the dryer in front of it. I was never a strong woman, but believe me when I say I found the strength to move that machine. I huddled in the corner of the room holding the bleach bottle as a weapon. They pounded and yelled, but for the moment I was safe. I saw movement and looked up. The spider, now the size of a dinner plate had flattened its body the way bugs can and was squeezing out of the room under the door that led to the garage.

Now, I was really safe, at least for the moment, that monster was gone and the other monsters had given up trying to break down the door. The garage entry was bolted from the inside so I could relax for the moment. I heard Troy yelling, "Forget it for now boys, she'll have to come out sometime. Then we'll take care of her."

Can you imagine how sick a family they must be to have a forty-year-father plot to kill his wife with his two thirteen-year-old sons?

I fell asleep, my body and mind exhausted. When I woke the room was dark, darker than I remember any place being. Suddenly, I needed to get out. Get away from the dark, the spider, the madmen. Slowly, I moved the heavy dryer, so heavy I don't know how I got it there. I made a space big enough to open the door. I listened at it, not breathing to hear better. Silence. Finally, with bleach bottle opened and aimed, I went out to find the house dark and quiet. Too quiet, I instinctively knew I was alone.

Diane Arrelle

I crept out the back door and stopped. A funny odor tickled my senses, strong and dangerous. Gasoline! I silently walked toward the front hugging the wall. Turning the corner by the garage I tripped over two large white rocks, soft and sticky rocks! I had to know what they were and why the fire that was to kill me had never been lit.

Gathering all my courage, I purposely tripped the movement sensitive floodlights by the garage door.

Horrible!

I doubled up and gagged. I may have hated them but I never wished a fate like this on anybody. Nicky and Ricky, wide-eyed and dead, were bound from the neck down in cocoons of spider silk. There was blood on the ground, but it looked like there was very little left in them.

They were going to torch me, yet I started to cry for them. I say started because something large and furry and velvet black was blocking the garage door. She was now the size of a medium sized dog. Yes, now I'm sure she thrived on hate. Twisting her head in my direction, it took a hesitant step toward me, than another.

It seemed like there was going to be no end to this nightmare! As she closed in on me, I saw Troy inside the garage behind the monster. He had his hunting rifle. Wildly, he swung the barrel, pointing it first at me then at that mutant spider. He was so disturbed he couldn't decide who to kill first.

He started to laugh, a high hysterical giggle. "This is all your fault, Bitch!" he mumbled between bursts of laughter.

Without thinking, I ducked down and picked up the cigarette lighter on the ground next to Nicky. I hadn't even realized that I'd noticed it. I flicked it on and threw it.

POOF!! That house went up like a piece of old newspaper. Troy too. I heard his screams as I ran. I had the grocery money and our automatic bankcard in my pocketbook so I was set for a while.

Now here I am, a hunted woman in a cheap motel right off the interstate outside of town. To think that a week ago I was just an unhappy housewife who only dreamed of running away, not being on the run.

That was two nights ago and my nerves are frazzled. I hate the cornfield outside my back window. I keep imagining that the spider survived the fire and is out there waiting, hiding, in the tall brown cornstalks. I know she'll find me because once a victim, always a victim.

I hear a crash in the bathroom. The window! Oh God, the bathroom door is opening . . .

Sept. 21

I thought I'd written my last, last night. I thought I was really a goner when that door opened. I dropped my pen and jumped off the bed where I had been writing when I saw a long thin black hairy leg reach out. I wanted to run, only I couldn't, fear has locked my feet to the floor. In a wave of weakness my knees buckled and I fell backwards onto the bed. I lay there and waited for the end, praying it would be painless.

Filled with a deep sadness, filled with regrets, I closed my eyes and waited, and waited some more. Finally I opened them and saw her, now the size of a very large dog, standing beside me. I quickly squeezed my eyes shut, held my breath and went rigid with dread.

Instead of eating me, she just stood there and nudged me with her good front leg. And she whimpered. I opened my eyes, let out my breath and sat up. I forgot to be afraid. This wasn't in the script; victims and losers never get a second chance.

She nuzzled me, rubbing against me and I couldn't believe it but I swear she was doing the spider equivalent of purring! I gingerly reached out and touch her soft downy back. I don't know what I expected, but it felt nice like a cat. She responded by shivering, then rubbed me harder.

What do you know, somebody finally loves me. I guess kindness does pay off. I only have to wonder, did she grow from the hateful vibrations that filled our home or did she grow from my need. Could my sparing her life make her respond physically to my desperate situation? I think she too felt that brief moment of empathy and came to my aid.

I'll never know, but in the meantime I think it's time to end this journal for a while and start finding my new life. So until I settle into my niche, I think I'll take my new friend and move in with Mom. I know she won't care. She won't dare!

Bloodsport

ALANNA BELAK

i. First Phase

IT **BEGAN WHEN** I was twelve, when I awoke in a pool of blood. Actually, I was eleven. Eleven years and seven months. It was four in the morning of August 31st, my first day back at middle school after a two month long heat wave filled with muck and mosquitoes and combated by Freezy Pops and trampolines. The full moon was still out, high in the sky, searing through my partially open blinds as if to reflect the utter horror of my discovery.

It was four in the morning of my first day back at middle school, and I thought that I was going to die.

By the time my heart stopped thudding and my ears stopped ringing, I gradually realised that to call it a "pool" of blood was probably a gross overstatement. Highlight "gross." I switched on the bedside lamp, casting glare on the window and blocking out the condescending moonlight.

I examined myself. Nothing hurt. Nothing oozed. For a moment, I considered that it was all a bad dream. Then I noticed the deep red-brown stain on the back of my nightgown and everything started spiralling out again. I dropped my underwear around my ankles and began to quiver, eyes welling up. I was dying. I had to be. And if I wasn't, there was only one explanation.

Quickly, I formulated my master plan. I'd throw everything out, conceal and destroy the evidence; I wished I could burn it all, but that would be too obvious. I would have to sneak out to the dumpster at the back so no one would find my underwear in the trash. Maybe then I'd just dump bleach on the bed sheets and no one would be the wiser.

Just as I decided I most definitely wasn't going to wake up my parents, of course, the light in my room did the job for me. It was my father who opened the door.

"Honey, what's the . . . "

And then he saw me and the bed and my fallen underwear and he bolted from the room like he wished he'd never entered in the first place. I sobbed, staring numbly through my tears at the dried, cracked stain on my panties like it was the Devil. Red was his colour, after all.

Mother whooshed in then and started wildly cursing under her breath at the mess and muttering in a voice so low I was sure I had a right to be ashamed—even if the entire situation was well out of my control.

"It's all right, honey, we'll just change the sheets . . . You need to put one of these on. I'm sorry they aren't thicker. I just can't believe there's so much blood already . . . "

And just like that, I felt I had to be abnormal.

She handed me a box of sanitary napkins, which I looked at blankly. Of course I knew what they were—I'd seen her badger my father about the correct brand to buy on more than one occasion—but it was so unreal.

"Why do I need to?" I asked, frozen to place.

Mother just made a hissing sound like I was being ridiculous as she began to tear away the bloodstained sheets from my bed. "Don't worry," she said, "your cousin Ellie wears them too. Just read the box. It's okay."

My cousin Ellie was four years older than me. I was so young compared to her. We didn't even like the same kinds of music. It absolutely wasn't okay. I peered sadly down at the box of pads and started to turn away.

"Oh, and honey?"

I turned back to Mother, who was still speaking in an urgent, hushed tone. She was pointing down at my discarded underwear from across the room, as if the garment was a poisonous serpent.

"Just throw those out in the bathroom."

ii. Second Phase

It didn't take long for me to begin to feel like an alien. At school, whenever it was my Time, which seemed to be more often than not, I would watch the other girls closely to see if they waddled the way I did, if they ever cringed quietly because of the cramps or the sudden flow, if their seats were ever smeared with crimson when they rose. Of course, they didn't. I was all alone in my time of suffering.

I remember there was a time in my youth when I leapt at the opportunity to join the other girls in games of soccer or softball. Unimaginable now. I would always end up with stained underwear in the end, and I'd have to wait until the change rooms were empty to remove my pants for fear of being noticed. Discretion got to be the ultimate strategy. The only sports I played now were blood-sports.

Of course, there were dispensers in the girls' washrooms for sanitary napkins, but they were always broken, and that lead me to believe that no one else needed to use them. Besides, I was afraid to use the facilities at school to change napkins, because the wrappers were loud and the smell was awful and I was convinced that everyone would know, if they did not already. As result, I often waited too long and the blood would overtake the napkin, just as it was slowly overtaking my life, and I would be left to return home with one more deep red stain between my legs.

One day, Mother emerged from the laundry room, clutching my soiled underwear, and as I knew what was coming, I cowered.

"Again?" she cried. "I can't keep throwing these out. They're expensive, you know that? I'm going to have to bleach them. Why can't you just keep yourself clean?"

"I have."

Mother just rolled her eyes and went to return to her task. I barricaded myself inside my room and wept. What more could I do? When the flow was regular, sometimes I would wear two, or even three napkins simultaneously. Whenever my napkin supply ran low, which sometimes it did, and I couldn't bring myself to ask Mother for more, I simply stuffed my underpants with folded toilet paper. Everything bled through in the end. The Thing was clearly unnatural, and it wanted me dead.

I couldn't take it anymore. The next day, after school, I went alone to the drugstore. I rushed inside, quickly, never making eye contact with anyone. It was like I was buying rubbers. If only I was just buying rubbers. Just spending five minutes in That Aisle was comparable to an eternity in hell. Mother had never offered me any option other than the puffy, stiff napkins she used; I assumed she had a reason for it, and that she would punish me for even considering the other option. But enough was enough. Hastily, I located the box I was looking for, and shoved it into a basket full of candy, as if enough junk food would conceal its presence when I brought it up to the counter and spare me the shame.

When I was home, I ran into the bathroom, sat on the toilet, and unwrapped one of the tubular devices, like a tiny missile. The instructions were clear enough. I positioned my fingers on the cotton so that they were well in range of becoming stained with sticky, black blood. I told myself it would be over soon.

Sucking in my breath, I thrust my fingers inside, gasping when I felt the burn against my unbroken barrier within. I hadn't accounted for that. The hurt. It was unfathomable to me, how it could be so difficult for me to access my own body, when so much of my bodily fluids did not hesitate to slip out, even as I sat there.

However, as my eyes watered, and blood trickled down my wrist, I realised it was a good kind of hurt, because it meant that there was finally something dividing me from It. I closed my eyes and spread my legs and shoved my fingers up until my mind went blank from pain and I could picture the Thing inside smothered and dying, and I smiled.

iii. Third Phase

Adam, who was only three months older than me, held me down, scratching my bare torso with his beard stubble. I fought back against him, clawing him at some point, but in the end, we both giggled like idiots.

"Come on," he pleaded, "why not?"

"Just wait a few days. Like three. Four, tops."

"This is so stupid, you know."

"We can still do other stuff. Come on, just . . . lay back."

"I know we can," he sighed, "but . . . don't you . . . trust me?"

I sat up, folded my legs under me, still clad in jeans. My eyes fixed on a tear in the fabric of one of the thighs. I'd somehow always managed to avoid this conversation before.

"Yes," I said. "Of course I trust you. I love you. You know that."

Adam slid up next to me and rested his chin on my shoulder. "Hey, they're just sheets. I can wash them."

Just sheets. They were never just sheets. I pulled away, heart pounding, pulse throbbing in my temple, nausea building in my gut at the mere thought.

Sex was both a blessing and a curse. It meant that I was free to maintain cleanliness by whatever method I wished without fear of pain. It had been well over two years since I'd had to throw out or bleach a pair of underwear, and even longer since I'd had to confront Mother about the Thing inside. Suddenly, I'd felt like every girl in those stupid advertisements I'd come to hate—the ones who weren't afraid to live life just as though it were any other day. Everything was finally normal, how it was meant to be.

And now, in one fell swoop, I was about to have that all ripped away from me.

I muttered, "You don't know what it'll be like."

"But don't you want to? I don't want you to just make me happy. I want to make you happy."

"I told you, three days."

"But you didn't say you didn't want to." Adam smiled wolfishly.

I paused, struggling, pressing my thighs together.

"Maybe," I said softly, "maybe I do want to. But I don't want you to . . . think badly of me."

"Why on earth would this make me think badly of you?"

"It isn't something you'll understand."

"Now you're the one who thinks badly of me."

"No, I think everything of you. I'm just afraid."

"You don't need to be afraid of me."

"No, I know," I said, knowing fully well it wasn't him I was afraid of. "You're right. I just want to make you happy. And me happy."

Adam laughed and kissed me, a bright gleam in his dark eyes. "See, we'll be careful. I promise we'll be careful. I love you."

And so he removed my jeans and undressed, and I forced him to turn away when I removed my undergarments and hid their stained, clotted nature from sight. Maybe it would be all right after all. I laid back on the bed, trying to keep myself elevated so as not the stain the sheets, and waited for him.

"Adam," I said.

Adam turned to me, respected me by not looking in between my spread legs, instead peering straight into my eyes. "Tell me if you want me to stop," he whispered. Then he kissed me ravenously, and I shut my eyes tightly in wait.

I was tense. It was going to hurt. It had to hurt, I thought. I knew it.

But it didn't. Adam slipped inside and fell into rhythm easily, instantly. I kept waiting for Its dull throb, the kind that scalded me every month, unwarranted, but it never came. I relaxed. It was so smooth; a sensation that felt like it would never go away, like being dragged along an endless, hazy red tunnel. I let myself be taken by Adam, but it wasn't long before I realised I wanted more. I shoved against him, tried to push him over.

"Are you—"

"Shh . . ."

I forced myself on top and as I kept rhythm, barely conscious of any movement but my own, I felt the adrenaline rush through my veins, sweat form on each pore. I peered down between us, but saw nothing remarkable. No smears of disgusting, sticky, horrible, wet, sensational, magical blood. Suddenly, I wanted to see it. I needed to see it.

Faster, I moved, breath wracked, imagining the fluid pouring from me, streaming like a gruesome waterfall, painting us both, making Adam's belly slick, feeling it on my fingers as I pushed him back, the warmth, the strings of red like cobweb, picturing the bed . . .

Soon, everything erupted at once, like a fountain caused by a split artery. It gushed impressively with some vague sense of familiarity, and yet, like nothing I'd ever experienced before. It seemed to last forever. And then it was all over.

When Adam came out, I saw everything. Not quite what I'd imagined, but it was wonderful. Adam didn't say anything. He tried a smile and I smiled back at him.

"It was okay," I panted. Then I went to retrieve my underwear.

iv. Fourth Phase

It was a full moon, and I felt the hunger of a wolf. I felt something in me had changed, something feral. The curse . . . Maybe I had accepted that It was no longer a curse. I was reborn.

I was in the bathroom, preparing myself to feel like a woman for the night, when the doorbell rang. I beamed, knowing exactly who it was. I practically jogged out to answer the door.

Adam stood there.

"You're early," I smiled, feeling like I could run a marathon. I planted a kiss on his lips. "And you don't look nearly ready for a night on the town." I had expected him to be a little more dressed up.

"No, I guess not."

"What about that?"

"Listen, um." He shuffled his feet. "I'm not sure we should do that."

I frowned. "What do you mean? Do you want to stay in? Are you sick?"

"No, I'm not sick. Listen . . ."

"Stop saying that, Adam. I am listening."

Adam didn't even smile. "I can't really do this anymore," he said dumbly.

"Are you—" I stopped. "Are you saying we should . . .? I don't understand."

"It's . . . I just feel like this isn't working anymore. I'm sorry." And Adam turned away, ready to leave. I stepped out after him, voice shaking, eyes stinging, throat tight.

"Is this about what we did?" I lowered my voice to a hoarse whisper, like the one Mother used so many nights ago. "What . . . what you talked me into doing? The other night? I told you. I told you, you wouldn't understand. You shouldn't have let me say yes. You knew I didn't want to . . ."

"What? No. No, of course not. Don't make this about that. It isn't like that at all."

"Then what's it like?" I wasn't crying, not yet.

Adam shook his head. "You're different. You're different and it's . . . making me different."

"But I love you."

"I'm really sorry," Adam said. And then he left.

And I was left standing there, shaking, eyes tearing, going over the same thought over and over and over again, going numb. Adam said no, Adam said no, Adam said no, it wasn't because of the Thing inside, it wasn't because of the Thing inside, it wasn't—but I knew better. I just knew.

I returned to the bathroom because I had nowhere else to go. Just stood there, staring at myself in the mirror, expecting something. Nothing happened. Nothing happened and I had been betrayed. By Adam; by my own body. I felt it. My body was rejecting me. Trying to claw itself open, push itself out from the inside. Bursting free.

Before I could stop myself, I cried out. I tore off my clothes, which I'd so slaved over in preparation for the evening. I scattered them everywhere. Soon, I was standing in the middle of the bathroom, naked, standing stock-still in front of the mirror. I watched, as though I were a complete stranger, as a trickle of blood rolled down my inner thigh. Was it taunting me? The Thing inside . . .

What happened then happened in a blur. I saw myself stumbling through the apartment, shadows of rooms and strewn drawers, the only sound being the echo of my throbbing pulse, assaulting my veins with increasingly vile lifeblood.

Then I was back in the bathroom. I couldn't be sure where I got the knife. I was doubled over myself, standing on the tile, thrusting the blade up, easy as inserting a tampon. Sometimes I stopped and watched myself in the mirror. There was so much blood, but I kept telling myself that I'd seen more, I'd always seen more, the Thing had always given me so much more.

The tiles were splattered, not red, but black. The mirror became smeared. But there was more, there had to be more, I had to get the Thing out. It wouldn't be over until It was out, it would never be over. I was giving us what we both wanted. I told myself that. It was for the best. I deserved it.

I never felt anything. I had always felt so much pain, every time It returned, every cycle of torture. Tonight though, I felt nothing. This was how it was meant to be.

Suddenly, I was in the bathtub. My legs were spread, dangled over the rims like I was waiting to get fucked. Getting fucked, all right. I was sitting in It, with my surgeon's blade. I had an angle on It, and soon it wasn't just fluid. Tissue. Muscle. Clots. I dug them all out fiercely; I was so close to emancipation. I would be normal soon. My head buzzed with the glorious knowledge. I was so close. I faintly heard myself laughing. Tears streamed down my cheeks. I'd never known such happiness. Mother knew, Mother knew something was wrong right from the start, but she didn't know how to fix it. Now I knew how to fix it. I knew how to fix It.

With one final wrench, the largest fleshy piece came out. The entrance was much larger now, though it was indistinguishable due to all the gore, like I'd just given birth. That was it. I'd exorcised myself.

I dropped the knife in the tub and my head fell against the rim and slumped over to the side. I was left staring at myself in the crimson-splattered mirror. That was it, I thought, smiling. And then it all ended when I shut my eyes and lied down in the pool of blood.

Alanna Belak

Black Bird

NIKKI HOPEMAN

Drive a nail into the blood of the murdered
to stop the formation of the ifrit . . .
-early Arabic folklore

THE BLACK BIRD crossed her line of vision again: ebon wings tilting on the updrafts of the city, unforgiving gaze persecuting her. She lifted her face to the overcast sky, and pulled her sweater closer around her body against the chill wind brutally biting her skin. Gray clouds marred her view of the blue sky she knew must be above.

It'd been so long since she'd seen the naked sky she could hardly remember the proper shade of blue. If she tried to think back to the last time the sun shone on her skin, she'd waste the day.

"Excuse me." The man behind her shoved her shoulder as he pushed past, coffee cup in one hand, a folded newspaper in the other, on his way to whatever job occupied his hours. She hunched over, shoulders folding in on her torso, to shield herself from the man's touch, his words, his gaze, the slow, burning stare of the bird in flight somewhere overhead.

Could he tell? Did anyone else see the bird stalking her? Could the other people in the street feel the malice oozing off the ink stain in the sky?

After long seconds, she straightened, ignored the pall over her head, and walked on. The hazy light surrounded her, choked her, but she shut it out with no small effort, and shoved through the glass doors of her office complex, anxious for the shelter of her windowless cubicle. A day to pretend the sky shone blue, dotted with robins and sparrows instead of the black wingspan against the drab cloud ceiling.

On the eleventh floor, she stopped in the break room, grabbed a cup of black coffee, and headed to her workspace. She walked around the partition, started to put her coffee on the desk, but found all her belongings packed into three cardboard boxes. Panic welled in her chest.

"Darcy?" She turned to the speaker. Jason trotted toward her down the aisle made by the rows of cubes.

"Yeah?"

"Don't get comfortable." He shuffled the papers in his hand. "Don't panic either, we're just moving you." He smiled. "You'll like it."

She smiled back, relief flooding through her. "Whew. You scared me there for a second."

"Sorry! Just figured it would be easier to get your things packed up by the night crew."

"Yeah, that's great." She grabbed a box.

Jason led the way, the other boxes stacked to his nose. Darcy followed him through the office maze.

"Here you go." He dropped the boxes onto the desk.

Darcy's heart fell.

"You're lucky. We've resorted to drawing straws over this one in the past. Boss says you need to be closer to the print room. Lucky you." He grinned and bobbed his head.

Two sides of the cube were windows. The angry sky, so much closer eleven stories up, crackled. She would be surrounded all day by brooding grayness.

The huge black bird glided past the window. It could see her here, could watch her working. She felt its eyes on her; felt the black gaze on her neck.

She shuddered.

"You know, if this spot is so popular, I'm happy to take my old one. Someone else can have this."

Jason frowned. "Seriously? You don't like this?" He waved an arm at the window. "It's gorgeous."

"I . . . " She thought fast. "I'm afraid of heights."

"Oh. Well, I'll talk to the boss, but I doubt we'll get to reassignments until late next week."

Darcy felt her eyes well with tears.

"I'll try. No promises." Jason patted her on the shoulder as he walked by. "Maybe you'll change your mind."

Darcy dropped the box on the desk. "Doubtful," she muttered.

One peek out the window left her breathless and anxious. She could see her parking garage, two blocks away, and dreaded the walk she knew she'd have to endure.

She spent the morning rearranging her new desk for work and studiously ignoring the broad expanses of glass to her right and, worse, behind her. She fled to the windowless break room for lunch and to escape the bird riding the thermals between the buildings.

Finally, the clock turned to five and the sounds of her coworkers gathering their belongings and discussing their weekend plans filled the space. She turned to grab her bag from under the desk and her blood froze. The bird stood on the sill just outside the window, not two feet from her. He stared at her from one eye, then the other, silent.

Her throat constricted and her hands shook. She couldn't bring herself to approach the window to retrieve her bag from the shelf under the desk. She leaned back in her chair, stuck out a leg and hooked a foot under the strap.

It tumbled to the floor.

She stifled a sob and peered frantically over the cubicle divider. No one in sight.

Back at the window, the bird paced. Back and forth, back and forth, never taking a black eye off Darcy. He seemed larger than before, like her fear increased his size. She watched him, panic rising.

He watched back.

"Go away." She only managed a whisper. "Go away, you son of a bitch."

"What? I didn't hear you."

Darcy whirled, hissed.

"Sorry!" The woman from the next cube over held her hands up, palms out. "Didn't mean to startle you."

Darcy breathed heavily, tried to laugh. "It's okay. Just jumpy. I talk to myself when I'm nervous."

"Me, too. See you tomorrow." The red-haired woman walked toward the elevator.

Darcy turned back to the window. The bird was gone. She reached down and snatched her purse, then joined the group at the elevators.

The claustrophobic environment of the tiny space gave Darcy a respite from the bleak atmosphere outside. She relaxed a tiny bit, leaned against the back wall, and listened to her coworkers' conversations.

"We're finally getting the grill out this weekend. Come over for a steak."

"Sounds great. I'll bring the beer."

"Make it cold!"

Laughter swirled around her.

Grilling. Steaks and cold beer. A knot formed in her stomach and she squeezed her eyes closed. They sounded so normal, backyard parties and all.

Darcy's eyes flew open. Backyard parties? In this weather? She eyed the man talking about his grill, wondering at his lunacy. The sky looked ready to burst, like those sinister clouds would rupture at any moment and unleash a flood on everyone not under cover. The clouds blotted out the sun all week, keeping the temperature in the chilly range.

She hated it. Wanted the sun, longed for warmer weather.

And that bird . . . but the bird had nothing to do with the weather.

The elevator doors opened and Darcy had no choice but to exit. Her coworkers jostled out of the lift, laughing, too loud for the echoing acoustics of the marble lobby. Darcy dipped her chin and pulled up her collar. She hesitated just before the doors, desperate to avoid the gaze of that malicious bird.

The automatic rotating door spit her out into the sidewalk as thunder cracked from above. Darcy flinched and resisted the urge to look up. She trotted the two blocks to the parking garage and barely kept herself from sprinting to the stairwell. Once inside, she paused, chest rising and falling with her heavy breaths. She leaned against the block wall, enjoying the safe feel of the enclosed space.

Two flights stood between her and her car. She climbed them leisurely, other commuters passing her on their way up or down. When she came upon the door to the third floor, unease prickled her again. She'd be exposed to the sky on the other side.

She shoved it open and a chill wind whipped through the garage, grabbing at her coat and legs. It whistled among the concrete dividers, filled her ears with the sound. It spoke to her, carried a name to her ears, and a cloying, sickeningly sweet odor to her nose. She suppressed a gag, and stumbled toward her car, trying to block the howling sound and putrid odor from her senses.

The sound of the wind died for just a second and she heard a dry flutter, like fabric rustling . . . like feathers in flight, the feathers of a large predator taking wing.

Panic threatened to overwhelm her and she made a mad dash for her car, frantically clicking the remote to unlock it. She yanked the door open and dove into the driver's seat, wrenching the heavy door closed behind her, gulping in air. She pounded on the master door lock, and sagged across the center console for a long moment, eyes shut tight, mind focused on the fact she was closed safely in the car.

When she'd calmed her racing mind, she admonished herself for her paranoia, her stupid paranoia, the *Darcy, you're a fucking spazz* paranoia; she forced a deep, cleansing breath, sat up with hands on the steering wheel, and opened her eyes.

The black bird sat on the hood of her car.

She screamed, a high-pitched thread of sound that tapered off into a burbling sob. "Go away, you fucking son of a bitch!"

The bird walked on those clawed feet toward the windshield, head tilted to the side, eyes watching her. His shiny beak opened and closed. The clicking sound of that giant beak shredded Darcy's nerves.

She jammed the key in the ignition, turned it hard. The engine caught, but the bird didn't move. It wasn't until Darcy shot backward out of her parking space that the bird took flight. She watched it alight on a car about twenty feet away.

Her stomach turned over. She would have to pass it to get out of the garage. After flinging the transmission into drive, she sped forward, well past any safe speed limit for traveling in the garage, and careened around the corners. The exit bar lifted in response to her transponder, and the tires on the little silver car squealed as she took the turn onto the main road.

Still sobbing, she wove her way through Friday afternoon traffic and onto the highway.

Fucking bird. Fucking, fucking, fucking bird. She cursed the avian stalker all the way home. There was a time she would have had all the windows down and the sunroof open, singing at the top of her lungs on the drive home.

That was before.

Just . . . before.

Now, she sobbed and wondered where that black monster would show up next.

She turned onto her street, a beautiful tree-lined lane she once appreciated. The shade offered by the trees was a welcome respite from a hot summer sun. Now she saw too many places for that fucking bird to hide. Gray leaves against gray sky, no warmth left in the world.

She pushed the button on the garage door remote as soon as she hit the driveway and did not stop, but pulled smoothly into the garage and hit the remote again before she got out of the car. It took a few minutes of sitting in the car to convince her the bird didn't fly in behind her while the door was up.

She got out of the car, an adrenaline crash making her movements sluggish. She dragged her workbag out behind her and dropped it on the concrete floor next to the vehicle. A flip of the light switch on the wall illuminated the garage.

Something on the hood of the car caught her attention.

Dark footprints. The distinct four-pronged footprints of a bird.

Bile rose into Darcy's throat. Fucking bird. She pulled her coat tight around her against the cold of the garage and went through the door leading into the dark kitchen. A quick circuit around the tiny one story cottage assured her all the curtains were pulled tight against the bleak sky and the bird.

Except the bedroom. That door stayed closed and locked.

She grabbed a roll of paper towels from under the sink and went back out to the garage.

The footprints spanned the middle of the hood to the windshield, the path she'd watched the black bird take in the parking garage. She leaned over to take a closer look and caught a whiff of rot, the scent of decay.

She gagged, ripped a handful of towels from the roll and started scrubbing. The prints came off the paint, but Darcy swore she could still see a shadow of them.

She looked closely at the substance on the paper towels, trying to identify what the bird had tracked on her car. Something dark. She touched the wet stuff, rubbed it between her fingers, held her them to her nose.

Dark red. The scent of iron wafted into her nostrils.

"Shit!" She dropped the towels in the can by the door, and then ran inside. She threw the big deadbolts, all four of them, then stumbled to the sink. She washed with the hottest water she could stand and lots of soap. She squirted dishwashing liquid directly onto the stains. Her hands burned.

Impossible.

She grabbed the vegetable brush, squirted dish soap on it, and scrubbed at her hands. She brushed and brushed, applied pressure at the places she'd touched the stuff, but couldn't get rid of it. Her skin looked clean, but a dark shadow remained, like on the car.

Stains?

Fucking impossible.

She drew blood from her fingers with the stiff brush, but kept scrubbing. She'd take the skin off if she had to.

When the water from the tap ran red and she couldn't feel the heat of the scalding water anymore, she put the brush down. Her breath came fast and shallow.

Blood from her wounds mixed with the water dripping from her hand. Detached from the pain, she examined the brush burns on her fingers. In the junk drawer she found antibiotic spray, and applied it liberally, then she wrapped her hand in a dishtowel, and went to the bathroom in search of a better bandage.

She struggled to swathe her bleeding fingers in bandages, then grabbed a bottle of bleach cleaner and a steel wool pad. Back in the garage, she sprayed the foaming cleaner on the bird footprint stains. While it treated the discolorations, she looked over the rest of the car. Nothing else.

The steel wool scraped the hell out of the paint, but the stains seemed to reach down to the metal. She could not remove the deep red footprints, no matter how much damage she did to the silver finish.

Blood-red bird tracks all over the hood of her car. She scrubbed, leaning her weight on both hands even while the needle-like tips of the steel wool burrowed into her wounds. The fluid on the hood of the car turned red by degrees, running down the sides and onto her clothing. Sticky, metallic-scented liquid covered her skin, climbed up her arms, reached toward her neck and face, blotting her pale skin color with deep red. She wiped it away, pushed it back down, over and over again, scraping at the stains on her car as they reached for her skin.

By the time she gave up, she was sweating and sobbing. She'd done some serious damage to her car for nothing. Her hand throbbed, and when she flexed her fingers, blood leaked from under the bandages. She stripped out of her clothes, jammed them into the trashcan in the garage, and then went inside to the shower.

After scrubbing her body with a loofah, she patted her raw skin dry and pulled on sweatpants and a tank top. She dug some gauze out of a bathroom drawer and rewrapped her injured fingers before putting a kettle of water on the stove.

Her hand shook as she poured boiling water over a teabag in her mug. She carried the warmth of the drink along into the living room, where she pulled the curtain aside to peek outside. Drab clouds hung low, blocking sunlight. Tree branches and leaves dangled, listless in the still air. Where the sun should be, low in the western sky, a red ball glowed behind the cloud cover.

Storms. The atmosphere bristled with static; the charged air felt just like it always did before a big storm. Great.

She squinted at the yard across the street. Her neighbor's kids sat

---

in a kiddie pool, splashing and shrieking. She shook her head and wondered what kind of mother allowed her kids to play in a pool with a nasty storm hanging over the city.

She dropped the curtain and walked to the front door to check the locks. After she assured herself that each of the metal bolts was in place, she perched on the couch, facing the window. She used the remote to power on the television, which sat off to her left since she'd moved the couch. She couldn't bear to sit with her back to the window anymore, so she'd turned the sofa to face the window and taped drapery weights to the bottoms of the curtains to keep them in place in front of the clear glass panes.

The volume on the TV stayed low, so outside noises could be heard. The newscaster murmured something about rerouting traffic around the marathon set to take place this weekend. A race? In this weather? Darcy shook her head. Crazy people.

She waited to see a storm warning ticker go by along the bottom of the screen, but didn't. Maybe this one wouldn't be bad. The other storms so far this week hadn't caused any damage around town that she'd seen despite all the noise. Maybe these were "all bark and no bite" storm clouds.

And maybe Darcy hadn't lost her mind. Sure.

Thunder rumbled, low, far away. Darcy sipped her tea, and leaned back on the couch. The low lighting and soft noises soothed her; the hot drink calmed her nerves. She examined her arms, expecting to see dark red stains where her skin came into contact with the substance on the car, but saw only her own pale color.

She really needed some sun.

Her favorite movie was in the player, so she clicked the system over to DVD and listened to the familiar opening music. Every night for the last week had been the same—come home, hide, avoid the windows, and fall asleep on the couch. The weather seemed to darken with her mood, finally culminating in tonight's impending storms. Maybe the sun would come out tomorrow and she could break this desperate melancholy.

Or not.

The sun couldn't change what she'd done. Every moment of this despair belonged to her and her alone.

Even that damned bird couldn't change it.

She pulled her legs up off the newly bare floor. She missed the thick Persian that once cradled her feet, and now cradled someone else.

The movie was a welcome diversion, and soon she set her mug on the floor next to the couch and nodded off, warm and secure in the cocoon she'd created.

***

For a long moment she didn't know where she was, and lay perfectly still, her heart beating a heavy staccato in her chest, breath coming in shallow gasps.

She struggled to pull herself out of the grip of sleep, the horrible sleep of the last weeks.

Dreams colored her perception of reality, washed her vision red and scented the world with sulfur and burning chalk. Darcy rubbed her face, tried to bring herself back to the present.

Rain lashed the windows outside, and lightning flashes illuminated the narrow gaps around the curtains. Thunder crashed, no longer the mild rumbling, but a furious rending of the sky. The walls shook with the force of the wind, and Darcy shuddered with fear, an echo of the chaos outside.

She walked to the bay window at the front and pulled the curtain back just enough to peek outside. The swaying streetlights were still lit, but heavy rain dimmed the weak yellow light they gave off, and she had trouble seeing anything but her own tiny yard. Tree branches swept back and forth through her field of vision.

The tree in her yard came into stark relief with the next flash of lightning, its skeletal branches black against the bright white light.

The big black bird perched on a thick branch, hunched against the wind and rain, watching the house.

Darcy gasped and dropped the curtain, a chill running through her body. The hair on the back of her neck stood on end, whether from the proximity to the electrical strike or the bird in her dogwood tree, she couldn't say.

Fucking bird.

She ran her hands through her hair, tugging hard, letting the pain clear her mind. The bird couldn't get in. She would be fine as long as she stayed in the house.

Back in the kitchen, she turned the heat on under the kettle again. The chamomile blend always helped her nerves. She thought of the shrink they'd made her see a couple of years ago and wondered if he would be willing to prescribe some sort of anti-anxiety med. Couldn't hurt to ask.

He might ask why.

She'd lie. That was easy.

The wind outside increased its intensity, and she tucked another pot onto the sill to hold the curtain down. While the water heated, she ran to the bathroom, never even glancing at the bedroom door. On her way back through, it was more of the same. She refused to look.

One day she might. But not yet.

Steam flowed from the nozzle on the kettle, and she turned the heat off. Before she could pick it up to pour a fresh mug, something hit the window over the sink.

The glass rattled, but did not break.

Darcy backed away from the sink, hands shaking. She stood still for a long moment, ears alert to any more noise or any indication of danger.

Nothing.

She inched closer to the sink, breath coming in shallow gasps. With caution, she removed a heavy pan from the sill and peered through a tiny gap in the curtains.

Nothing.

Tree branches lashed the yard, flailing wildly in the force of the storm. The clothesline to the left of the patio spun like a top, the vinyl-coated wire rope loose and thrashing.

Must have been a branch. Maybe even just a rock or something.

She leaned against the counter and pulled the curtain open a bit further to get a better view of the yard. The storm had pushed the patio table to the far side, and the chairs were strewn around the concrete slab. All the potted plants were destroyed, having been ripped from the soil and flung about the fenced-in space.

Darcy sighed. She couldn't believe the news hadn't issued any warnings. Maybe it was a surprise to the meteorologists, too. That sometimes happened in the storm belt of the Midwest.

Just as she was about the drop the curtain and pour another mug of tea, something crashed into the window again with a deep, heavy thud. She jumped backward, and fell, kettle spilling its contents all over the counter and dripping onto the floor. The steaming water splashed onto Darcy's bare feet, burning her.

She did not feel the burns.

Whatever crashed into the window cracked it, leaving a jagged spider web of damage in the center.

It was something big and black. She felt certain, and the certainty transformed into fear.

She fumbled backwards toward the wall. Once she felt the wall at her shoulder, she slid up, careful to keep the solid barrier behind her. Her heart pounded, and her hands shook.

It was black, she was sure of it.

She dragged her gaze away from the cracked window and peered around the kitchen, making sure she was still alone in the house.

A laugh burbled out of her throat, tinged with panic. Who could possibly be here? She had a bird for a stalker, not a machete-wielding, lock-picking man.

Wind whistled through the cracks in the window above the sink. She dug through the junk drawer, grabbed a roll of duct tape and, as fast she could work, ran lengths of the silver tape over the cracks. As she smoothed the final end onto the glass, the black bird appeared at the window.

His talons scraped the brick sill, struggling to find purchase in the grooves to support his weight. Horrified fascination gripped Darcy. The wings flapped to maintain his balance and the shiny black expanse blocked her view of the yard. His wingspan reached from one side of the window to the other. The inky plumage closed her off from the rest of the world, and the furious rain ran off the sleek feathers in thin streams.

She could not run, could not look away from its onyx stare. Those eyes stared back at her, full of accusation. As she watched, they turned from cold black to the bright blue she knew so well. The pupils dilated and her own reflection stared back.

The bird opened his mouth and she steeled herself for the harsh call. She winced, knowing the sound would pierce her soul.

When the sound did not come, she opened her eyes. The bird cocked its head, beak still open, and uttered a word in a terrible, grating whisper.

"Darcy."

Warm liquid ran down her legs.

She stood, urine pooling around her feet. The bird clung to the brick, seemingly growing larger as she watched. It butted its head against the damaged window, pushed against the tape holding the glass together.

The sound of the glass crunching under the weight of the bird brought Darcy to her senses.

She screamed.

The sound drove the bird into a frenzy and it beat the window with its enormous wings, shrieking a mix of bird sounds and human voice.

Darcy fled. Her first instinct was to run to the bedroom, lock the door, and wedge herself under the bed until the monster retreated.

The bedroom was not an option.

She ran to the bathroom, the only other room in the house with a lock on the door. She slammed the door shut, turned the lock closed. She swept toiletries off the wire cart next to the sink and jammed it under the doorknob. She backed into the tub and cowered, terror overriding every other thought. Sobs wracked her body.

The crash of broken glass from the kitchen tore a scream from her throat. "Go away!"

She strained to hear, willed her body to stop shuddering so she could listen for signs of the bird in her house.

It grew. The first time she saw it, not quite a week ago, she'd thought it was a small crow. Each time after that it seemed larger, somehow, although at the beginning she thought maybe it was a different bird. It got larger, it followed closer, and it lost all fear of her, stalking more and more blatantly.

This unnatural creature possessed the freakish size and enough strength to break through windows.

The sounds of glass landing on laminate countertops reached her ears. It was coming through. She forced herself to inhale and exhale.

For the first few days she pretended it was a fluke, a weird coincidence that she saw a black bird everywhere she went. She figured one caught her attention, so now all of them would. But this bird inched closer and closer every day, staring at her, showing less and less fear. It could be no coincidence that this bird followed her home, knew her car, sat in the tree just outside the bedroom window.

She didn't see it from the bedroom, of course. That room stayed locked.

More glass tinkled onto the counter and floor in the kitchen. Scratching noises grated her nerves like fingernails on a chalkboard.

If it was coming in; she had to get out. The door was not an option. Her cell phone was probably still in her purse, which was in the kitchen.

Who could she call? The police? Even in the grips of terror, she barked a laugh at that thought.

A loud crash followed by a thud came from the kitchen. Something scrabbled on the tile floor.

Darcy labored to breathe. She turned around in the tub to look at the window. Hail hit the glass with clicking sounds and the heavy rain obscured the outside. She stood to get a better look at what she might be dealing with if the window was the only way out.

"Darcy."

Her legs went weak and she dropped back into the tub. That voice came from right outside the bathroom door.

Nikki Hopeman

Light scratches on the door followed.

Panic overwhelmed her. Her rational mind could not concentrate on escape, but her instincts kicked in and she crept out of the tub and to the window.

The metal rod holding the short curtain midway down the window barred her escape. Between sobs, she tugged on the rod, determined pull it down or break it in the attempt.

"Darcy." Ponderous thuds on the bathroom door fueled her frantic efforts. It sounded as if the bird were throwing himself at the thin piece of wood separating them, separating him from his prey.

Strangled sobs tore through her lips as she put her weight behind bringing down the curtain rod.

"No, no, no!" she screamed as the pounding came faster, changed in tone from the low thud of a object on the wood to the higher, tighter pitch of a sharper, smaller object striking the door.

"Darcy," came the voice, no longer a guttural whisper, but something more menacing, more articulate.

Darcy hesitated with the curtain rod, turned to see the doorknob turn and rattle.

Adrenalin and disbelief flooded her system, and she wrenched the rod off the wall, plaster and dry wall erupting. She flipped the lock on the window open and wedged her fingers into the groove before she pulled up.

Nothing. The window was stuck shut.

She screamed, a high-pitched burble that ended with saliva dripping down her chin. She tried pushing from different angles; she broke fingernails and wood splinters lodged in her skin, but to no avail.

The thing on the other side of the door pushed hard on the knob, rattling the door on its hinges. The wire cart, jostled loose from its place under the knob, fell to the floor with a clatter.

"Darcy . . ." Her name came in a singsong tone, taunting, mocking. It spoke with confidence, assured of success.

Darcy peered around the small room, vision tinged by hysteria. Something heavy, something heavy . . . she had to get through the window.

She pushed a box of tissues off the back of the toilet and picked up the lid. She heaved it at the window, but it merely cracked the sturdy glass and bounced off. She picked it up and swung it like a baseball bat. Bits of porcelain fell to the floor, but the window bent outward. A few more hits and she would have it. Hope flared.

A crash of wood behind her replaced the hope with terror. Splinters hit the back of her head and the rush of cooler air told her the thing had gained entrance. Toilet lid held high, she turned to face her demon.

He stood well over six feet tall, a fusion of avian and man. Bird legs and feet supported a male torso and head, all covered in the inky black feathers. The familiar blue eyes peered out at her from under a tufted brow. Bloody tears dripped from the eyes, landing on the floor at his feet where he tracked talon prints as he drew closer to her.

"Darcy . . ."

Whimpering, she fell to her knees, and the toilet lid clattered to the floor.

"I swear, I didn't . . . it was an accident . . . "

"Hush. No lies."

His soft voice caressed her. "I'm sorry. It was an accident."

"I said no lies." He reached out a feathered hand and touched her cheek.

The fringe felt silky and tickled her skin. "Michael, I—"

Her head snapped back with the force of his slap and she tasted blood.

"I told you no lies." His voice turned hard. "Do not speak with your forked tongue, bitch."

She looked up at him, stunned into silence. In all their time together, he'd never struck her. Not even . . . not even when she killed him.

"You know why I'm here." His voice was soft again and his gaze stroked her soul.

"Yes." Her voice came out only as a whisper. "Please, I love you so much."

His eyes turned cold. "There is no love in your heart."

He knelt down to her, covered her mouth with his. He tasted like Michael, but the feathers on his face stroked her cheek. His hand grasped her breast, hard, twisted. She tried to back out of his embrace, but he pushed and the momentum carried her to the floor.

He peered down at her from above, bloody tears dripping onto her face. He raised one hand to her neck and squeezed as the other hand dragged talons in a line from the hollow of her throat to her belly.

The pressure on her neck prevented her from screaming. Her heart pounded as he split her ribcage to expose it. The feathers on his hands grazed the pulsating muscle, then gripped tightly and yanked the still beating organ from her torso.

His expression remained mild when he kissed her heart.

The last thing she saw was azure blue sky through the shattered bathroom window.

Playdate

DAWN NAPIER

TAMMY WATCHED HER daughter run around the back yard. Molly laughed as she scampered here and there, chasing imaginary friends and kicking up leaves. The fallen leaves were everywhere. Tammy used to rake every day, but the leaves were back every morning when she woke up. She had finally given up. Molly loved playing in the leaves anyway.

She's so happy, Tammy thought. It must be the sunshine. Rainy days make her grumpy.

Then Tammy smiled. Sunny, happy days like this one were so much easier on both of them. The last time it had rained, Molly had cried inconsolably from dawn until dusk.

Molly ran up to her, and Tammy's smile froze. Molly had that serious look again, which mean that she was about to ask The Question.

"Mommy, can Addison come over to play?"

Tammy sighed and ruffled Molly's curly hair. "I don't know, hon. I've got a lot to do today."

A total lie, but Tammy wasn't about to tell Molly the truth—that Addison and her snooty mother were snubbing them and had been for weeks. Joanne never called anymore, not even to just say hello, and when Tammy called Joanne, the other woman always brushed her off and hung up as quickly as she could. Bitch.

"We'll play in my room and we'll be really quiet!" Molly cried. "You can do whatever you gotta do, and we'll play in my room! Please Mommy?"

Tammy sighed. She dreaded making that phone call, hearing the inevitable no, and seeing Molly's crestfallen face. It hurt Tammy's heart to see her daughter so hurt and disappointed. But it was such a nice, sunny day—maybe she'd cheer up again quickly. Tammy thought there might still be ice cream bars in the freezer. Ice cream was always good for getting over disappointment.

Tammy went to the phone and dialed Joanne's number from memory. She felt like she'd called the woman every day for a week, though that surely couldn't be. The days just ran together, now that she and Molly were alone so much.

Joanne picked up on the second ring. "Hello, Tammy," she said. Her voice wasn't angry, but it wasn't welcoming either. She sounded wary, almost afraid. What was she afraid of?

"Hi Joanne! How are you?" Tammy forced cheer into her voice, as though her entire life wasn't collapsing around her.

"Just fine, Tammy. And yourself?"

"Oh, I'm all right. A little bored today, though. Would it be all right if Addie came over for a playdate?"

A long silence. Tammy wondered if Joanne had hung up already. She'd done it before.

"I don't think so, Tammy. I'm sorry, but Addison's got a lot to do today."

The same bullshit excuse Tammy had tried to use on Molly. Her hands clenched with anger. Who did this uppity bitch think she was, treating Tammy like a four year old?

Well she was done letting it go; that was for damn sure. Molly's feelings were going to be crushed—again—and Tammy was going to dish it out a little.

"Look Joanne, what is your problem? It feels like I've called you a dozen times—"

"Ten," Joanne said. "You've called ten times."

"Ten times. I've called you ten times, you say no every time, never an explanation. You never tell me why Addie can't come over, you just say no and hang up and you need to tell me why right now, or I swear I will call and call until hell freezes over! What is your problem?"

Another long silence. "You probably would, wouldn't you?"

"Damn right I would. Now tell me."

"I've tried telling you before," Joanne said. "I don't know if you can't hear or don't understand. But I did try."

"Try again." Tammy was adamant. She was tired of getting the brushoff, and surely Molly was too.

Joanne sighed. "Well—look. It's your house. It's not safe for little kids to play in anymore."

"What are you talking about?" Tammy looked around at her sturdy little house. It was the safest thing with four walls, neatly decorated, okay a little messy, but no house with a child was going to look like a museum exhibit. "Are you saying my house isn't good enough for your precious daughter to play in? Not clean enough? Not new enough? Jesus, when did you become such a snob?"

Joanne's voice was sad. "Tammy, you need to stop calling me. You need to move on, and find whatever else there is out there."

Tammy started to cry. She hated herself for it; crying was such a hormonal-weak-woman thing to do, but she couldn't help it. She was so alone, and so damned tired.

"Move on to what? To *what,* Joanne? Jeff's gone, and he's not coming back. I got laid off from my job, the only job I'm qualified for. I have no money, no degree . . . All I have left is Molly, and you're hurting her. It's bad enough that you won't talk to me, but think of what you're doing to my little girl. Please."

Joanne sighed. Her voice sounded choked, as if she were crying too. "I'm sorry, Tammy. I'm really sorry for you, and for Molly. I don't know what comes next. But don't you think you owe it to Molly and yourself to find out?"

"I have to go." Tammy's tears were pouring now. Joanne's kind voice was only making her feel worse. She would have preferred that Joanne be a total bitch so that Tammy could fight instead of crying. She hung up the phone.

Joanne had put an end to their friendship. Tammy didn't know why, but it was plain that she and Molly were on their own. They were alone.

Tammy went out to the back yard to give Molly the bad news.

***

Joanne hung up the phone and leaned against the wall. She felt drained and empty, and she was fighting not to cry.

"That was her again, wasn't it?" Addison asked.

Joanne turned and looked at her teenaged daughter. "Yes, that was Tammy again. She wanted you to go over and play with Molly."

Addison shivered. "How many times has she called now?"

"Ten times," Joanne said softly. "Every year, on the anniversary of the fire."

"You've even changed our number."

Joanne nodded. "Twice. I guess being dead is the ultimate Yellow Pages."

"I'm gonna go for a bike ride, okay? I need to clear my head." Addison was out the door before Joanne could even nod.

Addison rode her bike across town to Tammy and Molly's old neighborhood. She was officially forbidden to go this far by herself, but what her mother didn't know wouldn't hurt her. Dad worked at the car wash nearby, but he wouldn't say anything if he saw her. He would understand.

Addison rode down James Street and stopped in front of the empty lot that had once held a neat little brown Cape Cod. Until the fire.

She had only been four years old when it happened, barely old enough to understand the concept of death. All she'd known at the time was that Molly was gone, and there would be no more playdates. Much later, Dad had explained that Tammy had gotten drunk and fallen asleep with a lit cigarette in her hand.

Molly's body had been found in the upstairs closet. Smoke inhalation. She probably hadn't suffered. Addison supposed that this bit of information had been intended to be comforting.

Thank goodness it was pouring rain that day, Addison thought, looking up at the clear, sunny sky. If it had been a day like this one, every house on the block might have been toasted.

Addison got off her bike and walked around the empty, leaf-strewn lot. The house had been torn down rather than rebuilt. Probably too old and beat-up. But nobody had ever done anything with the lot. Addison didn't even see a For Sale sign.

"Molly?" she said. A cool breeze ruffled her hair. The street was silent.

"Molly, I know you're here," Addison said. I can't see you, but I can feel you. Can you feel me?"

Another light breeze. A few autumn leaves swirled.

"Molly, you need to tell your mother that it's time to let go. I think she feels guilty about the fire, and that's why she keeps calling my mom. But she needs to let go and move on, and so do you. Can you tell her that?"

Silence. Not even a whisper of a breeze. Addison felt like she was standing in a closed room.

"You were my best friend," Addison said softly. "I hope you can hear me."

Then she got on her bike and rode away.

Moths

MAGNOLIA LOUISE ERDELAC

(with Edward M. Erdelac)

IT WAS WELL past dark by the time Markos told Mr. Anthony and Ms. Jenny that two of the nine Campfire Kids that had left the camp on the hike were not with the group when they returned.

"Mike went off the trail and Jasmine went back for him," Markos said.

"Where?" Ms. Jenny asked, fighting to keep the shrillness out of her voice.

"Back there," Markos said, pointing to the trail at the edge of the campground.

Now she fought down the urge to grab Markos and shake him. Mike and Markos were tent partners. They were supposed to stay together.

"Why didn't you say something earlier?"

Mr. Anthony spoke up. His voice was much calmer.

"When did they leave the trail, Markos?"

"It was when we were all looking up at the shooting star."

Mr. Anthony put his hand to his face and looked at Ms. Jenny.

That had been about a half hour ago, when Tamara had pointed up and squeaked and they'd all stood on the trail and watched the streak of light flash across the darkening sky in the direction of the campground. Mason had said it looked like the star was pointing them the way home.

Ms. Jenny stood up and clapped her hands.

"Ok guys, change of plans! We gotta go back on the trail right away!"

There were groans of protest all over camp.

"What for?"

"I thought we were gonna light the fire!"

"I'm hungry!"

Mr. Anthony took Ms. Jenny by the elbow and spoke lowly. "We can't take these kids back out on the trail after dark. Aren't there bears out here?"

"All right, I'll go. I'll go by myself," she said.

She picked the hissing kerosene lantern off the picnic table, leaving a halo of wheeling little bugs in sudden darkness.

"You can't," Mr. Anthony said. "Not by yourself."

"Well then what do we do?"

"I'll call a ranger," Mr. Anthony said, taking out his phone. He flicked it open and scowled at it after a minute. "No bars. I'll drive down to the Ranger Station."

"I don't think we should wait that long. It'll take you a half hour to get down there and back up. In that time we could be back to where they disappeared."

"I don't know about this. Do you want to risk losing another one?"

"We didn't lose these!" Ms. Jenny nearly shrieked.

"All right, all right, calm down." Mr. Anthony said. "You're right. They can't have gotten far."

Markos had been standing there watching them quietly the whole time.

Mr. Anthony looked down at him and felt like the boy had gotten a look behind the curtain and found a doddering little medicine peddler pulling switches. He knew all the kids looked up to him,. They thought of him as this big strong outdoors type. They all knew he had been in the Army, though none of them knew he'd never been overseas.

"Why did Mike leave the trail, Markos?" he asked, as Jenny went and rounded up the other kids, deflecting their protests and explaining what had happened.

Markos shrugged.

"He said he saw a big bug."

Mike and his bugs. The kid collected them. He'd brought three mason jars along on the trip in his backpack, and broken one when he sat down on the bus.

Mr. Anthony had cut his thumb picking all the glass out of his bag, making sure nothing had got in his lunch.

"And Jasmine saw him go and went to get him?"

Markos nodded.

Jasmine was like a little mother hen, always fussing over the other kids, making sure they had their stuff, that they were in line. The trouble was, she tended to cut out the chaperones, taking things into her own little hands.

"Ok, Ok." He patted Markos reassuringly on the shoulder, though the kid didn't seem to be the one that needed it.

Ms. Jenny came over, wide-eyed, the kids in a line behind her, flicking their flashlights on and off.

"Ok listen up!" Mr. Anthony boomed. "We gotta go back down the trail a little ways because Mike and Jasmine may have gotten lost. I want everybody to buddy up and follow me, boys in the front, girls in the back. Ms. Jenny is gonna walk Tail End Charlie. You guys know what Tail End Charlie is?"

"Way in the back."

"In the back."

"Behind."

"That's right. Nobody walks behind Ms. Jenny, understood? Flashlights on!"

Seven little flashlights, ranging from Mag-Lites to pink and white Hello Kitty lamps clicked on.

Mr. Anthony made a mock commando signal with his hand to get the boys following, and went off toward the dark opening, his lantern casting a bouncing light ahead of him.

Maybe they would find them on the trail, walking back.

After a half hour, they did not.

Mr. Anthony thought they had reached the spot, and he told the kids to take out their canteens and drink and rest. Then he waved Ms. Jenny up.

"Start looking along here."

"For what?" she hissed. She looked very upset. Her hair was a mess, breath coming out in huffs.

"For anything."

He turned to the kids then.

"Guys? Everybody start calling for Mike and Jasmine, ok?"

They had been calling the whole walk back, and there were more groans at that suggestion.

"Aw come on!"

"I'm tired!"

"I'm *still* hungry!"

"Come on gang, sound off!"

"JASMINE! MIKE! MIIIIKE! JAAASMINNNNE!"

They shined their lanterns up and down the trail. Nothing. It all looked the same.

Then Markos was tugging on Mr. Anthony's pant leg.

"What is it, Markos?"

"Found something."

Markos led Mr. Anthony to the side of the trail and pointed.

Laying maybe eight feet into the bush, which was slightly flattened, was one of Mike's empty mason jars. The light from the lantern caught the glass and the coppery lid.

Mr. Anthony studied the spot for a minute, looking at everything. He knew he looked like he was scouting for sign or something, but really he was just trying to convince himself Mike had passed that way. The leaves, the bush was flattened, one of the dry sapling branches was snapped. Sure. It looked like somebody might've gone this way.

He called Ms. Jenny over.

They cupped their hands and called Mike's name in that direction, as if it would make a difference there.

Nothing.

"It's definitely one of Mike's jars?" Ms. Jenny asked.

"Yeah."

"Well, let's go then." She started to walk off the trail.

"Wait a minute. We can't take these kids off the trail."

"What if they're just laying out there a few feet away unconscious?" Ms. Jenny said. "Maybe they fell in a gully and hit their heads, or maybe they ate some poison berries."

"Kids don't really do that, do they?" Mr. Anthony said.

"I didn't think kids wandered off into the woods until now," Ms. Jenny said. "We have to try."

Mr. Anthony sighed.

"All right. Hey kids!"

Seven heads turned towards him.

"We found one of Mike's jars. We're gonna go into the woods a little ways."

"I don't wanna!"

"Off the trail? Cool!"

"There's bears!"

"Awesome!"

"I'm scared!"

Two of the kids started to cry: Peter and Amy.

"Come on now, guys. We're just walking a little bit in there to see if we see them and if not, we're gonna turn right around and go get the ranger."

"Why can't we get the ranger right now?"

"Because he's too far away! Don't you wanna find Mike and Jasmine?" Ms. Jenny snapped.

"I guess," sniffled Amy.

"Not really," said Peter at the same time.

It took a bit more cajoling, but Peter agreed to go if he could ride on Mr. Anthony's shoulders, and Amy said she would go for Jasmine and Mike's sake.

It was a hard walk with a lot of complaining as the branches and stickers clawed them. Their lights lanced out in every direction like a real life search party, glancing off the gigantic trees and sending sleeping birds flapping out of the branches.

All the while they called the kids by name over and over again, and the only answer was their own voices echoing in the stillness.

They came to a kind of clearing, and the kids fanned out a bit, shining their lights all around.

"Stay together!" Ms. Jenny urged, coming last into the clearing. She looked at Mr. Anthony as he set Peter down.

He shook his head.

"Wow! Look at this tree!" said one of the girls.

They had seen Sequoia trees all day long. They had even gone to see the General Sherman, a giant among giants that was supposed to be thousands of years old.

This one was bigger. It was like a dinosaur. The kids could have stood hand in hand and not been able to reach either side of the trunk.

The kids shined their lights up it, talking all at once.

"What are we gonna do?" Ms. Jenny asked, on the verge of tears.

Before Mr. Anthony could answer, the kids started screaming.

Both adults rushed over to where the kids had gathered around the tree. No bears were attacking them, but several of the kids were hugging each other and crying.

Only Amy stood apart from them, pointing her Hello Kitty flashlight straight up at the lowest branch on the big tree.

Something was hanging from the branch. A big silvery bundle like a huge cocoon.

Mr. Anthony held up his lantern, the stronger light fully illuminating what the Hello Kitty flashlight had only hinted at.

There were two big cocoons.

Out of the bottom of one, a pair of red Converse tennis shoes poked out between the strands, out of the other, the toes of purple gym shoes.

Mr. Anthony's eyes bugged and he looked at Ms. Jenny, who was shaking her head. Then he looked for Markos.

"Markos?"

"Those are Mike's shoes," Markos confirmed, eyes big and wide.

"And I think those are Jasmine's," said Tamara.

Mr. Anthony thought they were right. You couldn't mistake those big red shoes. Bozo The Clown shoes, he'd said when he'd seen them, and Mike had just blinked. He didn't know Bozo The Clown from Ronald McDonald.

"What?" was all Ms. Jenny could say.

"Never mind that," said Mr. Anthony, crashing around the clearing with a purpose to keep the kids from seeing him shake. He found a sapling and uprooted it entirely, shaking the dirty roots before walking back under the cocoons.

The more timid kids were gathered around Ms. Jenny, hugging her legs as she pushed their heads toward her and stared up in disbelief.

Mr. Anthony handed Amy his lantern.

"Hold this for me, Amy."

The girl needed two hands to keep the light steady, but she did.

Mr. Anthony held up the long sapling. It barely reached Mike's shoes, and he had to stand on his tip toes.

He batted the cocoon like a piñata. It wavered on the branch and shook horribly, as if Mike had been sleeping inside and the poking had woken him up.

"Careful, Mike! Careful!" Mr. Anthony called up. "We've got you! Don't . . . "

But the thin strand holding the cocoon to the branch tore, the cocoon shifted, and fell.

Mr. Anthony rushed to catch it, but he was too late. It crashed to the ground, and the children screamed.

Ms. Jenny put her hand to her mouth and whimpered. It was such a long drop!

Mr. Anthony rushed over to the cocoon. It was dry to the touch, and it was squirming and trembling on the ground. Mr. Anthony waved Amy over with the light and felt all around the cocoon, praying the boy inside hadn't broken his neck.

When the lantern light bathed the gray silken bundle before him, he saw that the fall had partly broken it open. There was a black space torn over where Mike's nose might be, just wide enough to get his fingers in.

He did, and pulled. The gap got wider. He saw puffs of breath coming out of the hole. Mike was still alive inside. Still breathing.

He tore it wide enough to get his other hand in, and using all his strength, pulled.

"Hang on, Mike!" he grunted.

The cocoon tore open, coming apart in two pieces in his hands, and Mike flopped out onto the dry leaves and lay there, curled up with his knees and arms bent.

But Mike wasn't Mike.

Or at least, he wasn't how they'd all seen him last.

His body was covered in bristly white fur, wet all over like a new kitten. A pair of spindly white antennae were quivering like skinny daddy long legs limbs above his bushy eyebrows, and two clawed, buggy legs had torn through his shirt at the ribs. His fingers were growing together, and poking out of the back of his shirt were a pair of glistening brown spotted wings, like a moth's.

Mike's eyes opened. They were completely normal, all the more startling in that weird, fuzzy face. They seemed to plead for help.

Mr. Anthony stumbled back, and Ms. Jenny and the kids all screamed.

Amy dropped the light.

It was hard to see what happened next.

Amy dropped to her knees and covered her ears.

She heard rustling sounds overhead, and Ms. Jenny screamed again, and this time her scream got quieter. It sounded like she went up into the air.

Mr. Anthony yelled for the kids to run. He grabbed Amy by the shoulder, but Amy pulled away sobbing and crawled away into the bushes.

* * *

Amy saw Markos' shoes get sucked straight up out of the light, kicking. He screamed the whole time.

She saw the flashlight beams swinging wildly everywhere. When the lights pointed up towards the tree, she saw big winged things that looked like pale kites dropping down out of the top of the tree where the leaves were thickest. They passed in and out of the light; big brown spotted wings, and once she saw a hint of segmented legs, like a bug's, but enormous, curled around Peter as he kicked and screamed.

Above all the yelling and crashing, she heard a weird chittering sound.

Then something sharp and bony touched her shoulders, and she felt a fuzzy something close in her ear, twitching, moving.

She shrieked and struck out at it, feeling a big papery something, she guessed one of the wings. Then there was a breeze that knocked her flat and she was hoisted into the air.

She wailed as she saw the flashlights and the lantern rolling on the dark ground, the whole scene swirling as whatever it was swept her up towards the top of the tree, the wind blowing the hair across her face.

Mike's pale, fuzzy body still trembled down there somewhere.

She shut her eyes.

***

The seven flashlights and the two lanterns lay scattered in the clearing before the giant tree all night and all day, their light invisible in the sun.

A black bear snuffled at the edge of the clearing, smelling humans and their food, but then it smelled something else and decided against entering.

The flashlights were dim by the next night, but the lanterns still burned bright enough to make the big cocoons in the tree glow silver in the dark.

There were ten in all now, eight relatively little ones and two very big ones.

All the flashlight batteries began to die then, and the lights went out one by one, including Mr. Anthony's lantern and Ms. Jenny's, as the kerosene finally ran out.

Only Markos's Mag-Lite still shined, and one of the cocoons rustled and split, one big brown spotted wing unfurling before the battery finally expired and the light winked out.

There was a rustling among the leaves of the huge tree, and the sounds of big wings flapping.

The Keeper

AMANDA NETHERS

TOM SAT NERVOUSLY in his idling car outside the large prison complex, trying to steel his courage. "Remember not to show fear," he told himself, "and withhold judgment. You're there to listen." Why had the condemned man chosen him? He was no reporter, no writer. He had only snapped the photos that accompanied the sensational headlines. His job was to capture the moment, not comment. Words were another man's game.

He thumbed the letter again but did not open it. The message had circled his mind all week.

I am ready to speak now. Come Alone.

Aaron Lucas

They had called him The Keeper. Tom could no longer remember who had so named the butcher, but he agreed that it was appropriate. He had kept their hearts, their tongues, their eyes, and their hair. He dehumanized them and left his naked angels in visceral display, begging the world to see. Tom, an unwilling vehicle for the madman's message, had obliged.

The last tongue The Keeper kept was his own. Throughout the trial he remained stoic and silent. He did not meet the gaze of weeping families. He did not smile for those who stood in judgment. He did not flinch at the angry accusations or tearfully request mercy upon his sentencing. The killer had only shown emotion once during the trial, a movement so slight that, had Tom's lens not found the moment, it would have been lost in the tide of the court's proceedings. The next day the front page of every newspaper featured the grim picture of The Keeper looking blankly at the court as the prosecutor displayed his handiwork to the jury. The only sign of emotion was the slight upturn at the corner of the madman's mouth. He was smiling.

The guards buzzed Tom through the outermost gate and he walked briskly through the long fenced walkway to reach the doors of Cell Block D. The warden met him inside and walked him to the interview room.

"You're not the first, you know. Others have tried to pry a word from The Keeper." The old man grabbed Tom's arm as they stopped at the door. "What makes you think you're any different?"

Tom shrugged. "He asked me to come."

The warden eyed Tom for a moment before radioing to control. "Mr. Levy is ready. Open the door." The thick door buzzed as the warden pushed down on the handle to let Tom into the room. "Here you are Mr. Levy." He gestured to a panel on the wall by the door. "We will have cameras on you during the interview, but should you need to request immediate leave, please press this button and control will unlock the door." The old man spared a withering glance towards the prisoner shackled across the room. "You should be fine. He's hardly moved in twenty years." The door clicked shut and Tom was left alone with The Keeper.

Cautiously Tom walked to the table and chair left for him in the middle of the room. He sat down and pulled his notepad and recorder from his pockets. The prisoner watched him, but said nothing. Tom pushed the button on the recorder and heard the little device hum to life. He gulped back his fear and in a calm, steady voice said, "Shall we begin?"

At first, it looked as though the prisoner wasn't going to say a word. He sat silently for a moment before starting to move his jaw. The first words escaped his mouth in dry rasps that sounded like a worn engine trying to turn over, "You are Levy, then?" He reached for the bottle of water on the table but the chains kept it just out of reach. Tom moved the bottle closer and watched as the prisoner gulped it down.

"Yes. I received your letter."

The Keeper finished his water and broke into a coughing fit. "Please excuse the cough. My voice has grown idle. The vines of age are strangling me back to silence."

"Take your time."

"I suppose you would like to know why I wrote to you, and what I have to say after so many years." Tom handed him another bottle of water and said nothing. "I am dying, Mr. Levy. I have kept the truth long enough. She cannot hurt me now." He swallowed another gulp. "I'm sure of it."

***

I noticed her right away. I'd been living in that old courtyard motel down on Sycamore in the Fens for over five years. Do you know it? Yes? Well, then you know that life is faded down there; reds turn to rusted pinks, whites turn to sallow yellows, and blacks turn to dusty greys, but not her, every inch of her gleamed. Her eyes sparkled, her hair caught the moonlight just-so, and even her laugh sounded like a tinkling bell. She was a sparkling oasis in a desert of pawn shops, pay-day loans, and liquor stores. My starving eyes feasted as she walked across the courtyard to her new apartment. I had been painter years before, when I still had belief and passion to cling to, but my well had run dry as reality rusted the armor of my youth.

You can be anything you want, that's what they tell you, but it's what they don't say that's important. They don't say that the forty-year old alcoholic behind the gas-station counter had a dream once. They don't say that the mother clinging to the last vestiges of sanity as her kids squall around her wanted to be a dancer. They don't say dreaming is easier than doing. Yeah, we're the snowflake generation all right, but all those snowflakes forgot that most end up mixed with salt and left in a dirty pile by the side of the road.

Dreams die slowly. It was an unfortunate series of compromises that led me to the courtyard motel with my canvas and brushes stashed in a forgotten closet. I won't bore you with the wrong turns and missed chances. Suffice it to say that as I watched her stroll across the courtyard, I felt a stirring I thought had long died and my fingers itched to give it form.

That evening, after she had finished moving into her new space, my new neighbor strolled into the courtyard of the old motel and settled into a chair to bask in the warm night air. It didn't take very long for my fellow tenants to emerge from their own caves and make their way to the dry patch of grass in the center of our home. She was glorious to behold in the moonlight and they flitted around her like tired gypsy moths circling a welcome flame. Her laughter filled the night air and I could tell she had them all enthralled.

I didn't join them on that first night. Instead, I opened my long-forgotten closet in the back of my apartment and dragged my old friends back into the light. I set my easel on the balcony outside my second-floor digs and went to work. At first, my strokes were clumsy and ill-formed. Art is just like any other worthy endeavor; your body falls out of practice if not used regularly. Soon though, my mind and brush found a rhythm. I painted late into the evening until spent. I dragged my work back indoors and collapsed upon my bed in content exhaustion.

Now I can see what you're thinking. You're wondering what any of this has to do with my body count. I assure you it has everything to do with it. Please bear with me and you will come to understand why I had to do it; why I had to kill them all.

I woke up around eleven the next morning and started to get ready for the day. I was doing the three-to-eleven over at the bottling plant on King so I had a few hours to chill before I had to catch the two-fifteen bus. I showered, ate breakfast, and watched a little Maury before my morning-fogged brain remembered my painting. I opened the curtains to let in the light and gently set the canvas on my kitchen table to view my handiwork. It was not at all what I expected.

Instead of a pleasant moonlit scene depicting a warm evening gathering, I had painted something horrible. The background looked just as serene as I remembered but the people were all wrong. They were not standing and gaily chatting as I had witnessed the night before. No, in the painting they stood around my new neighbor's chair blank-eyed and slack-jawed. From the eyes of each person, I had painted a golden light flowing outward and joining into a powerful beam that poured into the chest of the figure sitting in the chair. And into their open mouths I had painted a stream of darkness that rushed down their throats and encircled their hearts in shadow.

But that wasn't the worst of it. In place of the stunning woman with golden, flowing hair I had painted a horrible and twisted creature. Its skin was a purplish hue that stretched across its bony frame like old, worn leather. Its gray, matted hair hung limp upon its slumped shoulders ending in uneven strands that framed its flat, sagging breasts. In place of her hands I had painted long talons that gripped and pierced the faded chair on which it perched. And its mouth, oh God, its mouth! In place of sensual, inviting lips I had painted a gaping maw filled with row upon circular row of pointed teeth. They dripped with a yellow slime and framed a darting forked tongue.

I lost my breakfast. How could I not? Then I hid the painting behind the couch so that I could mull it over without that *thing* staring at me. I tried to remember what I had seen the night before. The warm air, my old neighbors, the moonlight, the sad little courtyard, I could see all of those things clearly in my mind's eye. But when I tried to think of her, I only saw the demon.

Of course, I'm a rational man. I wondered if it was something I ate. Can burritos do that to a man? I mean, lord knows what's in those things. Sycamore doesn't really do five-star, ya know? Anyway, I thought about it on the bus ride to the plant, all through my shift, and on the way home. By the end of the night I had concluded that I must have hallucinated, like maybe I had gotten so tired or so into painting that my mind created something that wasn't there. I was okay with that reasoning; I could accept that. At least, that's what I thought before I walked into the courtyard that evening.

The tenants were gathered around as they had been the night before only this time instead of hearing the silvery laughter of my new neighbor, I heard a rasping cackle. As I tried to sneak up the stairs to the second floor, I risked a glance toward the courtyard and to my horror I saw the living image of what I had painted. Tendrils of bright light were once again streaming from the eyes of my neighbors and being funneled towards the chest of the decrepit monster. Just as in the painting, a thick smoke of darkness emanated from deep within the belly of the beast, flowing up through its open mouth and down into the slack-jawed tenants. At that point, I ran.

I never said I was a brave man. My feet took those stairs two at a time until they brought me breathless to my door. With trembling hands I worked the lock and rushed inside, quickly shutting the door behind me. And there I sat in the darkness, wondering if it was I or the world that had gone mad.

Now, I don't know about you, but when I was faced with my possible insanity . . . well, let's just say I took it rather *unwell*. This isn't exactly the type of thing you call the police about. In my part of town, that would just be inviting them to commit me. Besides, I was a bit scared they'd be right to do so. Nope, the police were out of the question so I did what any thinking man would do in a similar situation; I dead-bolted the door and then I got drunk, black-out drunk.

If Jim Beam is good for anything, it's good for crystallizing your core thoughts. It punches through all the bullshit and really gets down to it. I woke up the next morning with a dry mouth, a splitting headache, and a plan. After chugging some water, eating some toast, and main-lining some Folgers Dark Roast, I got to work.

My first stop was the door of my next-door neighbor, Harry. Both in the painting and in the courtyard the night before Harry had been front and center for the festivities. I wanted to know what he had seen. I gave a sharp rap on the door and heard Harry rustle awake.

Amanda Nethers

"Who's there?" From behind the door I heard him banging things around as he stumbled in the dark. "Christ, what time is it?" I knocked again. "I ain't got religion and I don't want none!" I knocked a third time as a smile crept upon my lips. "That's it! You creepy bastards ready to meet this God you're always going on about because I'm gonna . . . " He opened the door, bat in hand. "Oh, hey Aaron. What gives?"

He invited me in and I gave him the quick version. When I was done he gave me a look quite similar to the one you're giving me now. His face said I was crazy, his eyes told me he was thinking about whether he put the bat away too soon. "So, you didn't see anything like that, then?"

He shook his head. "Nah, I think I'd remember beams of light shooting from eyes", he shrugged, "You sure you didn't get some that ecstasy stuff the Bowman kids are always going on about? They say it makes you see things." He walked over to his kitchen counter and poured himself a cup of coffee and then poured some vodka in the glass. His hands were steady as a rock.

This is a man who's had the shakes for as long as I've known him. Fens Bends, he called them. That early in the morning his hands should have been vibrating like a car driving over railroad tracks. Instead his whole body seemed perfectly relaxed. "Say Harry," I tried to sound calm, and nonchalant, "what's with your hands? I thought those shakes of yours were about as regular as that old tom that visits Mrs. Holson's each night."

"Well, I'll tell ya," he said, "That new neighbor of ours sure ain't a monster but the sight of her does calm my nerves." He took another sip of his coffee, "it's that or the cancer that's finally catching up to me. It's like my organs are fighting over which one gets to kill me off first." He started to laugh and got to hacking. I waited patiently as the coughing fit subsided. "Truth is, I don't think I have very long." He raised his glass, "Might as well enjoy it, right?" I nodded my agreement and said my goodbyes.

My visits with the other neighbors went much the same. No one had seen anything close to what I had described. In fact they only had good things to say about the young woman in 2A. The only thing that seemed at all odd was their health. It was after I finished talking to Mrs. Holson that I realized all of them had mentioned feeling unwell. Jim, up in 10B, he called it *faded*, like his energy had just slipped away.

Since that avenue had brought me to a dead end I figured the next thing I ought to do was look it up. I mean, surely if there are demons in the world I can't be the first to have seen one, right? If I was looking for something normal I probably would have gone down to the Super's apartment and just used his old Britannica set but I figured looking up stuff about demons might raise his dander a bit. I'd had it hard enough with that guy; I didn't need him looking at me sideways. So instead I hopped the twelve-thirty down to the city library.

I'm sure you remember that things were a bit different back in 1986. You couldn't just pull a device out of your pocket and ask it a question. How the hell does that even work? I'm locked up in here because I save the world from a demon and *that's* too much to believe. Meanwhile it's common practice nowadays to carry around all-knowing magic boxes in your pocket. Yeah, that makes perfect sense.

Back then I wasn't exactly the type of man who spent his days in the library. I'm sure that before I began my slow descent into bitter adulthood some perky broad had taught my young self about dewey decimals but I had long since replaced that knowledge with much more important facts. I was going to need help and I didn't want some book Nazi giving me strange looks about my topic of research. So, on the bus ride over, I concocted a back-story.

I waited patiently in the line at the front desk and when it was my turn I opened my mouth prepared to lay out a glorious and intricate lie. It was not needed. The bored librarian hardly even looked at me. With a worn sigh she said, "What are you looking for?"

"Demons," I answered.

She tilted her head back and curtly said to the woman behind her, "Chloe, show this man to the nonfiction paranormal. He wants demons."

Chloe led me to a full row of books and at first I felt overwhelmed. I just took it one at time, reviewing each title and pulling the ones I thought might be useful. Ten minutes later I had eleven books sprawled across a wooden desk and was carefully thumbing through each one.

Those books were fascinating to me. I had never been one to believe in the things that go bump in the night but my new neighbor had changed all that. Consequently the books now read like the hidden history of the world instead of the ravings of people with too little wits or too much imagination.

It was in the eighth book, an old tome filled with pencil depictions of each named demon, that I found her. Well, it wasn't her exactly, but the drawing could have been her sister, it was that close.

Amanda Nethers

Succubus, that's what she was. She was stealing the life of all those around her and filling those empty vessels with tendrils of her darkness in place of their souls.

Once I knew exactly what I was looking for, it was much easier to get the information. Chloe helped me pull several more books that specifically covered succubi and I poured over them late into the evening. I left the library knowing what I must do.

I am not a religious man but I stopped at St. Michaels on the way home. I sprinkled holy water on the small knife I had always carried with me for protection and I asked the Catholic God to help me succeed. I wasn't sure he heard me but I figured it was worth a shot. That's how they get you, you know, when you're scared. They've built up these fabulous painted castles that exude authority with only one true message in mind. *"Come to us, we know."* I was still wary enough of religion to duck out before a priest could spy me. No use trading one soul thief for another, am I right?

I reached home at about nine-thirty. They were all in the courtyard and there were even some new people I had never seen before. They all stood there in the same trance I had witnessed each night before. My heart wept for what I had to do but the books had been quite clear. To save their souls I would have to kill their bodies, the only way to loose the anchor of that foul she-beast.

I struggled with the decision for weeks as I watched my neighbors further wither. Soon they were pale shadows of themselves. They seemed to haunt the dry courtyard night and day, waiting for the nightly ritual to begin. As the days went by new people began to join my neighbors and they too began to fade before my eyes.

I know now that it was fear and disbelief that stayed my hand for those weeks. I don't know that I would have ever acted on what I had learned if the children hadn't shown up. Seeing the Bowman kids, slack-jawed and glassy-eyed, spurred me to action. She had to be stopped and I was the only one who could do it. Harry was the first to die. He didn't even acknowledge my presence as I walked toward him with determined knife in hand. I knocked him to the ground and he fell over like I was tipping a board. The lights continued to flow from his eyes, the darkness continued to fill his heart.

I took the eyes first. The books hadn't warned me about how slimy they were nor how easily they popped from their sockets. My stomach turned as I set them aside. They truly are the windows of the soul. As soon as his eyes left him the windows were shut and the beam of

---

golden light ceased. The demon shrieked behind me as it happened but did not move. I could only hope the books were right, that she was just as caged as they while she consumed them. I swallowed my fear and continued

Next, I took his tongue. They're longer than they look and quite hard to hold unto when you're trying to saw through them with a small pocket knife. It helped my nerves that he did not struggle but nothing could ease my mind as I carved through the bloody slab. I managed it nonetheless and tossed the still wriggling meat next to his eyes. The books had been very clear about the order of things. The tongue needed to be removed so that the darkness could not return to its master. She had shrieked again as I severed the link but still she did not move.

Finally, I took the heart. I crudely carved into his chest again and again until at last I managed to wrench the heart from his body. That's when I knew I had done the right thing. He expended a last bloody, gurgling breath and died upon the courtyard grass. The blood trailed down my arm as I held his heart and envied his serenity. Some part of me already knew that my end would be much more unpleasant than his. That the heart still beat as I held it, was my only consolation.

I set the beating heart away from Harry's eyes and tongue and went to work on the others. Each fell as easily as he and each death hardened my resolve a little more. Except for the children, nothing can prepare you for killing such innocence. Her shrieks after each death drove me onward, even as the blood of the Bowmans dripped from my hands.

She did not move until I had severed the final cord. Once that link was cut, she launched herself from the chair and rushed upon me with all the fury of a demon scorned. But she did not strike me for in my hand I held the Super's heart and behind me set the beating pile of her dark anchor.

She howled in anger instead and, in a moment of fury, she let slip a roar of fire that swept the hair and clothes from their bodies. I stood my ground and found that the books had been correct. Because I held a part of her, the fires of her rage could not touch me. I saw her eyes grow desperate and watched as she wove a veil around her, thinking perhaps that she could still capture me in her thrall. It was, of course, no use. What is seen cannot be unseen. You know that just as well as I. She saw it as well and dropped all effort of the illusion. She took off running instead.

I didn't chase her right away. That she still lived told me other fingers of her darkness still gripped this world but I had to see to my friends first. I took care of them as best I could. I placed their hands over their hearts to cover the holes I had made. The curtains from Mrs. Holson's home made good blindfolds for their eyes. There wasn't much I could do to bury them so I left them naked and hairless upon the moonlit grass.

She led me from city to city over the next few months as she retreated to those she had already enthralled. I slaughtered them each time and I am sad to say I took less care with those who were not known to me. It was dirty work and her vessels became the object of my rage. How could they be so easily fooled? How could they not see the demon before them?

She grew weaker with every den I raided until at last, in Boston, I held her last beating toehold to the living in my hand. You wouldn't think that demons could cry but they'll do anything to meet their ends. She could not harm me so she begged instead. It was no use of course; she had made me a killer. My heart had filled with its own darkness; there was no room for hers.

I burned them, all of them, after piercing each with the blade to still their beating. A great belch of black filled the air as they turned ash and then dissipated in a rain of orange cinders. Her howl of pain was exquisite as she was dragged back from whence she came.

For that brief moment I saw the fires of hell. They're not as you would imagine. To one whose heart has been filled with cold and black, the warm fires offer a solace you cannot find in the naïve laughter of the blind masses. Only duty held my feet to the floor.

I kept them, the tongues and eyes, so that their souls would be safe. I locked them away to keep the vessels forever shut. They shall wither as the bodies but stay separate from them until the windows are no more and the soul is free.

***

There were no windows in the interviewing room but Tom's body told him he'd been sitting a long while. The recorder had gone through three tapes and the prisoner through eight bottles of water. He wasn't quite sure what to make of The Keeper, the old man was not at all what he had expected.

"That's quite a story, why tell it now?"

"You know I am to die tomorrow by the hands of righteous men. I wished them to know me as I am, not as what they see."

"Why me? Surely you could have found someone better, someone who could give your story the proper treatment."

The prisoner laughed. "To bend my words through their prism? No thanks." The Keeper placed his chained hands upon his knees and looked at Tom with earnest eyes. "Why you? Because you are a seer like me. You see things as they are."

"What . . ."

" . . . the pictures, Mr. Levy."

"The pictures?" Tom's mind raced through the photos he had taken and fell upon the last one he had snapped of The Keeper. "You smiled. Why?"

The prisoner smiled at Tom. "Because sir, they were at peace. Your lens saw them at peace."

Amanda Nethers

The Way

ERIN EVELAND

"**IT'S GOT 'TA** *way* about it." Grandpa said, as the tobacco spit shot out of his mouth in one thick stream from the peak of the barn roof and down. The trail left on his chin wouldn't be wiped off. Through the duration of the coming night, the brown stain of it would linger there.

The thick drip of its plummet seemed to last forever. Jacob watched it finally splat and spread like a slug on the pile of manure below from the steep barn roof he sat upon. He was third, and last, in line of the pitiful posse out that stifling evening, waiting for *the way* to make its path towards them. Jacob's father was in the middle. Pa once said Grandpa's stories were something left over from the war, a proper way to avoid the subject of madness, but now Pa was a believer. Pa was on the barn roof as well.

Jacob caught himself tilting over the rooftop, watching the spit fall, thinking about mortality, when some of the cedar shingles beneath him broke free. Snapping his body back, trying to catch his balance, Jacob heard more shingles break off. They knocked in offbeat rhythm along the rooftop before dropping off the side in a silent descent. Afraid to look at their landing place, he tried to spread his legs farther between the peak of the roof, straddling and gripping the splintered wood tighter beneath his calves. As much as he didn't want to think about it, he wondered what sound, if any, his body would make if he were to fall. A haystack couldn't be pitched high enough to save him.

The three of them were on the rooftop about an hour, Jacob supposed. Earlier, they had the afternoon to prepare for the thing

---

coming their way. It was Grandpa's job to unload everything on the barn roof. Ammunition, wooden crates, and mason jars were among the things Grandpa hauled up to the peak with a pulley. Jacob and his Pa fetched everything Grandpa told them to, and the things Grandma insisted upon, causing the old man to mutter the first callous words Jacob ever heard come out of his mouth toward her. Now wasn't the time to question that though. Grandpa was trying to prepare, and he wouldn't give up hollering from the barn roof, even when his rusted voice cut to a struggling rasp in his urgency.

Later in the night, Jacob would think a flashing thought before the terror would sink in. He would think about the food Grandma had put together in haste, the blankets she gave him to bring up, and what a waste of time fetching all that stuff was. He would know, even before seeing it with his eyes, that it was all for nothing.

At one point, Jacobs's temperature spiked in the muck air, trying to appease the old man's irritation, but his legs were ready to buckle from exhaustion. He braced himself at the water trough where the cattle drank, watching the oils from their tongues swirl in the stagnant water. That was the only time Grandpa came down from the barn since noon when he went up. Before Jacob knew he was behind him, the old man threw him in. The water was warm but still the shock of it caused the boy's body to jerk in spasms as he sprang out of the trough. The old man's eyes were crazed as he looked at Jacob. He said in a raging stir, "It's a' coming. It's a' coming and it's headed this way!"

Way resonated in Jacob's ears.

Growing up, Jacob remembered Grandpa talking from time to time about *the way*. Usually late at night when the old man had been tilting the glass bottle back a little too often in the woodshed. "Tinkering and a drinking," his Grandma would say in simple manner. She was a quiet woman with limited words, who carried the same humming tune with her wherever she went, but her words were filled with truth.

When Jacob reached his early teens, he'd become accustomed to checking in on the old man late at night in the shed. Most times he'd miss Grandpa, or find him asleep on the torn recliner salvaged for the workshop. Jacob would turn off the only light bulb dangling in the center of the dusty room, and help the old man to bed. Recently however, he caught the old man on a rare night. At night he spoke more about *the way*, and the meaning of it. This night Jacob found the old man standing, paused in mid motion, just staring forward. It wasn't staring though, Jacob surmised, because the man had a blank look in his eyes, a vacant stare. Then the stare turned into something else, the sight of memory, but Jacob didn't know it at the time. He only saw the old man's pupils dilate and then twitch back and forth as if they were scanning something in the distance. It looked as though he was trying to get reception out of a rabbit-eared television, scanning and shifting for clarity through the static waves that seemed to block his sight against reception. Then they fixed on something only the old man could see.

It was on this night that Jacob heard of *the way* in regards to it being a creature of sorts, and not just the rambling kinks of an old man's tongue.

"Teeth," Grandpa said nodding his head in affirmation, looking ahead.

"Teeth, Grandpa?" Jacob asked at his side, leery of his Grandfather for the first time.

The old man swung his arm up, drink in hand, and tilted it toward the wall, sloshing its pungent waters over the glass rim as he replied, "It's got blades for teeth."

"Are you talking about a chainsaw?"

He didn't acknowledge Jacob but continued to view the wall, "Its body is its teeth and the hair of it don't cut off when it moves."

"What are you talking about Grandpa?"

"I'm talking about the way *it* moves boy!" He said, spinning around to Jacob's surprise, "When it moves, it grows, like a swelling tornado, growing and changing course when you least expect it. It's a whirlwind of gnashing metal – joining everything it destroys inside of it. The sound it makes alone," Grandpa scorched, "will cut ya ta pieces." He turned back to the wall in observation, taking another drink. He spoke again with words that were only for him to hear, before trailing off into his own thoughts, "Got 'ta watch the way it moves, ta know where it's a' heading."

Jacob turned to leave, not knowing what to say to the old man who appeared to be ravaged by time and life. He gripped the handle of the door to leave when his Grandpa's voice called to him.

"Sit down boy." He said with soft ease, "I need you to listen to something your Pa never would." Jacob hesitated, but then pulled up a stool aside of his Grandpa, whom for the most part appeared to be placated, compared to moments before. "I'm going to tell you this," he began, "because one day it's gonna come again. I thought it would 'a by now, but see . . . there's been a rule. A rule we made at the time in hope, but I think that's been the reason we ain't seen it yet." Jacob

---

eyes squinted, trying to understand. He nodded his head not knowing what to say at the old man's face filled with grave memory. "When I was a boy, much younger than you," Grandpa continued, "there was this thing—a machine like thing . . . some said it came from the ground, and those of us left that saw it, believe it returned to the ground." He shook he head for a moment as if to clear his thoughts of assumptions. "One thing is truth Jacob, and that's it came once, and it will come again." His voice rose and then smoldered back down. "Two things though." He said pointing his free finger at Jacob, "Two things, the rule and us. Never spill blood on the earth. That's the rule boy. Never spill blood, and if it comes again—we'll be ready."

The old man's finger was shaking as if it were a testimony of determination. Whatever the thing was that grandpa tried to describe, one thing was for certain. He believed in it. Jacob heard his Pa's voice in the back of his mind warning him about *the way*, and what it had meant to Grandpa before this night came about. Pa had told him, warned him, not to indulge on the old man's delusions the way he once had. They were nothing more than repercussions of his time in the war his Pa always concluded; the enemies afoot and Grandpa in a trench, but still . . . Jacob felt he needed to know. He thought for a moment, watching the finger in front of him bounce up and down as it seemed Grandpa was speechless, and the creature he spoke of paused on the tip of his tongue. Still Jacob wanted to know. He needed to hear it from someone else to confirm the story his Grandpa had sampled on him, even if that verification meant Grandpa was a madman after all.

Finally Jacob asked, "Did Grandma ever see it?"

The old man cleared his throat of some choked up memory and said, "Naw—well if she ever did see it, she ain't never said." He dropped his finger and drink to the bench in front of him and leaned against it. "It was her mama though who stopped it. Her mama was the one."

"How'd she stop it Grandpa?" Jacob questioned.

"Don't rightly know" Grandpa sighed, clearing his throat again of lighter gravel, snapping out of the vision he'd been under, "all I know is that there weren't nothing to bury afterward."

"How do you know she stopped it when you don't even know how?"

"Because we saw her walk straight at it. She just 'a walked as calm as you sittin there, out into the field and over the hill toward it."

"How do you know she was the one who did it then?"

"Don't know I guess, but if you was there at the time you would have thought the same. One peculiar thing was though, she was carrying a candle in one hand and a rock in the other—a rock with her name on it."

"Oh the rock." Jacob said now captivated. He'd seen his great grandmother's grave down past the farmstead miles to the small graveyard where she was buried in the center. The marker for her gravesite was a simple rock with her name on it. Jacob assumed this was some shame on the family at the time considering they didn't have money then to afford something else for her. He never considered a reason why they didn't buy her a new one, or the idea it was something sacred in the family eye.

"She was carrying her tombstone with her—and she knew it." Grandpa said, "How she did it, we'll never know, but she did and she was a strong woman fur it."

Within the year of Grandpa's tale, the rule would be broken.

It happened at daybreak, but from the smell of it Farmer Richards' son, Patrick, had been working through the night on his deceased parents homestead. Once dawn came, everyone in a five mile radius could smell the iron in the air. It carried itself through the fields, past the crops and drenched its gutted stench into the minds of the elder farmers, alarming their hearts with the dawn.

Since the Richards passed away, their only son Patrick was left to care for the farm. Stopping by to deliver grain with his Pa, Jacob witnessed how the ramifications of maintaining a farm could go astray. It wasn't the usual burden of sustaining a farm; it was what would become of it if left in a genuine madman's possession. On this delivery, Patrick came out wearing the same clothing he'd hung on himself five days before when Jacob saw him last. The grime imbedded in the stains smelled of feces; his or the livestock, Jacob wasn't sure. His face and breath however, repulsed all but the flies while his smile was the tipping scale toward lunacy.

The last time he saw Patrick, his Pa had been giving the Richards' son a low down on the conditions of the farm. It was the animals Jacob couldn't look at. They mirrored their caretaker, and their scaling hides and shrunken faces spoke of desolation.

When they left Richards' farm, Jacob heard Patrick's chuckling holler ring out to the back of Pa's pickup truck, "No one's gonna take it away," he shrieked, "No one's gonna take me away or them!"

Jacob never saw Patrick again but he heard about what the man did, this morning of the blood. His Grandpa was the first out of the house and down to Richards' farm. When he returned Jacob listened to the tale of the morning's events.

Through the night and into the dawn, Patrick slaughtered his livestock. Although it wasn't slaughter the way a farmer talks of it, meant for the purpose of the feeding a family and butchering for the market, it was massacre in senseless form. In huffing breaths, Grandpa had relayed to Pa the way he'd found the farm. Trails of feathers, claws, beaks and hooves were strewn about the farmstead while a path of their pieced out entrails led to one place; the back pasture where the steers had grazed. Grandpa found Patrick in the back eighty, next to a pile of livestock he was feeding into a wood chipper and shoveling the remains into the manure spreader. Jacob listened in, noticing Grandpa's right temple was gashed open and learned Patrick attacked him with the shovel when Grandpa tried to stop him. The old man said he was knocked out for a time, but when he came round he saw Patrick using the manure spreader; gushing blood and livestock remains across the field and over the scrap heap lying alongside of one of Richards' hills. The scrap heap was filled of old farm equipment, bed springs and wash tub drums along with other objects foreign to the eye, as time on the earth had imbedded them into its soil grave. Grandpa said there was nothing more he could do. The creature would be awakened, and soon it would be on the move.

Pa listened to the old man's words, inhaling the proceedings of the morning along with the tainted breeze blowing between them. He was concerned, but not convinced of Grandpa's warning, that is, til the ground was a tremor of spasmodic waves. It was then that the three of them started preparations for the creature to come.

Now they were on top of the barn and Jacob was not only afraid of falling, but terrified of the creature Grandpa scoped for along the horizon. "Gotta watch *the way* ta know where it's heading," the old man said again, scoping the distant tree line across the field to Richards' farm from the top of the barn. He sniffed the air, keeping his bloodshot eyes focused from reeling before tilting his body back, as if he wanted to snuff out the metal in the air.

Jacob and his Pa had climbed out through the hay loft window used to toss bales of hay down to the cattle. Climbing through to the rooftop, Jacob almost dropped his shot gun, but Grandpa snagged it in time. This evening, the gun seemed to be more important than the years of affection the old man had given him; the old man had been watching the earth, the air, the birds for any sign of *the way* since he was a boy, and now he looked for its movements coming from afar.

Erin Eveland

While the old man scanned the distance, Pa took out a mason jar filled with Grandpa's brew. Nothing went unnoticed. The old man swiped it out of his hands in irritation, took one long swig himself before pitching the firewater off the side of the barn. All was quiet for a time. The ground ceased to tremor, and hope filled the air. Jacob watched the final snuff of the setting sun's fire along the horizon as twilight took over. Pa stood up to take a leak, not able to arch his spill far enough to the edge. Jacob watched the piss bead off and down the side when he heard his Grandpa's solemn voice announce, "This way it comes."

In the distance, the standing hard wood timber fell to the wayside as toothpicks along its path. Black birds in the trees separated in one giant fold so that the sky looked like one great arc of winged feathers, and for each quill, a bird. Jacob could smell it, but before he could see it, he heard the sound it made. The sound Grandpa had spoken of, and with the sound it came into sight.

Jacob was horrified in morbid fascination watching the creature, and the way it moved, coming closer to the barn, and to him. They were still for a time, bewildered by the abomination they beheld not only growing in size but in substance. Even from afar, Jacob now understood the bite of what Grandpa tried to explain. The thing was on a methodical rampage. Anything living in its way was consumed in its destructive path.

It zigzagged and jolted in gyrations of fluid motion despite all its jarring. Jacob saw the creature folding and unfolding itself as the reverberations of its metallic scraping sliced metal shards into his racking bones. The slivers of its sound made Jacob feel like knives were being drug up and down his skin, sharpening themselves on his marrow and cutting fragments of his shins, cheek, neck and rippling spine in its workings. Soon he would understand why.

When it came into full view across the field, he saw a thousand blades of different proportions; all colors of metal, shapes and size formed into one giant mass, creating a spindling ball of steel. Metallic blossoms opened and closed, sucking in before folding back out again. Within the revolving metal flapped intestines around the blades, like snakes trapped in a pit. They writhed and slapped against each other while some of them shot out as if they could inflict a deadly bite in their thrashing wake, splattering what was left of their guts and gray matter as venom. The eyes of steers bounced through it, while the white and brown of their hides flapped in tattered pieces around the gyrating creature. Even at a distance, the scraps of flapping flesh were molding around the metal blades of the creature; hardening to it and

---

The Way

117

using the tallow of the cattle like glue, while leaving a fine shearing glisten along its edges.

The horns of steers came together in the middle. Like the eyes within the mass of tilling blades, they were not shred into fragments. The horns were knotted and twisted in the center but their prong-tipped ends protruded out as spears.

A scream bellowed from the west neighbor's farmstead where the Lipinskis lived. It could have been none other than Mrs. Lipinski, witnessing the same thing Jacob did now. The dicing blades veered directly toward her voice, cubing and ingesting all in its direction. Once the monster reached the homestead, her screaming ceased inside of the sound of a thousand chainsaws ripping their way through her two story house that cascaded into the air as easy as dandelion seeds from the bulb.

The creature suspended itself in the middle of the aftermath of what once was Lipinski's home. Jacob could see the tips of its blades revolving over the evergreens that lined a border around the old farm; it had grown and it was searching for more.

On top of the barn, none of them breathed, but the horses, cattle and other livestock, shut in the barn, suddenly became restless feeling the creature's presence near. The animals inside howled to be set free. The horses, along with the cattle and smaller fowl kicked their hooves, flapped their wings and butted heads against the barn wood. The barn rattled from the calamity within, attracting the attention of the creature that wanted nothing more than to consume.

Its tines and rusted spokes stopped for a heartbeat. It angled its attention straight for the blood-curdling barn Jacob sat upon with the wailing animals inside. Now the men breathed in panic. The creature was coming afoot.

Grandpa turned with a rifle in his lap, hollering for a crowbar even though the three of them sat side by side. Pa rifled through one of the bags, pulled one out and before the old man could take over, Grandpa pried open one of the crates they'd brought up. Inside the shimmied wood caked with dust, lay sticks of dynamite. Some were intact while others were covered in crystalline particles of nitro glycerin. The sticks were delicate to the touch, as their stability was no longer confined by shell and wick alone. Grandma saved crates of dynamite that her father had horded since his mining days at the limestone quarry, stamped with the mine name. Pa grabbed one and handed it to the old man holding a sparker in his hand. Before Grandpa could light the stick, Pa was holding another one for the assault.

Jacob sat, holding a shaking shotgun in his hands. In an abrupt bang, the latch of the barn door gave in and the animals within spilled out in random plight. There was no hope from them now. The creature weaved about as a spider making a web, picking them off the ground like fleas in its violent string of destruction. Devouring them, the earth was tilled up and spat out in its path, leaving everything in its way a gouged barren landscape. Even though the animals were nothing but a morsel for the amber bladed beast, it grew nonetheless. Hell's terror had a form, and it was close now; too close.

The first stick of dynamite was launched. Half way in the air the creature sensed it, tilting its blades on an axis to avoid the blow. Leveling itself back into proportion, it fixated on the old man on the barn roof and headed straight for him.

Grandpa sent another stick its way, only to miss, hollowing another crater in the ground. The creature was deterred for a short time, as the dynamite was now thrown at random spots around the front and sides of the barn. It jagged to and fro as if in search for a weak spot while the two men opened another crate in frantic haste.

"Shoot Jacob!" rang the old man's voice. The creature was now toward the back of the barn and towering just as tall. Jacob's reflexes did the work for him, pulling the trigger and racking the pump with instinct rather than thought. The slugs only caused the creature to recoil with each fire, but it did not rebuke nor hinder the blasphemous beast from advancing.

Now the old man and Pa each held a stick of dynamite in both hands. It was as if the creature snapped to the sparkling attention of the men waiting to launch the explosives its way.

For a moment, the creature retreated in one backward pull, tearing out the windmill and woodshed in its wake. They could see it milling a vast trench back and forth as it contemplated attack.

Suddenly it curved round and toward the backside of the barn. Jacob's Pa elbowed him with commands to move forward. On hands and knees, Jacob crawled along the peak trying not to drop his shotgun. He could hear the wick of dynamite sizzling in his Pa's hands behind him, even though the shearing sound the creature made almost drowned it out. They pushed him towards the creature, head first. There was no stopping. Before Jacob could make it to the other side of the barn, the creature's spindling blades started to tear away at the siding.

Two missiles of glowing flames sailed over Jacob's head, only to explode prematurely before complete impact. They did strike

---

however, one to each side on the cusp of the creature's metallic swiveling petals. The creature screeched an ear-deafening holler that made Jacob twist round on his backside from the pain of its howl. The shotgun in his grasp fell and dry fired; fortunately for Jacob he hadn't thought about reloading it in the rush. He looked up at his Pa behind him, standing with his hands over his ears, where the ignited dynamite was cupped within. In one great swoop of chipping wood, the backside of the barn started to buckle. Jacob was sliding toward the monster; head tilted back looking at it upside down while the peak of the roof trenched his body in thudding agitation. His vision thumped as he saw the mouthing horns of the creature separating to devour his flailing body whole.

In the barn's annihilation, Pa lost his balance and tumbled over Jacob. Jacob watched Pa's terror stricken face, as he free fell to the mouth of the beast. Before he would be caught in its grinding teeth, the dynamite detonated, sending fragments of Pa along with the explosion. .

The blast was close, but not close enough. The creature shrieked another howl of pain. The white horns of its mouth were chipped and colored now with soot and crimson particles of Jacob's father. Only Pa's legs were left, and they became a part of the creature the instant they touched its grappling mouth, jerking in time with the monster's roar.

Jacob hadn't time to think on what he just witnessed, but his bewildered horror was starting to work the thought process for him. With the explosion came a suspension; the barn ceased to fall, stuck midway between erect and collapsing. Jacob's head and arms were dangling off the roughage of century old timber, when his Grandpa gripped his shirt to hoist him up. For a flash they looked into each other's eyes with recognition: *This was the way of the beast, and no man could appease nor stop the way of it coming. No man knows how.*

Their gaze was broken by a sudden intake of the air around them. The old man looked up and past Jacob, still laying backside to the beast. His eyes brightened, fixated on the creature that haunted him through the decades. Jacobs head turned and saw what the old man did. The titanic spools of blades had somehow lifted off the ground in its fury, ready to come to a crash on the sodden earth below.

When it landed, the shockwave parted the earth beneath. The barn rippled in the quake, buckling studs, and sending Jacob and his Grandfather into a plummet of death. The old man fell on top of him as they rode the rocking surf, expecting the landing to be the last encounter they would have. Somehow, the sea of rippling cedar shingles stopped abruptly and the two of them hung over the edge, clinging to the barn as if they were on a mountain, too exhausted to climb and yet unwilling to fall.

The creature was upon them.

It spun around the side, gyrating within beckoning blades of merciless resolve. If Jacob understood anything about *the way* of it, he would have said it was smiling. He would have said the propelling wind asked one simple question; *who would be the first.*

Staring into the metallic bud of cascading knives, Jacob heard a faint sound, out of place, and time, behind the towering creature that paused just long enough to torment them in its gluttonous whirl.

At first Jacob thought it was his mind singing some lost melody to a tune he picked apart from the searing edge of the blades at work in front of him. Grandpa's eyes however, told him he was not alone in hearing the melancholy rhythm of an old woman's voice down below: It was Grandmother's voice ringing out in a song that only she knew the words to, but one Jacob had heard her hum all of his life.

They watched Grandmother walk towards them through the blades of the monster. Her white dress billowed as she came to a stance behind the creature.

She carried a slab of limestone in her hand, and a candle threatening to give out in the other. The creature folded in on itself, and then appeared to turn inside out, facing Jacob's Grandmother, whose calm demeanor appeared ready for this day more than the old man had ever been.

Her song started anew, and Jacob could hear the words to her ancient hum for the first and last time.

I am a miner's daughter
Who will follow my mother
Walk in her footsteps
Against the wrath of my father
His body is a heap of dust
Betrayed by the machine
Harvesting nothing more
But the ire I have seen
His spirit does linger
In the belly of the beast
Who rises with thunder
Which must be laid to peace.

With her melodic rhythm, the revolving blades of the creature vibrated in mid-motion, fluttering as if the machine was jammed with a spoke, coring deep within its lifeless heart. Grandma set the white stone down and advanced in willful strides against the towering beast in front of her, only her candle in front.

Jacob thought he'd heard it holler before, the deafening scream, but that was far from what the creature was capable of. Once again the air sucked in toward the creature. The intake pulled Jacobs breath away. He knew what was to follow. Now he understood *the way* of it, and it was getting ready to unleash its paralyzing scream on a helpless old woman and the candlewick flame she protected.

With the intake, he saw Grandma lift the first layer of her skirtings as if to shield the flame, but why Jacob couldn't comprehend.

Grandpa yelled out to her; a simple word full of meaning and echoing disbelief. He cried, *"Noooooo"*, reaching out to her on the crumbling roof, and lost his grip. Jacob didn't look. He couldn't after the old man went over the edge, lest he falter and lose his own nerve as well.

The creature had risen off the ground with the inhale and now it was getting ready to blast its deadening howl. It slammed down, sending boulders of earth, rock and tree roots in all directions. With its thundering crash came its demon cry. This time the sound didn't deafen Jacob momentarily, it blasted his eardrums out.

Jacob lay on his side, ears spilling blood, and he caught the last glimpse of his Grandmother and her fate.

Weakened, she managed to work herself into a stance, blood pouring from her ears as well. She'd made it up on heavy trembling legs. The candle was in one hand and the gathering of her layered dress was lifted up and bunched in the other. Jacob saw what was packed underneath: Dynamite. Layers stacked and strung around with precision only a miner's daughter would know. Within the bundle of her dress stuck out a single wick, uniting the sticks bound to her body.

The creature was on the advance, hungry from her defiance. The wick in her hand ignited, sizzling down her hand which burned a line in its pathway. The hardened eyes of the old woman didn't flinch, even when her dress caught on fire from the kindling wick in her mission.

Now the creature grasped her intentions but in its haste it hadn't time to slow down far enough from her. Skidding to a halt, the earth was spat up from its digging blades that attempted to retract the assault. The twisted burning wick instantaneously separated out along individual tracks, leading to different sections of dynamite strapped to her body. The creature might have been able to escape the coming explosion, if Grandma wouldn't have understood its purpose, but she did and she jumped right into its retreating blades.

Jacob saw the detonation, along with a thousand blades slicing through the air. He felt the searing heat of some of its metal fragments cut into him before all blacked out, and the day faded into recollection.

Decades later, when the earth was healed and time erased the memory of what happened on the farm; Jacob would find himself once again waiting on high. Scoping the distance, he would speak aloud to himself, more than to the others behind him, "It's got 'ta way about it, and this *way* it comes."

Out With the Old

LINDSEY BETH GODDARD

THE BODY OF Maxine Fischer's geriatric ex-husband stared lifelessly into the sky. It had long ago bled out, thick pools of crimson liquid congealing in the night air as a team of experts gathered information. A crime scene photographer circled the body, snapping pictures, as rigor mortis stiffened its features. Maxine had to look away when a mosquito landed on the white, chapped lips, searching—fruitlessly—for blood.

"Ms. Fischer," Deputy Jones said, like a puppy always at her heels. He stood at least a foot shorter than Maxine, his dark eyes too wide and eager, always searching for something more. "Is there anything else? Anything at all? You said Mr. Fischer was angry, attempting to forcibly enter the home—"

She cut the deputy short. "He *did* forcibly enter my home . . . "

The officer nodded, observing the shards of broken glass that lay splintered along the patio. "Yes, ma'am. I understand that. You are not under scrutiny here. I'm just trying to fill in the blanks." Maxine nodded her reply, pursing her lips and allowing the deputy to continue. "From what I can tell, Mr. Fischer has never been a violent man. He's never come into contact with law enforcement, anyway. There's not so much as a speeding ticket on record. Would you say this is a fair assessment of things, or was there another side to this man? A dark side? A violent streak that was never reported?"

"No, not Marty. He was a docile man. The spirit of the 1960's never truly left his heart . . . "

"Why then? What motivated him? Why did he lash out so violently? A recent argument, perhaps? Other troubles?"

Maxine sighed. She hugged close to the blue-eyed man at her side, snaking her hands beneath his jacket for warmth. He wrapped his long arms around her, gently swaying, as if comforting a child. He was tall, planting a kiss on her hairline as they slowly rocked back and forth. She laid her head against his chest, exhausted. "He wasn't happy about my leaving him for Rick. The divorce was finalized today. Maybe the reality of my absence was too much for him to handle. Maybe he couldn't let go . . . couldn't move on . . . " Her lip quivered as she recalled the look on his face as she had stared down the barrel of the shotgun, steadying her aim. She blinked hard, trying to erase the image.

Her eyes scanned a row of hard-jawed officers, bathed in the flickering glow of red and blue lights. She knew what they thought. The accusation on each cop's face was as plain as the badge on his shirt. Just look at the old man, his spindly fingers and liver-spotted hands smeared with streaks of his own gore. His balding scalp riddled with bloody fingerprints and pieces of decomposing flesh, from where he'd clawed at the wound in disbelief as he died, covering his face with his hands.

Marty had been approaching his seventieth birthday. Not a speck of black remained in his thinning, silver hair. His once broad shoulders were now bony and thin. His perfect posture had developed a hunch. The officers regarded his elderly corpse with a solemn pity, sizing up the new guy—the pretty boy Maxine Fischer snuggled up against as tears rolled down her cheeks, trailing mascara.

"Out with the old, in with the new," she overheard a young cop say. She looked up, shocked at the disrespect. She glared at him, eyes narrow and full of scorn. He seemed to feel the weight of her stare on his face, and swung his head in the other direction. Maxine scowled, eyes fixed on his back.

Rick cleared his throat. "Look, if there are no further questions, I think it's time for Maxine to get some rest."

"Yes, of course," Deputy Jones replied, tilting his head. "We'll contact you if we need anything else."

"Fair enough," Rick said, shaking his hand.

Yellow tape with the words "CRIME SCENE" written in bold, capital letters danced in the breeze as the couple walked side by side. Maxine paused, looking down at the corpse that lay in a puddle of excrement and blood. Exposed fat cells and muscle tissue surrounded the gaping wound in Martin's chest. His mouth hung open, colorless lips drawn into a postmortem frown. Maxine had to close her eyes to keep from crying.

Let the peanut gallery make their assumptions. Let everyone stand in judgment. The truth was, she hated to see him so mangled. She hated that *her finger* had pulled the trigger. Marty had once been a dashing professor, as brilliant as he was handsome, hounded by college girls, envied by colleagues. But age had not been kind to Professor Martin Fischer. He had grown ill, senile . . . burdensome.

She paused on the front porch, sliding her arm away from Rick's waist and turning to face the chaos on the lawn. Police cars lined the curb, some of their lights still flashing. Curious neighbors huddled in garages, or peered through the gaps in their curtains. She looked at Rick as he stood by her side, watching the coroner's van slowly inch up the drive. Her mind wandered, thinking back on a candlelit dinner they'd had just a few months ago . . .

In the glow of a candle, Rick's eyes gleamed a silvery blue that nearly took Maxine's breath away. He was poster boy handsome, right down to the dimple in his chin. Her eyes followed the line of his neck, past the sharp angle of his Adam's Apple. She lingered on the flesh of his chest, so tan against the open collar of his button-up shirt. His thick, brown hair always seemed to fall perfectly around his scalp, showing no trace of mousse or gel. He was a man of expensive taste, and it showed in the cut of his tailor-made suit. He smiled as he lifted a Whiskey Sour to his lips. It was a smile that said "I'm attractive, and you know it. Right down to each pearly tooth, I am perfect."

Maxine studied her own skin as she nursed a Vodka Tonic. Her hands were leathery, creased with wrinkles. Spider veins could be seen through her spray-on tan, though she had paid a great deal to "remove" them. There was a bruise near her wrist, though she didn't recall getting injured. She seemed to bruise easier these days, her body growing frail with age. She was reluctantly inching toward fifty-one, and all the Botox in the world couldn't bring back her youth.

When Rick was by her side, she saw the way people stared, sneaking glances when they thought her back was turned. Maxine understood how ridiculous it looked, her dating a man in his twenties. But she didn't care. To hell with their stares. He was gorgeous, full of life. Just what she needed.

"I'm leaving him," she said, swirling her drink with a straw.

Rick paused for a moment, donning his very best *concerned* expression. It reeked of bad acting, but Maxine didn't mind. When Rick feigned interest in her emotions, his eyes shimmered like glass, reflecting the apathy in his soul. She bit her lip and pretended not to notice. She gazed into those silver-blue orbs, knowing that this whole thing was a ruse: his interest in her, his attraction. His *love*. Maxine was loaded; she'd been loaded all her life. That's what appealed to Rick Huntley—her money. Not her body, not her soul.

But that was okay. None of it bothered Maxine. She felt at ease in his presence, full of hope. She found comfort in the moments of silence when Rick would run out of things to say (having talked about himself for an hour). It was peaceful here, sharing appetizers and drinks, admiring his gorgeous face as a cellist serenaded them with Bach. Most importantly, she was away from Martin and his obsessions . . . his ever-growing darkness and despair.

"You're leaving him? A divorce? That's a big step, Maxi. Are you sure?" She cringed at the sound of her name. Martin was the only man in her life who had ever called her *Maxi* and made it sound natural. Her nickname on anyone else's tongue seemed foreign, as if their lips had been forced to form the syllables. It fell flat, summoning mental images of feminine hygiene products. Or maybe she was frightened by change . . . by the sound of Martin's pet name on Rick's tongue.

"He's obsessed with the idea of getting old. It's all he talks about. All he *thinks* about! Mortality. Dying. I can't take it anymore, Rick, I can't!" Maxine sighed. It felt good to vent, but the words she spoke were only the tip of an enormous iceberg hidden just beneath the surface of her marriage. She didn't mention the strange rituals Martin had been performing, the black magic spells he'd collected after long, sleepless nights spent with his "research", flipping through timeworn books in the solitude of his den. She didn't tell Rick how one night as he chanted an incantation, the tiny pupils of his eyes began to widen, expanding. Darkness bled out from the center of his eye, past the light brown of his iris and onto the white portion, turning the entire surface black. It still gave her chills to think about it.

She rubbed the goosebumps from her flesh as Rick finished his Whiskey Sour. "Well then, I say it's time for a change." He gestured for a waiter with a wave of his hand. "We'll need a couple more drinks, because it's time for a toast. A toast to our new beginning."

Three months later they stood in front of the courthouse. The sky was a cloudless, brilliant blue, and sunlight poured over the parking lot, warming Maxine and causing a bead of sweat to trickle down her temple. Rick leaned against his silver Mercedes, frowning. "I thought it went well," she said, studying his expression. He only snorted in reply, tilting his bronze face toward the sun as he leaned on the hot metal car.

"I guess," he replied, after a moment of silence.

"What's that supposed to mean? It's over. My marriage is over. Now we can start something real. Something new."

Rick shrugged, arching one of his manicured eyebrows. "He put an awful big dent in your wallet, babe. I mean, all that money was yours from the start. He didn't deserve a dime." Maxine blinked, mulling over Rick's words before considering a response.

It was true. She'd been generous with Martin. Neither one of them had considered a prenuptial agreement when they tied the knot so many years ago. But the fact was, she was filthy rich. Parting with a small chunk of her fortune in order to speed up the divorce process was no problem. Plenty of money remained.

Her lips curled into a smirk. "Don't worry, Sugar Baby, Momma's still a millionaire."

Rick had to smile then, looking into her eyes, knowing full well she'd called him on his self-centered concern. He glanced around the parking lot. "Where's your driver?" he asked, referring to Maxine's hired chauffeur.

She checked the time on her diamond-studded watch. "He'll be along any minute. You don't have to wait around."

"I'll see you tonight," he said, opening the Mercedes door. He plucked a speck of lint from the spotless interior, tossing it to the side before sliding into the seat. He smoothed his jacket, fiddling with his keys.

A hand emerged from the back seat, snaking around his mouth. A dirty rag was shoved against his nose. He bucked weakly, like a tranquilized bull. The cloth obscured most of his vision, but Maxine saw the shock on his face. Rick put up a fight, but he was quickly losing stamina as the chloroform took effect. The writhing subsided, as his head lolled to one side. Maxine peered into the car and saw the top of Martin's face peering over Rick's shoulder from the back seat. His black eyes were fixed on her. "Get in," he said. "Let's go."

Maxine let out a breath she hadn't realized she'd been holding. The crackling of a dry leaf skidding across the asphalt caused her to jump. She looked around. A few cars were parked in a row of spaces parallel to her, but they were empty, most likely belonging to employees of the court—sitting behind their desks, blissfully unaware. A pedestrian stood at the intersection stoplight, waiting for the "walk" sign to flash. He faced away from her, drumming a beat to whatever song played on his ear phones, wires dangling from underneath his hat. And that was it. No sign of anyone else.

She climbed into the car as Marty pulled the unconscious body of her boyfriend into the backseat. He propped Rick into a sitting position. A thin trail of saliva dripped from the corner of his mouth. In the rear-view mirror, he looked like a washed up model who'd had too many drinks with lunch. She reached for Martin. She placed her hand at the back of his head. She kissed him deeply, running her French-tipped nails through the wisps of his thinning, gray hair. Her heart raced with excitement and love. She had missed him—the feel of him, the smell of him, his voice. She started the engine and eased the car into traffic, her right hand locking with his.

When Rick's eyelids fluttered open, Maxine was already staring at him. "Hello, lover," she said, mocking a tender voice. She smiled cruelly as he tugged on the restraints. Thick, braided rope was wound around his wrists, chafing the top layers of his perfectly tanned skin. Chains rattled against the handcuffs that sliced into his flesh. The metal gripped his wrists so tightly that his arms were throbbing with pain. Blood trickled from beneath the layers of rope. More of it wrapped his midriff and ankles. He squirmed helplessly on the cold, metal cot. "I'm so glad you're awake. I was hoping you could join us."

Rick tried to form words, but his tongue only scraped the dry, gritty rag stuffed in his mouth. He began to whimper, eyes pleading. He managed a few muffled grunts, coughing and gagging as he sucked a portion of the cloth down his throat. His eyelids were still heavy, and he fought the urge to close his eyes. The traces of an unknown drug coursed through his veins, making him dizzy.

Martin entered the room, his eyes as black as the hallway from which he emerged. The poorly lit den seemed to grow dimmer in his presence. Dark bags framed his eyes, as if he hadn't slept in days. His complexion was ghastly white, contrasted by the shadowy hall.

He held a book in his hands that chilled Rick to the core. Its cover was a patchwork of different colors and textures. It was roughly sewn, erratic in design. Seams intersected at odd angles on its surface. It was absent of a title. No text could be seen anywhere on the cover or spine. Rick didn't understand why the book, with its tattered yellow pages, was causing his heart to race. Martin flipped it open, and the lights began to flicker.

"You see, I never wanted a divorce. Not really," she said. Rick jumped at the sound of her voice. He fought against his restraints until the skin around them turned white. He shook his head when the struggle only caused him more pain. He turned to face Maxine, eyes startled. "But I never want to *lose* Martin, either," she continued. Her lips formed a guilty smile. She paced the floor in front of him, forcing his eyes to follow—back and forth. "So I had to find him a younger body."

She paused for a moment to study his reaction. His breathing became frantic, nostrils flaring with panic. "I was only interested in your body, baby. I told you that from the start . . . "

Martin started chanting. It was a low, rhythmic mantra at first, but soon it increased in volume. Rick wished he could cover his ears to block out the disturbing tone of voice. The air around Martin seemed to swirl and pulsate, like a heatwave permeating from his flesh. Rick noticed Maxine dousing a rag in chloroform. He bucked wildly, causing the chains to dig deeper into his flesh. She pressed the rag to his face as he fought her in vain. Rick Huntley's world, once again, went black.

Maxine could only imagine what happened when he awoke. They'd given him enough drugs to keep him unconscious during the ritual. He was sound asleep as they gathered the evidence, as they stacked Martin's collection of black magic books into a box and placed them in the trunk of Rick's car. They wiped the metal cot and folded it. They tucked it away, in a dark corner of the basement. They took the ropes and chains, leaving the house as it had once been—the hideaway of a brilliant, if somewhat aberrant, old professor. They left him there, on the floor of Martin Fischer's den, with only the dim light of a small desk lamp to greet him when he finally came to.

What happened when he awoke on Martin's stained area rug, surrounded by dusty bookcases? Was his first reaction to scoff at the dreary room, with its lack of designer decor? How long before he noticed his liver spotted hands? Or the bushy gray hair on his arms?

Did he look into the mirror, seeing the face of an old man? Did it floor him immediately into rage? Did he cry as he stared into those tired, brown eyes, set deep into the sockets of a wrinkled face?

Whatever the case, he had found Martin's keys. He had taken his car, driven home . . .

Rick had stormed up the path of his quiet suburban home, pounding wildly on the door with Martin's fists. He exhausted himself working a branch back and forth, until it finally pulled away from the bushes. He wheezed as he reared back, swinging the branch, shattering the bay window into shards. The frailness of his body seemed to catch him off guard, and he stumbled, landing palms down in the wreckage.

Had it terrified him to feel his old knees buckle? To fall backwards in the glass at Maxine's feet as she stared down the barrel of a gun?

No, Maxine could pinpoint his true moment of terror. She saw it in the way his eyes opened wide as the color drained away from his face. Rick stared, wild eyed, at his former body as it stood beside Maxine in the window. The handsome face that used to be his watched the scene with quiet approval.

But although Maxine knew the man inside Martin's body was no longer the man she loved, her finger hesitated on the trigger. She had to bite her lip, hard, when she finally pressed down, painting the porch with the old man's blood. Maxine shook her head, pushing the memory away. She didn't want to think about it. The dirty deed was done. Months and months of planning had paid off.

Still, the sight of Martin's body had disturbed her. Seeing the life drain out of his eyes. Or maybe it wasn't the body, or the blood and guts, that bothered her. Maybe it was the finality of things.

They had done it. Martin Fischer was inside of a younger man's body, looking at Maxine with brand new eyes. What did he see when he looked at her now? Did her flesh seem wrinkled pressed up against his?

She watched a group of neighbors gathered at the curb, her eyes lingering on a thin, fit blonde. "Maybe it's time I traded in for a newer model," she said.

Martin looked at her, his once brown eyes now a sparkling blue. He scrunched his eyebrows, shaking his head. "Don't be ridiculous, Maxi. You look great. You are absolutely in your prime."

He drew close to her, softly kissing her cheek, trailing warm breath down her neck. "Shall we go inside and celebrate, my dear?" His lips curled into a familiar grin. It was a smile that warmed Maxine's heart. Martin's face had changed, but he was the same man, somehow. In his eyes she saw a spark of attraction that had been absent in Rick's loveless gaze. He squeezed her hand the same way he'd been squeezing it for years, leading her through the doorway of their new home together.

"I love you, Martin Fischer. I always have. I don't know what I would do without you."

He closed the door behind them, sliding the lock into place. "I don't suppose you'll ever have to find out," he replied. "But just for show, I think you'll need to call me Rick."

Sometimes Monsters Are Real

KELLI A. WILKINS

*W*AKE UP. *Something is knocking.*

Janice blinked a few times, then rolled over and squinted at the clock on the dresser. The glowing numbers read 2:12.

She lay still, drifting somewhere between half-asleep and almost awake. Maybe she'd been dreaming . . .

Knock, knock, knock.

Her skin prickled, and she turned on the bedside lamp.

Knock, knock, knock.

She cursed and bolted out of bed. The noise had come from the ceiling.

"There's no reason to be afraid. It's a squirrel, or a branch banging on the roof."

Sure. Except a squirrel wouldn't knock three times. Squirrels can't count to three. It wants you to wake up. It wants you to know it's here.

It? What "it"?

She crossed the room and flipped on the lights. Dresser, nightstand, laundry hamper, bookcase. Everything was in its rightful place. Now what?

Check the house.

"Fine. Why the hell not? I'm already awake."

She pulled on a pair of gray sweatpants and opened the bedroom door. What if someone had broken in and was making noise in another part of the house? That might explain the knocks.

Burglars don't knock.

She crept down the dark hall and switched on the lamp as she entered the living room. The front door was still locked, the chain in place. Nobody had gotten in. Whatever the noise was, it had to be coming from outside.

Maybe it was a branch on the roof. Branches could sound like knocking. Besides, there was nothing over her bedroom except—

The attic.

Janice turned and headed back to her bedroom. The attic wasn't really an attic; it was more like a glorified crawlspace. How could something get up there? There were no windows, and the only access was through a small hatchway in her closet.

"To hell with it. Let it knock. I have to get up in four hours," she griped as she sat on the bed. She cast a suspicious glance at the closet door. It was still closed, like she had left it.

But what would you do if it was open a crack? Just enough so the thing could see out and watch you, but not enough for you to look inside? Monsters always lurk in closets.

Janice rubbed her temples. Why did these things always happen on weeknights when she had to go to work in the morning? Tomorrow was Friday, and Fridays were never good for her. Timmy's funeral was held on a Friday—a cold, dreary December Friday. To her, every Friday was a reminder of that horrible day.

It's after midnight now. It is Friday.

"Doctor Montgomery warned me about this," she muttered. "I should have taken a sleeping pill and dropped out of the world. Then I would have slept through—"

Knock, knock. Knock, knock.

Jesus! That noise wasn't on the roof. The forceful knocks came from above the bed. There was no denying it now. Some thing was in the attic.

Knock, knock. Knock, knock, knock.

Her skin broke out in goose bumps, and the hairs on her arms stood up. The rapping sounded . . . angry. Should she get dressed and leave? Call the police? No . . . she couldn't risk calling them because she heard a noise. This might be all in her mind. That's it, she reasoned.

This is a wild dream caused by those pills the doctor makes me take. These days, pills give you all sorts of side effects. People cook dinner in the middle of the night and don't remember it. Other people have vivid hallucinations. Why wouldn't I have strange dreams?

She nibbled on her thumbnail and eyed the closet door. Doctor Montgomery would tell her to face her fears. Be calm, cool, logical. Deal with one thing at a time. There was one way to know if this noise was real or in her head.

"Okay, fine, you, whatever you are. You want my attention? You got it."

Janice left the room and opened the hallway closet. A folding stepstool rested against the wall next to a flashlight. She carried them into the bedroom and glanced at the clock. 2:27. It had been fifteen minutes since she woke up, yet it felt like an hour. Time seemed slower. Maybe that's what night did—it played tricks on people.

She walked to the closet door and rested her hand on the fake brass knob. It felt cool in her sweaty palm. Should she? What if there was a man wearing a ski mask standing there? How many TV shows had she seen where women living alone were stalked by serial killers and murdered in their own homes?

She hesitated for a minute. What if I go sleep on the couch and ignore it?

Then you'll never know.

Screw that.

She turned the knob and yanked the closet door open.

Instead of a masked predator, all she saw were her clothes hanging in neat rows. Tension drained out of her shoulders. Okay, part one, done. Now I go up there, look around and—

And what?

One thing at a time.

Janice parted the clothes and set the stepstool under the opening to the attic. She aimed the flashlight at the two-by-three-foot piece of wood covering the hatchway.

To look inside the attic, she'd have to push up the wooden cover, slide it to the side, then climb all the way up the stepstool. Her head would be in the dark attic while the rest of her stood on the stool. If something attacked her, she would be utterly defenseless.

Janice climbed the first two stairs. The attic was quiet. Maybe that last batch of knocks meant it had left.

It. Like whatever it is has a consciousness.

Step three.

But what is it? Maybe a squirrel family had made a nest in the attic and was trying to get out. Or it could be birds. The roof was old; anything may have found an opening and crawled inside. Maybe bats.

Step four.

That's it! Bats are nocturnal. Maybe they were flying around and that's what made the noises. Bats flying could sound like knocking. She hated bats, but the thought of bats calmed her. Bats were a rational answer. Bats could be dealt with.

Kelli A. Wilkins

Step five.

She took a deep breath and placed her palm on the dusty wooden hatch. Okay. Give it a push and slide it over. Then go up and look. Be strong. This is your house. There's nothing to fear. One, two . . . three.

Janice shoved the board aside, then stepped up and peered over the edge of the attic floor. She aimed the flashlight into the corner. Demonic orange-yellow eyes reflected back at her.

She shrieked as the thing came toward her. Its arms jerked and flailed as if it was being manipulated on invisible strings. The creature's head was bent down, but she saw that it had a pointed nose, tiny ears, and a skeletal body covered with a coat of gray-white hair. Whatever it was, it had human-like hands and feet, except they were oversized and gnarled, with long black claws. A low rasping sound came from its chest.

She watched it, shocked and repulsed, yet oddly fascinated. "What the fuck are you?"

It came closer, lurching and twitching its way to the attic opening. Finally, it raised its head and locked its gaze onto hers. Its thin-lipped mouth opened wide, displaying rows of pointed black fangs.

Janice screamed and jumped back. Her right foot slipped off the stepstool and knocked it over. For a moment, she was suspended in mid-air, then she landed hard on a pile of shoes. The flashlight tumbled down through the closet, spinning light in all directions. She brought her arm up to shield her head—too late. The flashlight smacked against the side of her head and everything went dark.

***

Wake up or the monster is going to get you.

The booming voice in her head forced her to open her eyes. What the hell? Why was she on the floor?

She sat up and rubbed the side of her aching head. A second later, she heard a raspy, wheezing noise coming from the attic.

Everything flooded back to her in a flash. The knocking. The attic. The thing.

Don't look.

She forced herself to glance up.

The monster-thing sat perched at the edge of the attic hatchway, clicking its clawed fingers together. "Hello, Janisss."

She bolted from the bedroom and slammed the door behind her. Her knees shook as she ran into the living room and grabbed the phone.

Who are you calling? It's three in the morning.

The police. If she called the police maybe they would come out and look, to check, to make sure—

To make sure you're not crazy.

She plopped onto the couch, defeated. The police probably wouldn't come. They'd laugh and say Janice Petrovich is drunk and acting crazy again. First it's dead kids, then pink elephants, and now it's monsters in the closet.

Having a complete breakdown in a small town didn't do much for her reputation. Everyone knew she was nuts. Rumor had it that kids were warned to stay away from her house on Halloween.

Halloween. Why did she have to think about that? Timmy loved Halloween. Picking out the costume—what's better, a ninja, batman, or cowboy?—getting dressed up . . . parading at school . . . walking around the neighborhood collecting candy . . . She was thrilled to be with Timmy for that one year. That precious, gifted year. They did everything together and then—

A scratching noise pulled her from her memories. It was clawing at her bedroom door. It wanted to follow her.

"I should call the police. If they come here and see that . . . whatever it is . . . at least I'll know I'm not crazy."

But you are crazy. Only a crazy woman would throw herself into her child's grave.

She closed her eyes. Timmy was dead and he wasn't coming back.

"You have to face it. Admit it, Janice. You'll never see your son again," Dr. Montgomery had said during the last joint counseling session with Richard.

She had argued. Dear God, to think, she'd actually *argued* with the man, found some distorted logic to rationalize away the truth.

"How do you know?" she had replied. "If he could come back once, he could come back again."

The horrified look on Richard's face told her that she had crossed a line. To his credit, Dr. Montgomery calmly explained that this time was different. This time, Timmy wasn't in the hospital's critical care unit on a respirator—he was officially dead.

On the way home, Richard announced that he'd been seeing someone else, and he had filed for divorce. She wasn't surprised. Who wanted to be shackled to a thirty-three year old crazy brunette when you could start a new life with a perky twenty-six year old with big tits?

There was no point in trying to save the fragments of their marriage. They never talked anymore, and all Richard wanted was to "move on" after Timmy died. How could she forget her child? How was she supposed to pretend that life mattered when Timmy was buried deep underground?

She knew Timmy was gone, but she couldn't let him go. Without him, her life had no meaning, no light, and no purpose. She suffered through the daily grind of getting up and going to a job she hated, then came home to an empty, soulless house and cried herself to sleep.

"I should have taken more pills that night. Maybe if I'd drank the whole bottle of tequila, or if Richard hadn't come home when he did . . . " She stared at the phone. "If I tell anyone about this, they'll lock me up for sure."

A heavy breathing noise caught her attention and she looked down the hall. The creature stood there, staring at her. It was taller than she had expected, about four feet high.

"What the fuck are you?"

"A collector," it answered in a gritty voice.

"Get the hell out of my house or I'll—"

"Call the police? You won't. If you did, they wouldn't see me. They'd think you were crazy, right Janisss?" It grinned, flashing its evil, black teeth.

She shivered and wrapped her arms around her chest. This thing *knew* her. "What do you want?"

"What's owed."

"I don't owe you—"

"Me? No, I'm the collector," it said as it shuffled into the living room. "I've been sent by my master to take the debt to its rightful owner, tonight."

She frowned. What debt? What was it talking about? "I don't owe anyone anything. And even if I did, they wouldn't send a dwarf in a Halloween costume to my house in the middle of the night to collect it."

Her outburst shocked her. Why wasn't she afraid of it? Because monsters weren't real—at least that's what she had always told Timmy.

"The attic is sealed. How did you get in?"

"I slipped in, that's all you need to know."

"Why did you knock on the ceiling? If you can break into the house, why didn't you magically appear in my room?"

The collector cocked its head to one side. "I could have, but where's the fun in that? I wanted to let you know I was here and see what you'd do." It paused and took a wheezing breath. "I enjoy playing with my assignments. The other humans I visited tonight were boring. The CEO of a multi-million dollar pharmaceutical company lay in his bed, sobbing. The famous actress was so drugged out, she didn't know I was there. But you, Janice, you're a special case. You're different from the usual collections I make. You're interesting."

It came closer, and she smelled the faint odor of skunk. Or maybe it was rancid garbage, or old milk. Whatever it was, it was something bad. Was this thing death coming to claim her?

"You've got the wrong house. You want Mrs. Riley next door. Go haunt her attic. Go collect her. She's ninety-two years old."

"I'm not *that* kind of collector. Although we do have a referral service." It made a wet, gurgling sound that almost sounded like a laugh. "I'm here for your soul."

"My soul? Souls aren't real. How could I sell mine?"

"They are very real. And you did sell yours. Don't you remember? A year ago today you offered your soul in exchange for a particular service. The service was rendered. Now I'm here to collect."

The collector waved a clawed finger in front of her, and she was instantly transported back to the hospital.

Bright lights, nurses in soft shoes, whispers. Timmy lay in a tiny bed with his head bandaged. Tubes stuck out of his arms. He was a shell of himself. There was nothing inside him, no light, no life. Machines beeped and whirred, breathing for him. Someone was crying.

She turned and saw herself—God, she was wearing that ratty blue sweatshirt—and Richard at the side of the bed. Richard sat staring into space. She was wailing, sobbing into her hands.

"Why? Why my little boy? Why can't they bring him back? Make them bring him back. I want my boy back. I swear, I'll give anything to have him back again alive and healthy and normal and have that rotten kid who pushed him down the stairs die."

The image disappeared. She was back in her house. The living room seemed dim, almost hazy.

"Now do you remember?"

She nodded. "People say things like that all the time, but they don't really mean—"

"But you *did* mean it." The collector smirked. "And what happened next?"

"We left the room to fill out some organ donor papers." She smiled. "While we were gone, he recovered. Just like that." She

Kelli A. Wilkins

snapped her fingers. "Two hours later, a doctor came out of Timmy's room and told us he'd be perfectly fine."

A cold knot of fear gripped her stomach. How was that possible? In a few hours, Timmy had gone from barely existing on life support to sitting up and asking for a peanut butter sandwich. She wrung her hands in her lap. "Everyone said it was a miracle."

The collector chuckled. The sound reminded her of a cat trying to throw up a hairball.

"Not all miracles are made of goodness and light. Dark forces also have the power to grant miracles—bargains, deals, if you like. There's always a give-and-take at work in this world. You should know that."

"But Timmy isn't alive now. He's dead. So you can take your bargain and shove it," she spat. Her anger surged like a tidal wave, rising up from the depths of her soul. If she did unwittingly make a deal with the devil, it didn't count, because Timmy was dead.

Janice stood and marched to the sideboard under the picture window. Drink. She needed a drink. She rummaged in the cabinet, shoving aside stacks of unused Christmas dishes and tablecloths decorated with poinsettias. Christmas didn't matter when your kid was dead.

"Where the hell is it?"

Ages ago she'd hidden tiny bottles of Jack Daniels and vodka in here, tucked them back in the far corner in case she needed a fix in a hurry. If she could find one now, have one little drink, this would all make sense . . . somehow. She would wake up in bed and forget all about this nighttime visitor.

"Looking for something?"

"Whiskey, gin, tequila, wine. I don't care. I want something, anything—"

She looked over her shoulder. The collector winked at her. "Oh no. No way." She pushed past it and started pacing. "That's what you do, don't you? You ask people what they want. Then they answer, and bang! You get them. You know their weaknesses, the things to hold over their heads."

"You can have a drink. All you need to do is ask." It snorted through its narrow, possum-like snout. "But be specific. You humans always ask for grand sweeping favors like fame or money, but aren't specific about the details. That leaves room for—shall we say—interpretation."

"Like with Timmy? You brought him back, but then you took him away again."

The collector shrugged. "You said you wanted him alive and healthy and normal. And for the kid who pushed him to die. Easily done. That "kid" will die—when he's forty-seven. Heart-attack."

"That's not—"

"What you meant?" it spat. "Sorry. We're not in the business of asking for clarification. You never said how long you wanted Timmy back. Had you been specific and said eighty years, fine. He would have outlived you. But you didn't. You left that open to interpretation and we decided a year was fair."

"Fair? You have the nerve to tell me about fair?" She crossed the room in three strides and towered over the demon.

"Fair isn't having your child brought back from a coma after a bully pushed him down the stairs, only to have him taken away again, run down like an animal by some motherfucker on a cell phone. He was a kid. He deserved to have a life, play baseball, grow up, go on dates—"

Her voice cracked, and she burst into tears.

"If you knew he was going to die anyway, why bring him back? Why torture me into thinking that he would be fine and then take him away again?"

The collector shook its head. "That is not my area. Perhaps you should take that up with—" It paused and curled his thin, rat-like upper lip. "God. He took your son the first time. He started this, not us."

"God? To hell with God. I'm done with God. I'm not speaking to Him anymore. As far as I'm concerned, there is no God, and if He is out there, He can go fuck himself."

Janice sat on the couch and held her head in her hands. Why did this thing have to come here tonight and stir up all these memories? It was bad enough that she tortured herself over Timmy's death, but now this hideous beast wanted to make her feel worse. Every day the guilt gnawed at her. She had let Timmy go out and ride his bike that day. If she had kept him in the house, things would have been different.

The second time Timmy was taken away from her, it was over in the blink of an eye. The accident happened too fast for anyone to stop it. It couldn't have been prevented. At least that's what everyone told her. One minute, Timmy was alive and riding his bike. The next minute, he was a corpse.

When she got the call, she'd gone hysterical, cursing and screaming like a madwoman. This time, there was no going back, no miracle recovery, no hope, no chance.

Kelli A. Wilkins

"The second time . . . " it said, inching closer to her. "I imagine it came as a shock. There was nothing anyone could do. Timmy's head was caved in, broken to bits. His skull was crushed like an egg under the wheel of the SUV. There was no getting him back after that mess, no matter what you'd offer. Some things even we can't fix. Now come with me." It extended a gnarled hand. "It's time to collect."

"No. I'm not going anywhere with you." She ran down the hallway to Timmy's room. Once inside, she slammed and locked the door behind her.

She took a deep breath and gazed around. After Timmy died, she had kept his room just as it was the last time he'd left it—dirty socks on the floor, crayons spread all over, a half-finished drawing on the desk, his Little League uniform and new aluminum bat in the closet. Timmy's presence lingered in his room and made her feel less alone. The sheets and blankets still smelled like him. It had comforted her to know that a part of him was still here.

By the next Thanksgiving, Richard had had enough. He demanded that she clean out Timmy's stuff. He said it was unhealthy for her to keep the room intact. She refused, and that sparked another screaming argument.

"You're sick, you know that, Janice? You need help."

"Why? Because I want to remember him? Not throw him away, like you, and pretend he didn't exist. He was your son, for God's sake."

"And he's dead. I can accept that. Why can't you?"

When she came home from work the next day, Timmy's room was barren. Richard had packed up Timmy's clothes and toys and donated them. All that remained of her boy was a small box of photos and drawings. She had gone crazy when she saw that the room had been stripped bare.

"It's not a museum. He's dead and gone," Richard said. "Let him go. You can't hold him here."

That's when she started seeing Dr. Montgomery. She went once a week to discuss her thoughts and feelings, but it never helped. Dr. Montgomery listened politely and nodded in all the right places, but he didn't *know*. He didn't know what it felt like to have your heart ripped out. Lectures and books and therapy seminars talked about how to cope with grief, but it was only talk. Talking couldn't fix what was broken inside her. Four months later, Richard left her.

Janice closed her eyes and leaned against the door. Why had God killed her little boy? Timmy was always good. He'd never done anything wrong to earn God's vengeance. The bully at school who pushed him down the stairs, that spoiled brat who started all this, *he* was fine. Nothing happened to *him*. The cocksucker on the cell phone who creamed Timmy on his bike was alive and sitting in jail. Why didn't God punish him?

The doorknob rattled, and she backed toward the twin bed. "Go away you ugly thing. Get out of my house. Don't you dare come in here."

Timmy's room was her haven. Every night after work she spent a few minutes in here, talking to him.

The knob rattled again. "Don't make this more difficult—or painful. You owe us. We gave you back your boy."

"Bullshit. My son's dead. Any deal we had doesn't count. Now get the fuck out of my house."

"A locked door can't protect you."

She glanced at the door. So far, it had. But why? This hell-spawn had slipped into her house in the dead of night like a shadow. What was keeping it out of Timmy's room?

"Open the door and give me your soul."

"You're not getting my soul, you monstrous fuck. I never made a bargain with anyone."

"Do you think you did your boy a favor by saving him, Janice?" it hissed. "You should have let him die in the hospital the way your God intended. Timmy was unconscious and didn't feel anything. Bringing him back was a cruel mistake. He suffered the second time, Janice. Suffered badly. He saw the red SUV coming toward him. Felt the impact, heard the crunch of his own bones."

"Shut up, you son of a bitch."

That was it. She'd had enough. She yanked the closet open and grabbed Timmy's aluminum baseball bat. Last winter she had found it in the basement and brought it upstairs for protection.

It continued taunting her. "His bones were broken; his body turned to mush by the impact—"

"Here's some impact," she said as she whipped open the bedroom door and swung the bat.

It connected with the side of the monster's head and made a dull thud sound. She had remembered to aim low. The collector stumbled back and dropped to one knee.

"Don't you dare talk about Timmy like that, you prick." She brought the bat down again, as hard as she could, bashing it across the demon's back and skull.

It fell to the floor, making high-pitched squeaking sounds. She

Kelli A. Wilkins

stood over it, wailing away with the bat. "You killed my son, you twisted freak. Go back to hell where you came from."

After a few minutes, the squealing noises stopped. The collector lay still. Black goo oozed from its cracked skull.

Chest heaving, she stepped back and brushed her hair away from her eyes. So much for the collector. Now what? Should she call the police?

And say what? That you killed a monster with your dead son's Little League bat?

She closed Timmy's door, then poked the creature in the ribs with the tip of the bat. It didn't move. Was it dead, or pretending?

Still wielding the bat, she stepped over the body and ran into the kitchen. The clock over the sink read 4:45. The sun would be up in half an hour. She had to act fast.

***

Janice dragged the collector to the front door by its ankles. At first, she was hesitant to touch it, even with rubber gloves on, but once she got over the initial repulsion, determination took over. Using the baseball bat and a long-handled broom, she had rolled her midnight visitor onto an old plastic shower curtain and slid it to the front door.

She opened the door a crack and peered up and down the street. It was still dark out. The garbage men weren't making their rounds yet. Good. The last thing she needed to deal with right now was an early-bird neighbor putting out trash or walking a dog. It wouldn't look good to be caught sneaking a dead demon out of your house before sunrise. The coast was clear, so she lugged the makeshift shroud onto the porch.

As she hauled the shower curtain down the front stairs, she made sure the collector's head hit each and every brick step all the way to the sidewalk. "Serves you right, you bastard," she muttered, as she heaved it into the road.

Small and broken, the collector lay helpless in the street. If there was any justice in the world, an asshole on a cell phone would speed by and smash it to pulp.

She darted back to the house. A chill ran down her spine as she stepped into the living room. Although the thing was dead, or *seemed* to be dead, she didn't feel safe. It couldn't have been that easy.

She wandered into Timmy's room, locked the door, and sat on the bed. Her gaze settled on the box of Timmy's drawings and photos. She picked it up and rummaged through it.

After he'd "come back" Timmy had started drawing. He drew the same things—rainbows and sunrises—over and over. She reached into the box and pulled out a drawing. The left side of the page showed a black sky and an ominous gray funnel cloud. The other half of the picture had a brilliant golden sun showering beams of light over their house. "Sunshine kills all the bad things" was printed at the bottom of the drawing.

When did Timmy draw this? She had gone through the box a thousand times, but she didn't remember seeing this drawing before. She leaned closer and studied the gray tornado. Lines of wind resembling gnarled hands reached out from the cloud toward the roof.

A loud bang on the door made her jump. "Jesus!"

"Let me in."

It was back. How had it gotten in?

She examined the drawing again, then turned it over. It was dated the day Timmy died. Did he know what was going to happen? Was he trying to tell her something? The night before the dickhead in the SUV killed him, Timmy had woken up in the middle of the night, crying. She had rushed into his room and soothed him.

"What's wrong?" she'd asked.

"I had a scary dream. There was something bad coming for you, Mommy. It was ugly and lived in the dark."

At the time, she didn't think anything of it, but now—

Janice dumped the box on the bed and dug through the drawings. Almost every picture was of sunrises over the house. She smiled at the picture Timmy had drawn of his room. It was bathed in sunlight and his favorite sun catcher prism filled the room with rainbows.

After he came home from the hospital, Timmy always woke up early to watch the multicolored light dancing on the walls. His room faced east, and he slept with the shades up so the sun would wake him. She glanced at the window. The shade had been drawn ever since Timmy died.

The collector scratched on the door. "Let me in. Your time is up. I need your soul, *now*."

Its wailing cry sounded desperate. She thought back to what the ghastly thing had said earlier about being specific. The collector said it needed her soul, *tonight*—and it was nearly dawn. Was it running out of time?

"It's mine. You can't have it."

"I'll make a deal."

"A deal with you? I'd have to be crazy."

It laughed. "You can keep your soul, in exchange for something."

What else could it possibly want from her? "What?"

"You can keep your soul, but we'll go back to how it was at the hospital. You don't make the bargain for Timmy's life. You let him die."

"Die? He's already dead."

"But if we go back, he dies at the hospital. He never comes home. The devil's in the details. If you let him go at the hospital, he dies there peacefully, not splattered in the street. Your husband doesn't leave you because you went nuts. You keep your soul."

She frowned. Why would it make her a new bargain? What would that change? She spotted a photo of her and Timmy on his last birthday. Time. It would change time.

If Timmy died in the hospital, then she wouldn't have had that final year with him. All those fun times at the amusement park, going to his school play, Halloween . . . all of it would be wiped out. Those were some of the best times she had with Timmy. So grateful to have him back, she made the most of every moment together—and this monster wanted to erase them?

"Let me in." It rattled the doorknob.

She grinned. The devil *was* in the details. She clutched Timmy's tornado picture to her chest and stood. Would it work? Timmy believed it would. He had faith. He'd been to the other side and came back. Maybe he knew something she didn't.

Janice unlocked the door, then bolted across the room and waited next to the window.

"Come in."

The door opened slowly, and the collector shuffled in. Its head was bent sideways at an unnatural angle, and its left eye socket was crushed flat. It hobbled toward her, hissing and baring its pointed fangs.

"It's time."

"I know." She nodded. "Time for you to go back to hell."

Janice flipped up the shade. The morning sun flooded the room and the sun catcher prism threw rainbows everywhere. The collector bellowed and shielded its face with its broken, clawed hands. Its gray fur smoldered, giving off a stench like burning garbage.

"No! You can't do this. I must collect!"

She watched it fall to the floor, writhing and screeching as the light purified it. It convulsed and let out a final, high-pitched scream as it burst into blue-white flames.

All that remained of the collector was a pile of gray ashes in the center of the room.

Janice sat on the front porch sipping a cup of coffee. She closed her eyes and let the mid-day sun warm her face. After the collector had burned, she had sprinkled salt on its ashes, then vacuumed them up. She waited until the asphalt was good and hot before dumping the gray remains in the middle of the street. Ten minutes later, a truck sped through the pile, scattering the ashes everywhere.

At nine o'clock she called a realtor and asked them to send someone as soon as possible. There was no point in staying in the house now. A new life was waiting for her.

After killing the collector, her grief had been replaced with a calm acceptance. The past was over and needed to stay buried. She couldn't change what happened to Timmy, but she'd bet her soul that everything was going to be all right.

Someone coughed lightly, and she opened her eyes. A short man in a charcoal gray suit was standing at the bottom of the stairs. Where had he come from?

He flashed her a wide smile. "Mrs. Petrovich?"

She nodded.

"My name is Aton Moloch. I'm from the real estate office," he said as he climbed the stairs and stood over her. "I heard you're eager to sell. What would you give me if I promised I could sell your house in a week?"

She splashed her coffee in his face.

Heart and Soul

SUZANNE ROBB

GREG MAJORS STRIPPED off his shirt, and his jeans followed suit. The pool beckoned to him and he obeyed.

"Come on, Mary, the water's great," he called out to his wife.

A splash behind him caused a smile to spread across his face. He waited a minute for her to grab him, or try and surprise him, but nothing happened. Greg dunked his head and turned to see where she was.

The surface remained calm, but something made him uneasy.

"Honey, did you say something?" Mary said as she stepped out onto the back porch.

She put her hand on a column and swore when her fingers came back sticky.

"Sorry, I just painted those," he said with a nod toward the columns. "Come on in, we've been working all day"

Tiny shadows produced by the angle of the sun caused him to think something hid below the surface, waiting to attack him. An old childhood fear about secret openings that let sharks into the deep end of the pool plagued his thoughts.

"Greg? Did you hear me?" Mary said, and from the annoyed sound of her voice it was obviously not the first time she'd called out to him.

"Sorry, what was that? I think I inhaled paint fumes for too long."

"I said dinner's going to be ready soon; come in when you're done relaxing."

Greg sighed. Ever since they bought this house, it had been one thing after another. He and Mary used to love talking and being together, now it seemed as if she could barely tolerate his presence. He pushed off the side of the pool and did a few laps.

After fifteen minutes, he decided to go in. A few feet from the ladder something grazed his leg. He spun looking down but didn't see anything. Whatever it was felt slimy. He pushed his way to the stairs and managed to back out of the now murky pool making sure nothing snuck up on him. In the shimmer of sunset he swore he saw a face, and it wasn't happy.

***

Mary slammed the pan into the sink regretting it the moment the back logged water soaked the front of her shirt. She reined in her anger, which was getting more difficult with each day.

"Damn garbage disposal is backing up, but he decides to fix the pool first. What does he care if I can't make a proper dinner?"

Foregoing the rubber glove, she stuck her hand into the tepid liquid, ignoring the rotten bits of food circling her wrist, then forearm. She made sure the bottom of the sink was clear then shook her head as she pushed through to the drain to where the food was ground up. Only in this house, it didn't work, like everything else.

"Just once, can't something do what it's supposed to?"

She felt around as she stared out the window watching Greg in the pool. Of course, this served to make her angry and catch her finger on something due to lack of attention. She glanced down when the bits of meat, eggshells, and other grime formed a band around her arm and pulled.

"What the hell?" she said as she tried to pull her hand out.

A slow whir began and Mary panicked, the disposal was shorting out again. She pulled on her hand again, and watched in horror as the remnants of meals past enveloped her. A second before she was about to let out a scream, the disposal turned on and Greg came in.

Her arm was tossed out of the sink; she didn't pull it out. The point needed to be made, if only in her head, something *pushed* her arm out.

"You won't believe what just happened to me in the pool—" Greg started to say, but stopped. "Are you okay?"

Mary shook her head negatively while Greg came over and helped her sit down.

"The disposal is broken again. You need to take it out. I don't want it anymore," Mary said in a voice bordering on normal.

"Whatever you want. Why don't we eat and then I'll take care of it okay?"

***

Greg hated plumbing of any kind, but Mary wanted the disposal out. Of course nothing was that easy when it came to this place. Somehow removing the disposal caused a backup somewhere else. When he went to the shed the next morning to grab some tools to finish replacing some rotten deck boards he realized the ground was soaked with something unpleasant. Now he had to check their septic lines.

"Are you sure you don't want to have specialist do this?" Mary called to him.

Greg made a face at the comment and tried not to think about what was writhing next to him in the crawlspace.

"It's Saturday morning, we can't afford to pay overtime holiday rates, and we need the damn toilets to work."

He wriggled further until he came to what resembled a pipe that would carry waste to the septic tank. The reasons they bought a place in the country was beyond him. Privacy, space, land, and all that other junk seemed irrelevant when you had to empty a crap collector buried somewhere in your yard.

He got into position and felt something tickle his neck, thin and slender.

Like a blade of grass, he thought.

"Can you please keep the flashlight steady?" he yelled.

A beam of light moved his way and he saw a snake stick its tongue out at him.

"Jesus."

"You okay?" Mary asked.

Greg put a hand to his chest in an effort to calm his racing heart. "I'm fine, just got up close and personal with a snake."

More things skittered across his neck and face: spiders, ants, and other things he didn't want to think about. He wrestled with the pipe wrench until he got the upper part loose. He moved out of the way as he pushed it to the side to see if the blockage was here.

A sludge like substance spewed forth and coated him within seconds. The smell enough to make him vomit and dry heave as he started to pull himself out of the small space. Roots sprang up and twisted around his ankles and arms. Greg let out a scream and grabbed for his utility knife, slashing at them wildly.

"What's going on?" Mary yelled with worry.

The light showed him strange things, mad faces in the mud, human bones sticking out of the ground and wrapping around him.

"Calm down, I got your foot."

Greg felt Mary pulling, and used what strength he had to claw his way free. When he did, the events were a jumble in his head. He glanced down at his body and threw up once more at the stench.

"Get the hose," he said in a monotone voice.

Mary turned, but not fast enough to hide the smile on her face. He wanted to kill her, stick her face in a pile of steaming waste and see how funny she thought it was.

A blast of cold water snapped him out of his morbid thoughts. They worked together to get most of the offending material off of him.

"I'm leaving it as is, we can piss in the woods for all I care," Greg mumbled.

***

Mary scrubbed the floor for the five hundredth time. No matter how often she did it, the stain reappeared. Sometimes within hours; others days.

"What the hell is it about this place," she mumbled to herself, "It's falling apart more and more."

"I clean, scrub, disinfect, and wash this damn spot every day." Mary wiped her brow and sighed in frustration.

With the area clean, *again*, Mary stood and went outside to enter the small storm cellar they used as a basement to keep supplies in. She lifted the shutter style doors and waved away the stale smell.

The stairs creaked underneath her weight. She felt along the walls shivering at the coolness. When she reached the bottom she walked straight into a giant spider web and screamed; the gossamer strands sticking to her face and hands. The prickles of hundreds of little legs along her neck and face, down her shirt as she realized baby spiders were swarming her body.

She flailed even more when she felt hands grab at her, trying to hold her in place.

"Hey, calm down, I'm trying to help you," Greg said.

Ropy strands were pulled from around her neck, and she swatted at her body where she felt the arachnids invading. They scurried along her thighs, behind her knee, along her lower back, between her breasts, they were everywhere.

"Get them off of me, they're everywhere," she screamed as she stripped off her clothing.

"Jesus, let's get you in the house."

Mary let Greg lead her, modesty a thing of the past as she continued to feel hairy feet traversing her body. Inside the house Greg soothed her, assured her not a single one was left on her body. After glancing in the mirror from every direction she believed him.

Suzanne Robb

***

Greg sighed as he lowered himself into the pool. He made sure to go on days in which there was full sun so no shadows crept up on him. The fear of something in the water was irrational, he knew. Still, something about the face he saw a few weeks ago haunted his dreams.

Tomorrow the plumber would be there, after a week of delays. Not a day too soon. If he had to hear Mary complain about using the woods one more time he was going to freak out.

He let himself float along the cool surface, the warmth of the sun lulling him into a relaxed state. He thought of the months of fighting since moving into the house. The costs of unseen repairs were bankrupting them. The only solution would be selling the house, and he couldn't be happier to be rid of the money trap. All they needed to do was make it presentable, take the money, and run.

A slick of water oozed across his chest and he jerked back to reality. Slimy restraints were wrapped around his legs and arms, pulling him underneath the surface. Opening his mouth to scream, a surge of water drowned his voice, the smell of rot and decay overwhelming him.

As the putrid fluid travelled down his esophagus and into his lungs, Greg inhaled through his nose. More nastiness entered him and the face from before hovered above; the shape more apparent as he hung between life and death. Another form held him in place on the bottom of the pool.

Four arms, or legs, whatever they were, could hold him with no effort. He struggled even though it was pointless. As his vision darkened a voice echoed in his head, *"with death, rebirth."*
***
"Greg, if you don't get your ass in here you can forget about me reheating your dinner," Mary yelled for the third time.

She slammed the plate on the counter not caring about the ceramic chip that broke off. Haphazardly wrapping the meal in saran wrap she opened the fridge, the odor of rotten food assaulted her senses.

"Great, now the fridge is broken too."

Mary slammed the door and squeezed her eyes as tears formed. "Goddamn son of a bitch, I've had it with this place. Greg, if you can hear me we're selling this rat trap and getting the hell out of dodge. I'm not spending one more night in this place."

Mary tossed the plate in the sink, shaking her head as it floated to the bottom. The backed-up sink mocking her. She stomped through the living room and found the stain, bright red and spreading.

"What the hell is wrong with this place?"

Mary ran up the stairs and went into their bedroom. She pulled down her suitcase and started to throw clothes in mindlessly.

"It's not haunted, he said, guy has an answer for everything," she muttered to the room.

"Stains always come back when you replace the flooring, and septic tanks smell like dead bodies all the time, the hell it's some animal."

Mary shook her head in anger at all the bull she let Greg shovel to cover up the obvious fact there was something seriously wrong with the place. From the day they moved in, everything went wrong.

She entered the bathroom to grab some toiletries when a reflection in the mirror caught her eye. A woman with a serene smile and beautiful dress stared at her. Mary thought it odd, but felt her blood pressure lower as she took in the angelic-looking woman in white.

Mary approached the mirror and held out her hand, the other woman smiled and motioned her forward. The sound of shattering glass roused Mary out of her stupor. She sat on the floor, blood flowing out of her wrists faster than she thought possible.

The mirror lay shattered before her, but in a small wedge she saw the face of the woman, and she wasn't smiling anymore.

As Mary's life drained away she watched in fascination as the tiles and grout absorbed her blood and the things around her began to shine anew. A voice, far away from her now, *"with death, rebirth."*

***

David Hawkins looked around the immaculate home.

"Oh, honey I love it! There's even a pool," his wife Jane said with enthusiasm.

"Can you excuse us a minute?" David said to the real estate agent. The woman smiled, trust emanating from her.

"Honey, we can't seem too overeager. It's kind of pricey."

"I know, but it's perfect. We don't need to do a thing."

David gave her a lop-sided grin. "Whatever you want, honey."

The agent appeared at their side. "Have you made a decision?"

"We'll take it," Jane said with a smile.

The woman smiled. "Perfect, I think you'll like this place. The prior owners really put their heart and soul into this place," she said with an odd grin.

***

David slipped into the pool to cool down after working on renovations all day. Jane stepped out on the porch with an unhappy look on her face. He opened his mouth to yell out a warning, but was too late.

"I see you finally painted the columns?" Jane asked as she pulled a blue hand away.

"Come in here with me, we've been working like crazy. Who knew how much upkeep a place like this needed."

"Dinner's ready. I have more work to do, but you enjoy your swim."

David sighed, all they did was argue. He hit the water, surprised when something splashed him back. He made a full circle then dared to look beneath the surface as something grazed his leg.

Playing With Fire

SUZIE LOCKHART

ICONCEAL MYSELF amidst a cluster of bushes, watching the human woman.

She arrives nearly every evening, at about the same time. She wanders the docks, as if searching for something. All the while, her eyes remain focused on the entrance of the forest.

It always takes a moment to remember. I hold so many memories, absorbed with each one of my prey. It makes it hard to focus, but slowly images begin to take their shape.

Ahhh, yes.

It is a child's mother; one that I had lured many moons ago. The taste had been delectable. Children always have a particular relish, and are easiest to ensnare into my lair by the river. I wonder if the mother would have a similar flavor. My mouth waters at the thought, and saliva seeps through my teeth, dripping onto the bare branches.

The maternal bond is strong. The human woman yearns for her child. I feel my body shifting already.

Her child is long gone. Just one of the many meals needed for sustenance; for survival.

So hungry . . .

My insides rumble, and a small growl involuntarily escapes my throat. I crouch down lower as my form continues to change.

Winter is coming, and the visitors are all gone. Already, the mountain behind the forest is turning white.

But this woman; she is always here.

Watching.

Waiting.

I see her eyes skirt the edges of the trees, and it's as if she knows...

I hear a warning inside me. A chill runs through my body, instinct urging me to leave. Try again tomorrow.

Long ingrained instinct warning me not to tempt this woman.

But I am starving, and food will soon be in short supply. My tongue involuntarily licks across my black, bumpy mouth, and I feel the coarse gray hairs underneath my bottom lip disappearing. I take the form of the human child; the one that had been my victim so long ago.

The woman's eyes grow wide as I reveal myself, and her hand flies to her mouth. I use the soft tinkle of her child's sweet little voice as a siren; to lure this human woman. I will lead her deep into the forest and trap her near the water. Perhaps it is what she desires? To die, as her child had.

So hungry . . .

Slowly, ever so slowly, she makes her way silently across the fine sand that surrounds the island.

"Mama!" The child's voice cries out.

Ahh, it is working. She begins walking towards the trees. "Mama!" Her steps quicken. "I'm coming, baby. Mama's here!"

I smile as the child, looking forward to the feast ahead.

Every so often I glance over my shoulder; to be certain she is following, as I lead her deep into the woods. At the river, I shall reap my reward. It is almost too easy. Then that unsettling feeling returns, urging me to leave this woman alone.

I scoff. What can this human woman do? She has no weapons, like the human men that sometimes hunt. I sometimes play games with them, shifting as I weave in and out of the towering trees. But I never try to lure the hunters. I am too smart.

There is nothing the woman can do. I chide myself as she continues following me deeper into the woods. Her scent drifts through the air, and I savor the sweet smell.

Where has she gone?

I can smell her, but I can no longer see her.

I spot her wandering in the other direction.

"Mama!" I cry. She turns back for a moment, and then continues up a hillside. What is she doing?

Now, *I* am following *her*. I pick up my pace. It is difficult in this child's body. Frustration wells up inside of me.

As I near the top of the hill, I sniff the air. I smell it before I see it.

Cautiously, I creep around the towering spruce trees. My body quivers as the sight of a campfire comes into view.

The menacing flames lick at me. That's when I see her, on the other side of the reddish-orange blaze. She points to the tent beside her, and puts a finger to her lips before disappearing again.

My frustration turns to anger as I scurry around the outskirts of the campsite, trying to find her. What kind of game is she playing?

Again, I feel something stir inside, signaling a threat. The sight of the fire has shaken me.

I'm left with no alternative, as I tread behind her. How stupid can she be? I am her child! She should be on *my* heels.

It is beginning to get dark. The moon offers little light as it rises in the graying sky. I hear wolves howling in the distance; I need to grab this woman and get back to my lair.

A pack of wolves is the last thing I wish to deal with.

The only thing worse than the wolves is fire...

I haven't survived this long by being stupid!

I should not go this deep into the forest, but I am determined to finish this.

To finish *her*.

I whimper in the child's voice. "Mama, *please!*" I cry.

"Just a little further, baby." Her whispered words reach my ears.

I cannot turn back. I feel the need to flee, but there will be no satisfaction until I tear her apart.

I see that she has finally stopped in a small clearing. She sits on a rock suddenly looking exhausted. How I long to consume her. My stomach rumbles again.

"Baby," she coos. I start to lose my focus. The need to devour her is overpowering. I would have to be quick about it, and then make my way back to the river. I am disappointed that I am unable to savor the moment, but I smell the wolves closing in on us.

She is smiling at me as I approach her.

Perhaps I am right. Perhaps she wishes to die, as her child had.

I slide next to her, and her hand runs down my back. I begin to shift.

She screams.

No one is around to hear her.

No one, except those wolves.

The urge to leave has reached a fevered pitch, but hunger overtakes everything.

I sink my sharp teeth into her flesh, and my gnarly fingers grasp her arms tightly. A small squeal is the only sound she makes before the paralyzing poison I exude courses through her body.

I consume her quickly, ingesting her whole being in a matter of minutes. My hunger is satiated, but I am left with a certain dissatisfaction. The human woman had not tasted as I had expected. It was as though her blood had been tainted . . .

A feeling of dread slithers through my veins.

Something is wrong.

What has she done?

I begin to absorb her memories. I see her giving birth to the girl. I feel her joy as I watch all the loving moments the two exchange.

Then, a cruise to Alaska. She is on the island, with her mate and the child. I feel her pain as she realizes the girl is missing.

Aughhh! I can hardly stand the searing grief that grips me.

My vision becomes blurred. Charlotte is her name. She stays on the island, but her mate leaves her. More horrible pain.

I see her working in a book shop, in the little town called Sitka. She always stays late. She pours through books, until one day she finds it . . .

"Kushtaka!" She hisses. She has discovered my secret.

Always she works late; looking for something else.

Searching for a way to kill me.

I hear her reading to herself aloud as she says the words, "*Magnesium carbo-nite;* that's it!"

Then, I see her looking at a reflection of herself. She speaks to her replica. "For you, baby." A look of determination is plastered on her face.

Then she smiles. I'm forced to watch her plan unfold as she sits on this rock, and lifts her hand to her lips. She uncorks a small vial, emptying the liquid into her mouth just moments before I find her. She coughs and sputters, but promptly regains her composure.

The compound begins to burn me from the inside out.

Fire. She knew what would destroy me, and in my haste to eat, I'd senselessly ingested it.

I thrash around, screeching in protest as a liquid inferno oozes through my rough skin, and singes my pores. Steam emits from my body and the smell of burning flesh fills the air around me.

I throw myself onto the ground, but the small patches of snow aren't enough to extinguish the searing pain. The river is too far away; I would never make it.

The atmosphere around me changes and I feel them before I see them. My demise has come. The growls make me quiver in fear. Slowly, I move my head to face the carnivorous yellow eyes staring back at me.

The pack descends; coming to finish the job. They smelled their meal from a mile away. They clamp down on my flesh, tearing my body apart.

It is not quick.

It is not painless.

I feel every excruciating bite as the fire inside me rages. The only small satisfaction I take is the fire being passed on to the wolves. I listen as they howl in pain.

The last thing I see before my eyes close for good, is an image of the human woman, Charlotte, embracing her child.

She had bested the Kushtaka at his own game.

This time, it is I who screams . . .

Morning Sickness

MANDY DEGEIT

HE HELD HER hair back from her face as she regurgitated the contents of her stomach over the arm of the chair. Her partially digested food made sloppy, wet sounds as it ricocheted in and out of the plastic mop bucket he had placed there and splattered everything within a two-foot radius. She coughed and wheezed in a feeble attempt to catch her breath as a strand of drool stretched down from her bottom lip, nearly reaching the floor. Her skin was pink and sweaty and the loose blond wisps of hair that had fallen out of her ponytail clung to the sides of her face. He gently tucked a loose strand behind her ear and helped her back into an upright-seated position. Her head lolled back, loose and uncontrolled on her shoulders, as she stared vacantly at the ceiling. She blinked repeatedly, the accumulated tears streaming from the corners of her eyes and down the full curves of her cheeks.

He stepped carefully over to the sink, avoiding the bulk of the vomit and opened the kitchen window. He breathed deeply as fresh air usurped the rank odor of bile that lingered heavy in the air.

He choked back his own need to vomit as he cleaned up the mess with a mop that had been leaning nearby. He rinsed the mop out and leaned into the window for a deep breath of fresh air, before grabbing a glass from beside the sink and filling it with water. He steadied her head with his hand and tilted the glass, allowing the liquid to flow slowly into her mouth. She swallowed noisily as he pulled the near empty glass away. He offered her a sympathetic smile. She closed her eyes—lost in thought—daydreaming far behind her twitching eyelids.

He stood at her side, allowing her to come to her senses on her own. Watching her carefully, trying to figure her out, yet not understanding what pushed people to do the things they did.

Why was she here? He shook the thought away—it didn't matter why she was here—it never really mattered.

She hadn't moved from where he left her—she couldn't move—since her wrists and ankles were securely taped to the kitchen chair.

The taste of vomit was fresh on her tongue but her stomach felt empty. As the convulsions in her abdomen ceased, she knew she wouldn't be sick again. She rested with her head back and eyes closed and thought about what she was doing there. Fear and confusion were only part of the overwhelming flood of emotions wreaking havoc in her mind. There was so much more.

She was late . . . so late.

Her period was supposed to have come and gone by now.

It can't be . . .

(She was so careful.)

She brought the test home, freaking out as she flipped the box over in her hands.

She pissed on the stick . . .

. . . And waited a few minutes.

As she turned the test over in her hands, she started to cry.

As she opened her eyes, she squinted into the harsh sunlight as things came into focus. She saw him standing over her watching her every move. She looked up at him, silently pleading for what she couldn't ask for out loud. He avoided making eye contact with her and simply he shook his head. Sorrow creased her face as she frowned and bit her lip; fresh tears flowed freely down her face. She sobbed once and then fell silent. He sighed as she opened her mouth and waited, slack-jawed and silent. Her eyes looked longingly to him. He reached over to the table and grabbed a piece of wood, already dotted with her teeth marks. Holding it out, she bit down obediently, took a deep breath, and closed her eyes. He shook his head sadly and positioned himself between her open legs.

He righted himself between her spread legs and punched her hard in the stomach. Her teeth gnashed tightly onto the wood between her teeth. The slat helped her absorb the pain and save the enamel of her teeth. She strained against her bonds with a deep grunt; the layers of tape preventing her from moving. She slumped forward, her hair falling over her face, and spat the wood onto her lap. Her shoulders heaved as she tried to catch her breath. He watched her carefully as she coughed and sputtered, stealing the occasional glance between her legs but there was nothing there. He steadied himself with his left hand on her shoulder. She sobbed loudly between coughs, her cheeks soaked from her tears. He took the wood from her lap and held it out again. With a deep breath, she willingly gripped it between her teeth and leaned back, waiting. As his fist slammed into her abdomen, the red-hot pain momentarily blinded her. Her teeth ground down on the chunk of wood and a splinter dug painfully up into her gum line. A trickle of blood added a coppery tang to the flavour of pine, which already filled her mouth.

He doesn't wait. He can't wait. He simply wants it to be over; she is just like all the others. He hit her—in the abdomen again, but harder this time—not giving her any time to recuperate. *Just get it done, don't wait, just do it.* He thought as his huge fist slammed into her the third and final time.

The piece of wood muffled her grunts and groans as he pummeled her. Her face was scrunched in a grimace of excruciating pain, and then suddenly, the corners of her mouth peaked up into a tiny smile. She felt something change inside. She was sure something wasn't the same as before. At that moment, she knew it was done.

He stepped back, taking the hunk wood from between her lips. Tiny beads of sweat were beading on his forehead. She leaned back into the chair, panting heavily and smiling. *She's almost beautiful*—he admired her silently in the moment of silence before she spoke.

"Finally." Her voice cracked. She licked her lips and cleared her throat before trying again. "Finally . . ."

He looked down and saw the blood soaking through the crotch of her pants. He breathed a sigh of relief and grabbed the scissors from the table.

"There you go. It should be done." He cut her wrists free, careful not to slip and knick her tender skin. He crouched down between her legs and quickly freed her bound ankles.

She peeled the remainder of the tape away with a scowl as the tape clung to the tiny hairs on her arm. "Cool." She said quietly, as she massaged her skin in an attempt to coax the blood back to her fingertips.

He stood and offered his hand to help her out of the seat. She got up too quickly, and the room went blurry as dizziness affected her balance. She nearly fell back into the seat but he held her up, grabbing her hand and wrapping his hand around her waist.

"Thanks." She reached into the pocket of her skintight jeans.

"Here, this is for you." She slipped something into his hand and took a teetering step towards the door.

"Hey . . . are you gonna be okay?" He was concerned about the amount of blood as he looked back to where she once sat; the dark purple imprint stamped onto the wood of the chair. He shuddered, making a mental note to clean that up first.

"Yah, I'll be fine. I think I'm having a miscarriage." She winked and began rummaging around in her purse for a moment before finding her keys. "I should probably go lay down or something. Thanks again."

"Ummmm, yeah, thanks for coming." There was trepidation in his voice; he didn't feel comfortable letting them leave like this, but he did what needed to be done. She seemed much steadier on her feet as she walked past him out the front door he had opened for her. As she walked slowly down the path to her car, he couldn't take his eyes off the burgundy stains blossoming between her thighs.

They are like those ink blot tests. Hers looks kind of like a butterfly.

He watched her as she rounded the car, opened the door and sat down slowly. She buckled her seatbelt and started the car. "Uhhhh, yah safety first . . . " he mumbled sarcastically glancing back into his kitchen, "I'm sure she's always so careful." He shook his head sadly as he closed the door. "Just like all the others who come through here."

Glancing down at the hundred dollars she gave him, he shook his head and tucked the money into his wallet. *Gotta make rent somehow, I suppose.* He checked his watch and was relieved to see he still had time. Taking a deep breath he stepped into the kitchen to tackle the cleaning and hopefully be able to choke down some lunch before the next appointment showed up.

Mandy De Geit

And One for the Road

JOANNA PARYPINSKI

"**M**AGGIE?"

The voice pulled me from a dream. I snapped open my eyes to Dave hovering over me with a spatula in hand. "Morning, Ma. Looks like you dozed off again waiting for the coffee."

I yawned and hefted myself up from the stiff wooden chair while Dave shook his head and returned to the omelet he was frying up. The cooked-egg smell and gentle sizzling helped to center my reality. Good old Dave—he'd been the morning cook of Ed's Good Eats for five years now. 'Course, he had nothing on me, as I'd been waitressing at the diner for near to a decade.

Dave was a stringy fellow who made a mean strawberry crepe. I wasn't his Ma any more'n I was anybody else's, but he liked calling me that on account of how I liked to mother people—like my kid brother, who I took care of for twenty years. Anyway, mornings were just me and Dave and whoever happened to wander into our rinky-dink food stop in the middle of Nowheresville.

The coffee was done, so I grabbed the glass pot and squeezed through the doorway of the kitchen. There were four people and one cooing baby. The couple to my right looked about as straight-laced as they come—probably city folks. He was wearing a blue sports jacket and had the newspaper way up so that all you could see was his creased forehead and some slicked hair. She had orange hair pulled up tight as it would go so that it stretched her face and hoisted her eyebrows up in surprise. Neither spoke to one another.

In the next booth over was a woman maybe thirty years old

wearing a stained, ragged sweatshirt and pushing back greasy, dark blonde hair that tumbled out of a loose ponytail. She didn't seem none bothered that she looked like a slob; she was rocking an infant in her arms, blinking bloodshot, dark-rimmed eyes at the window.

"Coffee?" I offered the man in front of me, the only other patron. He looked about my age, with peppery stubble running over his square chin, dark sunglasses, and a cowboy hat on his head.

He smiled broadly, and I counted three gold teeth. "Why, thankya ma'am." His voice growled like the engine of a pickup truck. He paused holding out his mug, and I couldn't tell but it looked like he was reading my nametag. Or he might have just been enjoying the view. "I mean, Maggie. Pretty name."

I poured the steaming coffee. "You don't look familiar. Passin' though?"

"Why, yes ma'am. I mean, Maggie." Yeah, nobody did nothing but pass through here, and the couple of regulars we did have never showed up 'til lunch anyhow. "I'm on a road trip. Meeting my cousins up north. They live in Chicago."

"How nice," I said, heading over to the table with the couple. "Hey, there. What can I get y'all today?"

She stared me down over her freckled nose. "Coffee's fine for me." Her voice crackled like a dry winter breeze.

He said from behind his newspaper, "Eggs Benedict."

"Comin' right up." As I went to tell Dave the order, the bell above the door tinkled violently.

The baby started to cry.

The boy who walked in couldn't have been more'n sixteen. Kid looked like he'd gotten stuck in a blender: his face was scraped up, a dribble of blood snaking down from his left nostril. There was dirt on his torn leather jacket. Underneath was a faded black Lynyrd Skynyrd t-shirt. He held his stomach with his right hand like his breakfast hadn't agreed with him. "Excuse me," he panted, desperate eyes catching mine. "Do you have a phone I could use? My bike skidded on some rocks and I wiped out."

My insides panged, and I felt again like I was in a dream. "Sorry sweetie, but the storm last night took down some power lines. Phones still aren't working yet." His bruised face fell. "But I have a first aid kit in the back. Why don't you sit down and I'll see if I can patch you up, all right?"

"Yeah, sure. Thanks."

As I scurried to the kitchen, I felt a hand brush my backside, and

I flinched. The cowboy grinned at me, and I could see now there was more in that grin than gratification for pouring him coffee. My stomach went cold as I turned to escape the leer and get the first aid kit.

I passed Dave in the kitchen, throwing the clock on the wall a glance—8:47—and opened a cabinet. "Eggs Benedict for Mr. Snooty, and are the phones still down, do you know?"

Dave slid the omelet onto a plate and leaned against the counter. "So far as I know. That was one helluva storm, huh?"

"Yeah," I murmured, grabbing the kit in one hand and the plate in the other. "Hey," I snapped, and Dave shrugged his shoulders. "Eggs Benedict," I reminded him before striding out the swinging door.

Motorcycle kid was hunched over at the table closest to the front door, face mottled red and purple, hands plastered to his stomach. I set the kit in front of him and popped it open. "I'll be right back. Would you like something to eat?"

His breathing was ragged. I didn't like it; his lungs seemed to rattle. "I don't have any money."

Runaway, I decided. Took his daddy's motorcycle, didn't know how to ride it properly, and skidded on the empty stretch of highway beside the diner. "On the house." His head snapped up. "I'll bring you out some pancakes."

I turned away before he could say anything, setting the omelet down in front of the cowboy. He held up his empty mug, and when I turned away to get the coffeepot his hand grabbed my rump again. His grin was feral, lips pulled back from those gold teeth. My heart thumped uncomfortably, cold shivers racing over my tingling skin, and I skedaddled back to the kitchen.

"Eggs Benedict," said Dave as I walked in. I jumped at the sound of his voice, jittery all over, and took the plate. "You okay?" he asked.

"Yeah. Get some pancakes going, will you?" I grabbed the coffeepot, heading back out.

The baby was still crying.

Its repetitive wails crescendoed while the mother rocked and shushed, murmuring a continuous chant: "Shhh, don't cry, be quiet for mommy, just for a minute, please don't cry . . ."

My head was starting to pound. I set the eggs Benedict in front of the couple (neither looked at me; she kept her gaze glued to the window, and he remained hidden behind his newspaper). Then, reluctantly, I returned to the cowboy and his dark leer, filling up his mug as he grinned, bits of egg and cheese oozing from between his glittering teeth.

"Thankya, Maggie. Can't do nothing without coffee in the morning," he drawled. My heart skittered as I backed away from that terrible grin.

I returned to the runaway, the baby's cries echoing through the diner and my brain.

"Everything okay over here?" I asked, feeling the cowboy's bestial gaze burning into the back of my head. The kid looked up, blood wiped clean from his face. Still, his right eye was swelling up something fierce. He looked a little dazed, and for a minute I was reminded of my little brother Kevin, who'd once gotten into a fight at school so bad his whole face was swollen up like an eggplant. We all piled into the car to go to the hospital, but he grinned the whole way because he'd won the fight. I missed him.

The mother was still trying to shush the baby, her mutterings more frantic and strained now. "Oh please be quiet, shut up, stop crying, just for one minute, shhh, goddamnit, *shut up* . . . "

I could have gone for a drink about then, despite the hour. Ed's doesn't serve alcohol, but I knew Dave kept a bottle of Jack Daniels hidden away in one of the kitchen cupboards for himself. I thought it might help to drown the baby's cries.

The cowboy was leering at me from across the room, tipping his half-empty mug in my direction. "How 'bout one more for the road, huh?" he said, and I filled it again.

"If she doesn't shut up that little brat, *I* will," the freckly wife snapped quietly, and her words settled over the diner like a thick fog. Her eyebrows were dangerously close to her hairline. The man only moved to turn the page of the paper.

"Say, could you point me in the direction of the restroom?" the cowboy asked as he sipped his coffee, unperturbed by the bleeding boy and the shrieking infant. I pointed to the back by the kitchen before excusing myself from his presence.

A sickly pallor was sweeping over the runaway's face; his eyes were glassy. "Hey, are you feelin' all right?"

The baby would not stop crying.

He blinked slowly at me before pulling his right hand up from his stomach. It was covered in a thick, shiny layer of scarlet, and I hadn't seen it before because of his dark shirt, but I saw it now, and it was everywhere: it was gushing from the wound in his stomach and pouring down onto his jeans, dripping into little red puddles on the floor.

Joanna Parypinski

He opened his mouth, and what came out was a throaty gurgling sound. I stifled a scream by biting my fist. A bubble of blood popped between the boy's lips, and all I could think was, *oh now he won't be able to eat his pancakes, they'll just go in and slide right out onto the floor again!* All my thoughts were choppy and disjointed: *he can't eat his pancakes* and *Kevin, why are you such a reckless driver* and *who will eat the pancakes now* and *it's going to get you killed one day, Kevin, you've got to be careful or it's going to get you killed—*

The baby screamed in my head.

The coffeepot slipped from my grasp and shattered on the floor, sending tiny bits of crystal in every direction like glittering water; it settled over the spilt coffee, which fanned out black across the tile.

The kid slumped onto the table, eyes blank and dull, mouth open, teeth stained red. His dripping hand dangled beside the chair, gleaming ruby under the overhead lights.

"What the hell?" It was the freckly woman, standing and shaking her husband's shoulder, gaping across the diner at the bloodstained boy, and the baby was crying, *somebody shut up that little brat or I will,* and there was blood everywhere.

I bolted for the phone in the back hallway, the world jerking sporadically around me, and snatched it off the receiver, holding it to my ear for a full thirty seconds before I realized that there was nothing but dead air. The phone slipped from my sweaty, trembling grip and hung upside-down on its cord, swinging as a shadow fell over the entrance to the hall.

"There you are, Maggie." It was the cowboy. He grabbed the back of my neck and hauled me into the men's bathroom, shoving me up against the cold, smooth wall. The room reeked of disinfectant with undertones of piss that would never go away. He pinned me from behind, and his hot, stale breath that stank of cigarettes and coffee brushed the side of my face that wasn't squashed against the wall.

"Please," I choked out.

"I was waiting for you to come over here, Maggie. You were preoccupied with that kid, though, weren't you? Like 'em young, huh?"

The tiles in front of me blurred, and wetness pooled on top of my mashed cheek.

"Don't matter. The road gets lonely, you know." He chuckled. "And it's a long drive up to Chicago. So how about one for the road?"

No, I tried to say, *please,* but all that came out was a low moan. I could see the kid, bloody and slumped over on the table in his Lynyrd

Skynyrd t-shirt and leather jacket, eyes blank and dead, shards of crystal scattered over the floor amid the dark puddle of coffee, and the baby was crying, the baby was crying, the baby was crying—

He grabbed my hair in a fist and yanked my head down, twisting my neck like a gymnast doing a backbend, and a guttural scream erupted from my strangled throat before I passed out.

***

"Maggie?"

I opened my bleary eyes to a familiar voice.

"Morning, Ma. Looks like you dozed off again waiting for the coffee."

What? I couldn't seem to get my tongue around the question. I blinked, and Dave's words caught in my head and repeated like a merry-go-round. Hadn't he said that to me this morning? Yes, this morning, before—before—

I blinked and shook my head, trying to block out the feeling of cool tile against my cheek and the cowboy's hot breath on my ear.

"Hey, you feelin' okay?" Dave asked, crouching by my chair, one eye remaining on the omelet he was currently frying. I nodded, trying to shake off the sensation of déjà vu.

"Yeah . . . I'm fine . . . " I mumbled, standing up and grabbing the coffeepot.

I went to the cowboy's table, a bolt of fear zigzagging through my heart at the sight of his dark sunglasses. The world spun around me surreally as I offered him coffee.

"Why, thankya ma'am," he said, holding out his mug. His head paused in the direction of my nametag, and I couldn't tell if he was reading it or just enjoying the view, and hadn't this already *happened?* "I mean, Maggie. Pretty name."

My heart hammered in my chest. Yes, I'd done this dance. The cowboy didn't seem to know that he already knew my name. I blurted out, "How's your road trip goin'? Chicago's a long ways off, ain't it?"

His grin faltered. "How'd you know I was going to Chicago?"

"To meet your cousins, right?"

He gaped at me, and I counted three gold teeth.

Dashing to the city couple, nearly tripping over my big clown feet, I sputtered, "Coffee for the lady and eggs Benedict for you?"

The woman glared at me from beneath her raised eyebrows, and the man actually lowered his newspaper a fraction of an inch so I could see his eyes, narrow and discerning. "What are you, psychic?" he spat.

A wild bubble of laughter rose in my throat, choking me, and I giggled madly—much to the couple's evident discomfort. "Why yes, I *am* psychic, as a matter of fact!" I glanced at my watch. It was 8:44. "And in just a second or two, a kid's gonna walk in that door looking all busted up, wearing a leather jacket and a Lynyrd Skynyrd t-shirt—"

Not a moment after I was done, the bell above the front door gave a frantic jangle, and in stumbled the kid who couldn't have been older than sixteen, glancing around nervously until he spotted me. "Excuse me," he wheezed, but I didn't let him finish.

"No, our phones ain't working yet from the storm last night, and what the hell were you doing trying to ride a motorcycle you couldn't handle, anyhow?" I snapped. His eyes widened and he swayed slightly, his right hand clutching his stomach. "Just sit down and keep pressure on that wound. I'll get the first aid kit . . . "

The baby had started to cry.

I flew into the kitchen and nearly toppled over in my haste to get the kit. "What's going on, Ma?" Dave asked as he slid the omelet onto a plate and leaned against the counter.

My hands were shaking as I searched for the first aid. "Hey, the phones are still down, right?" I knew they would be, but I had to check. My pulse thrummed wildly in my throat.

"So far as I know. That was one helluva storm, huh?"

"Yeah, yeah," I murmured, finding the kit. I turned to exit, but Dave tapped me on the shoulder and handed me the omelet.

"Are you sure you're all right?" he asked. I snatched the plate from his hands and hurried into the diner.

The kid was sitting where he had been before, at the table closest to the door, and he still had his right hand against his stomach. I made a quick detour to the cowboy and dumped his plate in front of him with a clatter. The baby continued its wailing, the mother cajoling it to stop, and I wanted to tear my hair right out of my head, it was all happening again, *it was all happening again.*

"Shhh, don't cry, be quiet for mommy, just for a minute, please don't cry . . . "

The cowboy held up his empty mug, but I ignored him, and he reached out and grabbed my ass. I shook him off and went to the runaway. Setting down the first aid kit, I crouched down and said, "Okay, now take your hand away and I'll bandage it. We've got to stop the bleeding, or . . . " *or you'll die, it's going to get you killed one day, Kevin, you've got to be careful or it's going to get you killed.*

An image of my brother behind the wheel of his old car (careening down the street, one elbow crooked out the window, blasting classic rock) burst into my head. He looked just like this kid—a little older, yes, but they had the same face, the same reckless but apologetic face. And there was Kevin right in front of me, zooming down the back road at ninety miles an hour, tires flying off the asphalt for brief seconds, *Kevin, why are you such a reckless driver? It's going to get you killed one day.*

The kid took his hand away, and I saw the gaping tear in his flesh oozing blood; it gushed around his fingers, leaving his palm sticky and slick with the dark red liquid. I choked back vomit and pressed gauze to the wound.

He hissed. "How'd you know . . . all that stuff about me?" he panted, wiping at the blood dribbling from his nose.

The kid was so young. I could have been his mother. "Call it a lucky guess. What were you running away from?"

I applied more gauze because the blood kept coming and staining the first few layers of the white material. "My dad—" he hissed again "—can be a real pain in the ass. He wanted to send me to military school." He stared mournfully down at the hole in his stomach and murmured, "This was my favorite shirt."

The baby's cries repeated like a stuck record. I really wanted a shot of Dave's Jack.

Across the diner, the woman with the tight bun and the high eyebrows shouted, "Are we ever going to get our *food* over here? And somebody better shut up that little brat, or *I* will."

I swore, realizing that I'd never told Dave to start the eggs Benedict. The kid looked all right for now, so I got up and stuck my head in the swinging door of the kitchen.

"Hey, Dave, get some eggs Benedict going."

Everything was going to be okay. I was going to fix it. Things would be different this time. I grabbed the coffeepot where I'd left it and approached the cowboy.

"Oh please be quiet, shut up, stop crying, just for one minute, shhh, goddamnit, *shut up* . . . "

The baby kept crying.

"How 'bout one more for the road, huh?" the cowboy asked, tipping his half-empty mug at me. I filled it with coffee, telling myself, *he's not going to. I won't let him this time. I'll fix it. I'll stop it.* He sipped his coffee. "Say, could you point me in the direction of the restroom?"

"Sorry, we ain't got no restrooms here. You can piss on the side of the highway if you want," I replied swiftly, refilling the top inch of his mug until it was brimming. Sadistic pleasure washed over me as he spilled the dark, scalding liquid over his hands.

"Sonofabitch," he grumbled, sucking at his burned fingers. I smiled coldly and spilled a little coffee in his lap. He yelped, grabbing himself, and I chuckled, put down the coffeepot, and turned back to the runaway—

—who was now leaning over the table, slumped on the red and white checkered tablecloth, mouth open, blood streaming through the gauze on his stomach and onto his hands, which clutched feebly at his Lynyrd Skynyrd shirt, *Kevin, it's going to get you killed, it's going to get you killed . . .*

"What the hell?" came the cry of the freckled woman across the diner.

The baby was crying. The baby was crying. The baby was . . .

Numbness tingled at the tips of my fingers, and I choked on a sob as I knelt by the kid, trying to stop the bleeding, knowing that he was already dead, my hands slipping on the blood.

A strong arm grabbed me from behind and lifted me off the floor. I couldn't breathe as he carried me to the back hallway, towards the kitchen, and I thought maybe he was taking me to Dave to calm me down, but we made a turn and suddenly I smelled disinfectant and urine, and I knew what was coming.

The cowboy shoved me against a wall, a nice white wall which I smeared with the blood caking my hands. "Thought that was funny, spilling coffee all over me?" he spat. "Telling me there was no restroom?" He slammed my head against the wall, and I saw stars as my forehead cracked sharply on the tile. "I got to liking you, Maggie, but I see you like to play games. Don't matter. I got my own games. I'll make it hurt."

Tears streaked my face as I clawed desperately at the wall, bands of red running down it in rivers, and I sobbed like the baby in the diner.

"The road gets lonely, you know." He chuckled. "And it's a long drive up to Chicago. So how about one for the road?"

I screamed. There was red in my vision, red streaks on white like a candy cane, and there was my brother, twenty years old, wrapping his car around a tree, his face a mangled, bloody mess, *it's going to get you killed one day, Kevin*, and there was black coffee spilled everywhere, and then everything went white.

***

"Maggie?"

Round and around we go.

"Morning, Ma. Looks like you dozed off again waiting for the coffee."

I leapt from my seat, nearly overturning the wooden chair, and stared wildly at Dave. He raised his eyebrows and lifted his hands in surrender.

"Hey, what's wrong? What's going on?" he asked, but I hastened through the swinging doors into the diner, and there he was. There was the cowboy, smirking at me behind his sunglasses, *there he was!* Fury and terror made my hands shake, and I knew I had to do something, I had to stop it from happening again, I had to *stop* it, for chrissake!

Dave was behind me, peering through the door to the kitchen. "Can I get you some coffee, sir?" I asked over the thumping of my heart. The cowboy nodded.

I retreated to the kitchen, grabbing the coffeepot. Dave watched me warily.

"Finish the damn omelet, and then make some eggs Benedict or Mr. and Mrs. Snooty will throw a hissy fit," I ordered. He gaped at me for a moment before returning to his omelet, and while his back was turned, I rummaged in the cupboard and found his slim bottle of Jack. I slipped it into the big pocket of my apron, along with a small book of Ed's Good Eats matches.

Back in the diner, I held up the full pot of steaming coffee, and the cowboy grinned.

The bell above the front door shrieked like a flock of frightened birds, and the baby started to cry.

Here we go again.

Hopelessness fell heavy, like cement shoes. The kid was going to die. I couldn't do anything to stop that.

I leaned over the cowboy as if to fill his mug—and swung the coffeepot at his face. Glass shattered; dark liquid streamed; glittering shards dispersed like confetti, and he gave a terrible scream, clutching his face, which was now a mess of blood, coffee, and bits of glass.

The freckled woman yelped. The baby screeched louder than ever, and I wanted to shut that thing up, I really wanted to shut up that baby that wouldn't stop *crying!*

The runaway started forward, but I held up a hand. "No, our phones don't work, they haven't worked since the storm two days ago—*yesterday!*—so you can just sit down at your table and try not to bleed to death!"

Joanna Parypinski

The baby yowled like a dying cat. The mother tried to quiet the child, rocking back and forth in her dirty, ragged clothing, muttering madly, but her eyes were now trained on me.

The cowboy moaned and clutched his face. "How about one for the road?" I shouted feverishly. "How about one more for the goddamn road to Chicago!" I reached into my apron, yanked out the bottle of Jack, and dumped it out over the cowboy's head. Whiskey spilled over his shoulders, soaking his blood- and coffee-drenched shirt. When the bottle was empty, I grabbed a match and struck it, the fire as orange as the freckled woman's hair, and I chucked it at the cowboy. He burst into flame.

An agonized, unearthly howl filled the air, mingling with the baby's frantic bawling and the freckled woman's screaming, and I cackled with twisted glee as the cowboy flailed his arms and flames leapt over his body, incinerating his hat, blackening his skin—burning the smirk right off his face. The air was acrid with the scent of smoldering flesh. He screamed, and I laughed, and then he was just an ashy, skeletal mess on the floor.

"Don't move," came a low voice from behind me, and I felt a cold circle of metal press against the back of my neck. Glancing at the empty booth, I realized that it was the newspaper man.

I started to turn around, but he smacked me with the gun, and I fell forward onto my knees. The only sound now in the diner was the crackle of dying flames and the baby's constant keening.

"I fixed it," I mumbled, dazed, seizing upon the joy that rolled through my stomach where nausea had been before. "I fixed it. I fixed it."

But I hadn't. My eyes found the runaway, who was sitting at his table, pale and bloody and very much dead. The man above me—a lean man with slicked black hair and a blue sports jacket—pointed his gun at me.

Ignoring her crying baby, the mother finally cried out, "Somebody call nine-one-one!"

"You can't!" I shouted, staring at the kid, still dead, still dead. "The phones are down. The phones will be down forever. Nobody will ever be able to help us. We're stuck, don't you see? It's never going to end." My strangled voice rose. "It's never going to end. It's never going to end!"

I shoved to my feet, casting about for an escape—maybe if I could get out of the diner—or maybe it was over, now that the cowboy was dead—but the man with the newspaper dove forward, trying to catch me before I did something crazy, before I killed anybody else, and the butt of his gun cracked against my temple, and I was out.

***

"Maggie."

No. Please, not again.

"Morning, Ma. Looks like you dozed off again waiting for the coffee." I cracked open my eyes, feeling ancient and made of stone.

"I guess so." My limbs sluggishly obeyed my command to stand, and I grabbed the coffeepot and went to the cowboy. His sunglasses gleamed weirdly in the overhead light. The whole diner had spiraled into another dimension with me, reality as gray and lifeless as I was.

"Coffee?" Even my voice seemed flat, like a sheet of tinfoil. The cowboy tipped his empty mug towards me. Round and around we go.

I didn't give him a chance to compliment my name. Instead I leaned down by his ear and whispered, "You're never gonna make it to Chicago."

His face froze in a half-smile; I couldn't see his eyes behind the glasses. I drifted over to the couple and poured Orange Eyebrows a cup of coffee.

"Aren't you going to take our order?" she asked haughtily, even though she wasn't going to order anything.

"Eggs Benedict," I murmured faintly as I stared at the man's belt. He lowered his newspaper a touch.

My fingers loosened, and the coffeepot slipped from my hand, raining crystal on the floor once again—or maybe for the first time. The dark liquid pooled at my feet, and with the crash, the baby started to cry.

"Well!" huffed Eyebrows.

I bent as if to pick up the glass and saw the holster under his open sports jacket. The gun was in my hands before he could drop the newspaper.

Over the baby's crying, the bell tolled.

It never ends, I thought. *The baby's going to cry forever. It's never going to end.*

I swung around to face the runaway, who stumbled and raised blood-slicked hands when he saw the gun.

He was going to die anyway.

The bullet hit him in the chest. His battered face was a mask of shock as he went down, hitting the floor on his side, blood squirting out around him. He stared at me with blank, glazed eyes.

I was tired. It had been a long day.

The baby cried, cried, cried like it was broken.

Joanna Parypinski

The freckled woman was screaming. I went to the cowboy, who shook his head as if telling me, *no.*

Such a long day. It would never end. I had to fix it. But the baby wouldn't stop, it would never stop, it would just keep crying, crying, crying. Forever. It would never end.

I leveled the gun at the cowboy. My finger squeezed, and his head jerked back as the bullet lodged into his brain, leaving nothing but a small red hole above his eyes. He slumped sideways, hat slipping onto the floor, and I saw chunks of red and purple on the back of his chair. It took a long moment for me to realize that it was his brains, that the back of his head had split open as the bullet exited, and now his brains were splayed out on the seat. That would be a pain to clean up.

The cowboy fell from his chair. His sunglasses slipped off his nose, and I saw that his eyes were bright blue. Bright, blank, cold, and dead.

"Maggie!" Dave called from behind me. I turned, looked into pleading eyes. "Ma, please. Don't."

But the gun was already at my temple, right about where the newspaper man had hit me with it the last time. Or the time before that. I wasn't sure anymore. This time, last time, next time. It was all the same. It would never end.

Long day. It went on forever and ever and ever . . .

The baby was crying. The baby was crying. The baby was crying.

Somebody shut up that little brat or I will. Kevin, why are you such a reckless driver? Who will eat the pancakes now? The Lynyrd Skynyrd t-shirt was his favorite. It's going to get you killed one day, Kevin, you've got to be careful or it's going to get you killed. Morning, Ma. Looks like you dozed off again waiting for the coffee. That was one helluva storm, huh?

Fix it. End it. Long day. Never going to end. Don't matter. The road gets lonely, you know, and it's a long drive up to Chicago.

I smiled through cracking lips. "How about one for the road, Cowboy?" I asked the dead man on the floor. "Or don't you think you've had enough? Don't matter. It's a long drive up to Chicago. Well, here you go. One more for the road."

I pulled the trigger.

***

"Maggie." Here we go. Pause. I opened my eyes. "Morning, Ma. Looks like you dozed off again waiting for the coffee." Dave smiled. The omelet sizzled. It smelled like eggs and blood and burnt flesh.

I was on a merry-go-round with dark, snarling horses and poles made of bone. No off switch. Circles of hell.

Coffeepot. Cowboy's grin. Ragged mother. City folks. I tilted and the world tilted with me.

The bell chimed a deadly, alien chime.

The baby started to cry.

It never ends.

***

There's a symptom of PTSD called intrusion, where the sufferer is plagued by nightmares or daytime flashbacks. They say in severe cases, the sufferer can return to the memory continually to change the traumatic event. Reality is broken, so they try to fix it.

They say it might not have been so bad if it'd only been one thing, but the combination of the kid dying, the memory of my brother's fatal car crash, and the cowboy's attack triggered the intrusion.

At least that's what the doctors tell me, but I may have misunderstood. I can't really hear them over the baby crying.

Joanna Parypinski

Biographies

Diane Arrelle (Weaving Tangled Webs) the pen name of Dina Leacock, sold more than 150 short stories and has 2 published books. When not writing she is a senior citizen center director. She resides with her husband, her younger son and her cat on the edge of the Pine Barrens in Southern New Jersey (home of the Jersey Devil).

Alanna Belak (Bloodsport) Originally from Calgary, Canada, Alanna is a writing graduate from Vancouver Film School. She has written or co-written several produced short films. Her work has previously appeared in *Neon Magazine, The Eunoia Review, Criminal Class Press*, and *The Adroit Journal*. She is currently based in London, England working to launch her writing to the big screen. Her first professional feature screenplay—a remake of Orson Welles' *The Stranger*—is currently slated for pre-production with NGN Productions.

Chantal Boudreau (Orbs), an accountant/author/illustrator, lives in Nova Scotia, Canada. A Horror Writers Association member, she writes horror and fantasy, with several short stories published to date. *Fervor*, her debut novel, was released March 2011 followed by sequels, Elevation and Transcendence, and two novels in her Masters & Renegades series. http://www.writersownwords.com/chantal_boudreau/

Nadia Boulberhane (The Sadistic Chessboard) wants to set the world on fire, burn brighter than the sun. A writer that decided to step outside the bubble and take chances, mixed some different ideas and emotions for this work. She uses writing as a way to connect moments of the impossible and turn them into reality for just the smallest moment. She finds it a pleasure to be part of this work.

Mandy DeGeit (Morning Sickness), hailing from Ottawa, Ontario, Canada is awesome, outspoken and spends most of her money on tattoos and traveling. When she's not writing, she's thinking about what to write next. You can find out what she's up to here: http://mandydegeit.com

Magnolia Louise Erdelac (Moths) is in the third grade. She enjoys swimming, reading to her plants, taking care of her cat Noah, and playing with her mind. She has slept with the hall light on since she saw skeletons and ghosts in the dark above her little sister's crib. This is her second published story.

Erin Eveland (The Way) lives in Michigan, spending long winter nights writing in the garage, bundled in blankets and the occasional hat to keep warm. Summertime, she fends off insects and sleep to write the stories that come to mind during the day, enjoying the company of her four children.

Lindsey Beth Goddard (Out With the Old) is a dark fiction author living in the suburbs of St. Louis, MO. Most recently, her short stories have found homes in the anthologies: Night Terrors (Kayelle Press), Welcome To Hell (E-volve Books), and Tortured Souls (Scarlett River Press), as well as in webzines such as Hogglepot and Dark Fire Fiction. When not writing, she enjoys interviewing fellow authors, playing with her three children, and watching horror movies. For more information, you can visit her website at: http://www.lindseybethgoddard.com

Nikki Hopeman (Black Bird) loves the kind of horror that leaves her quaking in the back of the closet, the kind that won't let her close her eyes. She holds an MFA in writing popular fiction and shares her home in Pittsburgh with her husband, two sons, a cat, a couple of corgis, and a motorcycle. Her debut novel *Habeas Corpses* (Blood Bound Books) is due for release this year. She can be reached at www.nikkihopeman.com.

Hollis Jay (The Mistakes) has her BA in English and American Literature; an MFA in Creative Writing, and her MA in English. Find her books online: *The Ever* and *The Control Room or the Demands of Heather*. Follow her on Face Book and on her blog/ pod cast "Myriads of Thought."

Charlotte Jones (My Left Hand) promised herself she would do something more creative with her life after a twenty year career as a computer scientist and management consultant and began writing and taking pictures. Her work has appeared in over eighty literary and commercial magazines including *The Bellevue Literary Review* and *Nerve Cowboy*.

Suzie Lockhart (Playing with Fire) After high school, Suzie attended The Art Institute of Pittsburgh, but the gnawing urge to write always remained with her. Three years ago, she began working on an idea for a YA novel. When her son, Bruce, realized he had the same passion for storytelling, they teamed up. Together, they finished that book, which is presently being considered for publication. Their efforts have produced several short stories, including publications in *Dark Moon Digest* and *Sirens Call*.

Dawn Napier (Playdate) is a thirty-something married mother of three. She grew up in upstate New York and Waukegan, Illinois. She has been writing short stories, poetry, and novels for most of her life. Her genre of choice is horror, but she also writes fantasy and dabbles in science fiction.

Amanda Nethers (The Keeper) is a poet and short fiction writer living in Northern Maryland. She is a Pushcart Prize nominee whose recent works can be seen in *Scarlet Literary Magazine, Tales of Blood and Roses, EMG-Zine,* and *Off The Rocks Volume 14.*

Joanna Parypinski (And One for the Road) is the author of the horror novel, *Pandora,* and other scary stories appearing in *Arcane II, First Time Dead 3, Cover of Darkness,* and more. She is currently working on her MFA in fiction writing.

Suzanne Robb (Heart and Soul) is the author of *Were-wolves, Apocalypses, and Genetic Mutation, Oh my!* published by Dark Continents. She is also a contributing editor at Hidden Thoughts Press, and co-edited *Read The End First* with Adrian Chamberlin. Her work appears in several current and upcoming anthologies with Chaosium Inc., Coscom Entertainment, Post Mortem Press, and many others. In her free time she reads, watches movies, plays with her dog, and enjoys chocolate and LEGO's.

Kelli A. Wilkins (Sometimes Monsters are Real) divides her time between writing horror and erotic romances. Her speculative fiction has appeared in several anthologies including *Dark Things II: Cat Crimes, Frightmares, The Four Horsemen of the Apocalypse, Haunted, What If . . .,* and *Best of The First Line: The First Three Years.* Readers can learn more about Kelli and her writings on her website www.KelliWilkins.com or follow her weekly blog http://kelliwilkinsauthor.blogspot.com/.

Melissa Clare Wright (The Hangar) is the pen name of Melissa Mininni. She has degrees in Biochemistry and Neuroscience and currently works as a technical writer, though she'd rather be writing stories. She was born in Scotland, raised in Canada, and currently lives in California with her husband and a black cat who is gradually bleaching in the sun.

Acknowledgements

There are many people I need to thank for their part in helping with this book. First off, I want to thank Stan Swanson for believing in me enough to give me a chance at editing this. His faith this past couple of years has gone a long way in repairing the lack of self-esteem I suffer from. Second, I need to give a huge shout out to Jennifer Word who helped me initially read the over 300 submissions we received for this fabulous anthology. I never would have made it through all of them without her help.

Of course, I must give a huge hug to the authors of this anthology. They have been so helpful, proving that not only do horror writers stick together, but as women, we really do watch out for one another. This anthology brought me closer to the friends I already had, and has gained me some great new friendships as well. And I must extend my deep gratitude to the lovely Angel Leigh McCoy, who wrote such a fabulous introduction.

Last but certainly not least, I have to thank my other half, Max Booth III. Without him, I would never even have been in the horror world at all. I wouldn't even be in the writing world. Without his support, I would be nothing more than a shadow of a person. To him, I owe my life. Aloha Ia Au Oe Maxie.

Lori Michelle

CPSIA information can be obtained at www.ICGtesting.com
Printed in the USA
LVOW060824140313

323936LV00004BA/14/P